SECOND CHANCE OPTION

OPTION

By Elizabeth Spaur

First Print Publication: July 2018

© 2018 Elizabeth Spaur

ISBN – 10 is 1-7325343-1-4

ISBN – 13 is 978-1-7325343-1-5

Cover Art and Logo by Kristina Mull © 2018

Cover Photo © Sasa Mihajlovic | Dreamstime.com

Dedication

To my brother, Brad, who put up with all my questions and "what ifs." I couldn't have come up with this series without you.

AND

To my husband, my knight, my best friend. Without your limitless support, I wouldn't be where I am today.

Acknowledgements

Writing a story is a solitary exercise. Getting a book out to the world is a team effort. I couldn't have done this without my team: Beverly, Margo, Kristina, Diane, Mia, JoJo, Karen, Connie and Wendi. Thank you all for your critiques and beta reads.

Thank you to Bev Katz Rosenbaum and Jan Carol, my amazing editors.

Thank you to Kristina Mull, cover designer extraordinaire.

If you're interested in learning more about what's next for the Gridiron Knights and the folks who live in King's Folly, be sure to sign up for my newsletter (http://elizabeth-spaur.com/landing-page-newsletter/).

He was looking for a fresh start. She was looking for a new path. Love is what happens when they weren't looking for it.

At loose ends after a medical discharge from the Navy, a call from Cade Maguire's college coach gives him a new objective. Help save his alma mater's football program. A gut-wrenching betrayal drove him from the game once. Can he finally stop running long enough to let go of the past and find his future?

Veterinarian and genius Tess Gallagher has an abiding love for home and family. She's spent her life taking care of everyone else. Doing what was right always came before doing what she wanted. When her younger brothers enter her in the American Ninja Warrior competition, can she finally stop hiding her true self from the world?

Sparks ignite between Tess and Cade when she saves his injured dog and love is right on the horizon when Cade's new job is put in jeopardy before it even begins. Will Cade realize Tess is the second chance he really wants? Will Tess realize that Cade has always seen her for who she truly is?

Will they both realize that love is the only option that matters?

Chapter 1

It was a view Cade Maguire hadn't seen in almost fourteen years. The trees on the edge of the South Carolina National Forest showed signs of spring as the branches sprouted buds. If memory served, the forest would be a riot of color in a few weeks.

"What the hell are we doing here?"

Not surprisingly, neither of his Bernese Mountain Dogs responded. Sonny and Sam were great companions but hadn't mastered the art of speech. Yet.

Mostly black with patches of light brown and white, they were almost identical. The only way to tell them apart was the white strip of fur between their eyes. Sonny's was a little narrower than Sam's. Their light brown eyebrows sometimes made their expressions almost human.

He dropped the last of his boxes in the front room of his new cabin. All his worldly possessions fit neatly into the small corner between the bay window and the back wall. The boxes he was expecting from his grandfather would probably fit in the hall closet. Moving around his entire life had taught him not to hang on to things, but this was pitiful.

The year lease he signed made him jumpy. Especially because that agreement had him living in King's Folly, a town he'd never in a million years thought he'd see again, much less plant roots in. But stubborn didn't pay the bills and the chance to get back in the game was too good to turn his back on because things had ended badly here.

The room was bare except for the boxes. Someone had come through and cleaned recently. Hardwood floors shone in the early morning light. There wasn't a dust mote to be seen in any of the rays of sun shining through windows so clean birds might smack in to them. A fresh coat of white paint covered the walls and left behind a smell that reminded him of being transferred to a new base.

Thanks to the Navy, he'd had access to three squares and a place to sleep for the last fourteen years. Starting from scratch wasn't new. Usually, his assignments came with furnished apartments, not bare rooms with no amenities.

Shit. I don't even have a coffee maker.

He rifled through his duffle bag, which had the necessities and found his planner. It was an old school, leather bound, refillable notebook, a gift from his grandfather after his graduation from Officer Candidate School. A little something from one type A personality to another. The book was the one thing that had survived all his moves and deployments. The list of things he needed to make this

2

cabin more habitable was a mile long. It wasn't like he knew where to buy some of this shit, either. When did he ever think he'd have to buy kitchen appliances?

"I guess Maguires never say never, right boys?"

Sonny barked as if in agreement and Sam pressed against Cade's right leg burrowing close, careful not to put too much weight in to his comforting move. It always amazed him how attuned they were to the residuals of his injuries.

He reached down and scratched them both behind the ears. They were still puppies at almost a year old, but they were big. The three of them had been through a lot together since he'd gotten them six months ago.

"On to the next adventure."

They chuffed their agreement and followed him as he limped toward the door. Sonny and Sam danced around him, clearly looking forward to another chance to go outside and play. He didn't blame them. The three of them had been cooped up in his truck for the last three days driving from San Diego to South Carolina, only stopping long enough to get a few hours of sleep when he needed it or a bite to eat when they all got hungry.

As he opened the door, the dogs bounced outside like they were spring loaded. He inhaled taking in the smell of pine and yellow jessamine, trying to ignore the faint hint of sea salt in the air. The sound of woodpeckers in the distance was oddly soothing.

A pair of barks signaled that the boys had found something to occupy them. The muscles in his back and side pulled tight sending an ache along the edge of his nerves. It was one of those days that he felt closer to a hundred years old instead of thirty-six. Rotating at the waist helped and he studied his new quarters as he worked out the kinks left behind by the long road trip.

He'd deliberately avoided the beach properties. Too many memories. Instead, he'd found a two-bedroom cabin at the edge of the woods. Plenty of room for Sonny and Sam to run and fewer ghosts for him to trip over. Maybe he could figure out what it meant to make a place a home.

The first notes of Queen's "We Are the Champions" interrupted his thoughts. He pulled out his phone, then hit 'accept.'

"Ed." He greeted his former coach, first true mentor, and new boss.

"You in town yet?" The old man got right to the point.

"Yeah." Cade stretched, trying to work more of the pain and stiffness out of his right side. After so much time driving, his scars were tight. He was going to need to use that

4

lotion his physical therapist had hooked him up with. "The boys and I got here a little while ago. Just finished unloading the truck."

"The boys?"

"My dogs." An itch at the back of his neck made him go taut. He took a quick look around.

Where did Sonny and Sam go?

"Right. I hate to bug you since you just got to town."

The itching sensation intensified. "What's up?"

"We've got a situation brewing. We need to meet this afternoon in Ron's office."

"I'll be there." He needed to get off the phone. Something was up.

"Knew I could count on you." Ed disconnected the call.

Always a man of few words. It was one of the things that made the man a great football coach. When he had something to say, you listened because Ed King used his words so sparingly.

The dogs weren't barking anymore, which meant they were sniffing after something. Probably on the trail of some local wildlife. Still, he needed to find them. They weren't familiar with the area and there were wild animals in the forest around them and swamp land not too far from here. The problem was figuring out which direction they went.

5

A sudden screech of tires followed by a yelp and the sound of a vehicle peeling away came from the direction of the road and catapulted Cade into action. He ran down the driveway toward the sound. His heart beat like a pair of hummingbird wings and his chest felt like it might explode. When he got to the spot where his land met the road, he found them. Sonny lay motionless, but whimpering. Sam hovered over him barking at the retreating SUV as it screeched around the corner.

Cade dropped to his knees. Sonny's breathing was shallow, and there was blood. A lot of blood. Too much blood.

"Hey. That truck just took off." A lanky kid came out of nowhere and took a knee on the opposite side of Sonny and reached out as if to pet him.

"Don't touch him," Cade barked, fear coiling in his stomach like a viper waiting to strike.

"I know where the nearest vet is. It looks bad, but the Gallagher clinic is the best. If anyone can patch up your dog, they can." The kid sounded out of breath, but confident.

Cade nodded. He knew something had to be done, but he was, for the first time in his life, incapable of action. Things were moving too quickly for him to think.

The next few moments were surreal. It was like he was

watching the scene unfold through a Vaseline covered lens. The kid hustled Sam into the cabin and locked the front door after he'd closed it. Then he rushed back to Cade and helped him bundle Sonny into the backseat of Cade's truck. His dog's whimpers tore through his body like the IED that had ended his Navy career.

Looking at his buddy fighting for life made his stomach turn. He'd seen more than his share of blood, but this? This much blood? Because some stupid asshole couldn't slow his fucking car down?

Cade buried his fingers in the long black fur at Sonny's neck, careful to avoid his obvious injuries. He curled over until his mouth was next to the pup's ear.

"Easy, boy. I've got you. It's going to be okay."

Please, God. Please, let it be okay.

Sonny's whimpers echoed through the cab of the Avalanche. The truck must have been moving. He heard the engine and felt the movement as the kid rocketed around corners like a race car driver.

Cade didn't care about the truck. All he cared about was getting Sonny to help.

"We're almost there, boy," he whispered. His voice sounded like he'd been gargling shards of glass.

Please God, let us be almost there.

7

Sonny and Sam had gotten him through the worst days of his life. Recovering from career ending injuries had taken him to the edge. The puppies had pulled him back from it and helped navigate his new normal. There was no way he wanted to map out another one. He was too old for that shit.

The viper coiled in his gut balled up tighter and settled as if waiting for the perfect moment to lash out and destroy everything. He didn't know what he would do if Sonny didn't make it.

Please God, don't let me find out.

Ninety-nine point nine-nine percent of the time Tess Gallagher loved her work. Being a veterinarian was her calling. She loved animals and taking care of them was a joy and a privilege. Serving her community at the same time was the gravy on top of the French fries.

However, since hiring her part-time assistant, there was that other point zero one percent of the time.

"Is it just me or does this new cage make Mr. Wigglesworth look fat?" And there it was. Her former nemesis, unlikely new friend and recently hired employee, Delilah Derringer, and her total lack of a filter struck again.

Tess glanced over her shoulder to make sure she'd closed the door to the examination room. The last thing she needed was for Mrs. Milton to hear any insults to her beloved parakeet.

"Really?" These were the moments she wanted to smack the sass right out of Delilah. "You know how Mrs. Milton is about this bird."

Delilah shrugged. "She hates me anyway. I ran into her in the grocery story last week, and she spent fifteen minutes telling me what an embarrassment I am, and it was my lucky day when 'that nice Tess hired my lazy behind.'" She held up her fingers to make air quotes and mimicked the woman in question perfectly.

Tess closed her eyes, inhaled deeply and counted to ten, letting the slightly antiseptic smell of the room soothe her.

"It's hard enough to get some of our older clients to take me seriously. All we need is for Mrs. Milton to start telling the entire town we were making fun of her baby." She'd worked hard to build her reputation and didn't want Delilah's lack of tact to tear it down.

Delilah laughed. "You really need to lighten up. You don't want to main line Pepto-Bismol again."

It was probably wrong to want to strangle her. No, it was definitely wrong. Still there were moments, like this

9

one, where Tess gave it serious thought. Instead, she focused on Mr. Wigglesworth's annual physical, counting to ten again, and once more for good measure.

"How old is chubby anyway?"

Tess studied the soft pink plumage of the gentle bird and did her best to focus on her patient and not the woman who seemed to delight in tormenting her, even though lately it was good natured instead of nasty.

"He's fifteen. His initial appointment was one of the first ones I assisted Dad with before I started vet school." Tess smiled at the memory. She'd been thirteen and a mixture of excited and terrified that had made her want to shout and puke at the same time.

"Fifteen? I thought parakeets only lived like five years."

"Technically, this is a Bourke Parrot, but their called parakeets. The average life span is fifteen to twenty years, depending on whether they receive the proper diet and care."

"Well, the whole town knows Mrs. M is a fanatic about the care and feeding of anything but husbands."

Tess couldn't stop the giggle that escaped. She tried not to encourage Delilah's more outrageous commentary, but sometimes she couldn't help herself. The woman was funny. Unfortunately, halting one of her rants against some of the more disapproving citizens of King's Folly, South Carolina was like trying to stop the bulls at Pamplona. Since they had gone from enemies to friends, she had learned that it was essential to distract Delilah before she got on a roll and from the look of her, she was winding up for one hell of a tantrum.

"Speaking of husbands, any word on your divorce?" She felt a little bad using her friend's personal drama to change the subject, but these days it was the easiest way to put the brakes on the freight train that could be Delilah's mouth.

"Did I tell you what that cock knocker is doing now?"

Tess tuned out the rest of the speech, because yes, in fact, Delilah had told her what her soon be ex-husband was up to now. In excruciating detail. Three times. This Morning. By the time she finished her examination of Mr. Wigglesworth, the room had gone strangely quiet. She turned around. Delilah was standing in front of the door, arms crossed, a spark of irritation in her blue eyes.

"What?"

"You did that on purpose."

"I have no idea what you're talking about." Tess kept a gentle grip on the parakeet as she turned to put him back in his cage before returning her attention to her irritated friend.

"You brought up the lying, double-crossing bastard so I would stop making fun of the bird."

"That doesn't sound like me." She maintained eye contact with Delilah. There wasn't time for a staring contest, but there was less time for the drama. After a moment, her friend smiled and stepped away from the doorway to let Tess pass.

"I have no idea how I always got the better of you when we were growing up. Can't get anything by you these days."

"When we were growing up, I thought you were scary." Tess stepped outside of the exam room, knowing her words would, oddly enough, soothe her friend. Given that she was the one who had gotten Delilah worked up over her ex, it made her feel better to be the one to calm her down.

Tess had to admit that since she started spending more time with her three younger brothers and Delilah she was getting better at picking up on people's more subtle social cues and expressions. It was still a lot like trying to decipher an ancient, unknown language, but more and more she was building a translation key.

She took her patient back to reception where Mrs. Milton and Sheila were still trading the latest and greatest in local gossip.

"And do you know what the uppity English teacher said to me?" Mrs. Milton broke off from her tirade when she spotted Tess coming down the hall. Her pink tinted lips, the exact same color as her bird tilted up and, with a high-pitched coo, she moved away from the receptionist's desk and waddled toward Tess, who held the cage out for her client.

"And how's mummy's wittle baby waby?" She smashed her nose up against the cage and made kissy noises.

"Mr. Wigglesworth is doing very well, as usual. You're taking excellent care of him."

Mrs. Milton beamed at Tess and pinched her cheek. "You're a good girl."

Tess smiled and ignored the fact that Mrs. Milton spoke to her in the same tone she used with her bird. It was better than the people who spoke to her like she was still a child. "Thank you. You keep doing what you're doing, and we'll see you and Mr. Wigglesworth next year."

As Mrs. Milton and her parakeet left the building a black Avalanche screeched to a halt in front of the clinic, smoke blowing from the tires. Tess had a split second to appreciate the large, muscular man who jumped from the back seat of the truck before all her attention shifted to the large, bloody animal cradled in his arms.

She threw open the door. The bitter smell of burnt rubber filled the air.

"I need a doctor." His voice sounded raspy and thick.

"I'm Dr. Gallagher. Follow me." She led him to the nearest empty examination room and watched closely as he laid what she could now see was a Bernese Mountain Dog down on the table as if it was the most precious thing in the world to him.

With years of experience she ran her hands along the dog's body and found the source of the bleeding and looked up to see her veterinary technician, Charlie, and Delilah, standing in the doorway, waiting for instructions.

"Charlie, prep the OR and have the portable x-ray standing by. We've got internal bleeding and possible broken bones. Delilah, bring in the gurney, we need to get…"

She focused on the man, whose oddly familiar, piercing green gaze never left his dog.

"Sonny." He seemed to know what information she needed.

Tess nodded. "We need to get Sonny in to surgery."

The next few moments passed in a flurry of activity. Sonny was quickly transferred to a gurney, then wheeled back to the OR. There was no question that her staff would settle the distraught, and sexy man out front. This wasn't their first ball game.

Once in the operating room Tess and Charlie worked in concert to save the big dog's life. Delilah stood by the door, eyes looking anywhere but at the injured dog, hand over her mouth, doing nothing to disguise the gagging noises she was making. She waited for an update on Sonny's injuries that she could share with his concerned owner.

It took Tess a few minutes to study the x-rays they had taken while Charlie finished making sure Sonny was prepped for surgery. Tess hoped she could send Delilah out to the waiting room with an update before she tossed her cookies.

"Let him know Sonny has a broken right hind leg and some internal bleeding. The break is in two places, but it's clean so we are going to set the leg after we stop the bleeding and repair the internal damage. He's welcome to wait, but this is going to take a while, three to four hours at least."

Delilah left the room like someone lit her ass on fire.

"I still don't know why you hired her."

Tess smiled beneath her surgical mask. She and Charlie had been friends since infancy and she wasn't ready to give Delilah the same pass Tess had. "She needs the job and she's a hard worker."

"She can't stand blood, she's disrespectful to the clients, she's..."

It was a familiar refrain. Tess tuned it out momentarily when she spotted a bleeder. "Retract this."

Charlie didn't stop her litany of complaints against Delilah as they continued the surgery. She paused occasionally to take Tess's direction and the occasional breath. Lately Charlie reserved her diatribes for the OR because she knew no one would overhear her. Tess sighed.

"You do know the definition of insanity, right? Cauterize that."

Her assistant expertly followed her instructions. "Doing the same thing over and over again and expecting a different result."

"Right? How are his vitals?" They'd been growing steadier as the bleeding was controlled.

"Stable. So, I'm insane now?"

She set the last clamp in place, confident she'd identified all the bleeds. "Let's stitch up these bleeds. You do keep repeating yourself."

"What type of sutures are we using? I'm worried about you."

"Internal, absorbable." Tess held out her hand for the

sutures. "I know you're worried. I even understand why you keep bringing it up. I have, historically, been very slow with social cues and Delilah has, historically, been nasty to me."

"But you think she's changed." It was a statement, not a question. Charlie checked Sonny's vitals.

"I believe in second chances and I think she deserves one. If I'm wrong – "

"I'll kick her ass."

Tess laughed. Charlie had always been her biggest defender and was far from convinced that Delilah had turned a corner. "And if I'm right?" She scanned the now closed incision, pleased with her work. Sonny's vitals were stable, and he'd responded well to the anesthesia.

Charlie sighed. "I guess I'll have to be friends with her."

"You already are friends. I know social situations aren't my forte, but I believe the two of you enjoy baiting each other. Let's cast this leg."

The two women worked in concert to finish Sonny's treatment. Now that he was clearly out of danger and Charlie's latest issue with Delilah had been dealt with, Tess took a moment to focus on the man who had brought Sonny in. Those familiar green eyes had finally sparked a memory.

Cade Maguire.

He was back, and he had great taste in dogs.

Chapter 2

Cade paced the waiting room of the clinic. Eyes focused on the hallway where the blonde, he didn't think anyone told him her name, disappeared after explaining Sonny's injuries. It looked like she was going to puke. Weird, considering she probably saw stuff like this all the time. If he looked in a mirror, he was sure he'd see a similar look on his face right now. The truth was, he was barely holding his shit together and not having Sonny or Sam with him only made it worse.

Sam was probably going nuts.

The kid who'd stopped to help him after that asshole hit Sonny and took off was still here, sprawled out in one of the big chairs in front of the window that read "Gallagher Animal Clinic." Other than glancing up from his phone occasionally, he pretty much left Cade alone.

People and animals had come and gone. There must be someone other than the gorgeous brunette with the piercing hazel eyes treating them. He strode back to the reception desk where the blonde, looking like she'd either puked or gotten over the need to, and the receptionist, an older woman whose name he couldn't remember, even though she'd told him, were talking quietly.

"Any news?"

"Mr. Maguire." The older woman smiled at him, her kind brown eyes full of understanding.

"I know, it takes time. I just want…" What did he want? He clenched his fist. "I need an update."

The receptionist nodded and turned to the blonde.

"Sorry, one trip back there is my limit for the day. I'll watch the front desk." She moved towards the chair but was blocked by the older woman.

"You know you're not allowed to cover the front." She sighed.

The blonde put her hands on her hips. "Seriously? I can answer phones."

"Delilah, there are rules for a reason."

Cade could tell this was winding up to be one hell of an argument. Before he could intervene, the kid stood up and did it for him.

"Geez. What's the big deal? I'll go back and check for him." With that pronouncement, he disappeared down the hall.

Cade couldn't look away from the two women staring at each other like they were one second away from the kind of fight men pay to see, if it involved mud or Jell-O.

"Is he allowed to go back there?" It seemed like a reasonable question to him.

The older woman stared at him liked he was nuts. "Why wouldn't he be?"

"Um, because he's a kid and he's not trained." The kid might be local, but as far as Cade knew he wasn't authorized to go back to the operating room.

Both women laughed.

"He's clearly new," the blonde pronounced before sauntering off.

Cade didn't miss the subtle middle finger she flipped at the older woman, neither did the recipient of the gesture.

"That girl." Sheila clucked before focusing on him. "It's been a while since you've been in King's Folly."

He jerked back. "You recognized me?" It had been almost fourteen years since he'd put this town in his rearview mirror.

"Of course. I've lived in this town my entire life. I'm not going to forget the man who still holds the college record for completed passes. Most accurate quarterback that ever played the game." She winked at him.

Warmth crept up Cade's neck. "It's been years since I played. I'm old news."

"Not around here you're not, especially not now." She fluffed her hair then held out her hand. "Sheila Caldwell.

I'm the receptionist, office manager and all-around girl Friday here. I'm also a member of the town council. If you need anything, you let me know."

He shook her hand. "Thank you." He didn't know what else to say. On a good day, he wasn't that talkative. Waiting for news on Sonny's condition made him less so.

Sheila patted his hand. "Tess is the best there is." She glanced over her shoulder then leaned closer to him. "Don't let her daddy know I said that. He's sensitive."

"Her – " Cade tensed when he saw the kid coming back down the hall. "How is he?"

"Tess stopped the bleeding. They're setting his leg now. She said he's stable and they'll be done soon."

"So, he's going to be all right." Cade let go of the breath he felt like he'd been holding since he'd found Sonny bloody and whimpering at the edge of his driveway.

"She's optimistic. My sister doesn't make promises she can't keep, but if anyone can get Sonny through this, it's her."

"I heard that."

All three of them turned towards the sound of the voice. An older man came down the hall, the image of the kid.

"Hey, Dad."

Suddenly Cade made the connections he had missed

due to his panic. The gorgeous vet was the kid's sister, and this must be their father.

"Tyler." The man nodded at his son as he approached. "So, our emergency patient is going to pull through." He stepped forward and held out a hand to Cade. "Cade. Trevor Gallagher. Good to see you again."

"Again?" Cade tilted his head as he shook the man's hand. He looked familiar and Cade usually had good recall for names and faces. The problem was it seemed like everything around him was moving twice as fast as normal while his brain was at half speed.

"My wife, Tatum, is Coach King's daughter. We crossed paths a few times when you played for the Knights."

"Right, Dr. Gallagher. Good to see you again."

"You and Ed have your work cut out for you, rebuilding the football program."

Cade rubbed the back of his neck. "I'm still not sure why I agreed to it. It's the craziest plan I've ever heard." He wasn't sure he had it in him to put down roots, especially here, but if Ed needed his help, he was all in. And he couldn't turn down a chance to get back in the game.

Trevor laughed. "That's one way to describe it."

"I think it's awesome," Tyler said.

"I agree with young Mr. Gallagher." Sheila joined the

conversation. "It's awesome and just what the program needs."

"What's that?" Cade was interested in her thoughts. The idea of a group of coaches coming out of retirement to train a bunch of former players with no coaching experience to take over for them within a few years, had seemed a little out there when he'd first heard it. He wondered what other people thought.

"Coach King and his team will bring experience to the program. You and your team will bring honor back to it."

Cade was humbled by Sheila's assessment. He would have to make sure her faith in him was justified.

"You're amazing."

Charlie's words of praise sent warmth flowing through Tess.

"Thank you." She studied Sonny's vital signs. Everything was normal. "He's stable. You can bring Cade back to sit with him for a little while."

She had a meeting she was already late for. Now wasn't the time to let a pair of handsome green eyes, a tight T-shirt and mysterious tattoos peeking out from the edges of the sleeves distract her.

Fifteen minutes, three blown red lights, but thankfully no tickets, later she pulled into the parking lot outside the university administration building. It took another ten minutes to get to her destination.

"You're late."

The biting tone sent a chill down Tess's spine and the smell of Paco Rabanne made her want to gag. She closed her eyes and braced herself to turn in the direction the voice had come from.

There was no way she would apologize to him. "There was an emergency at the clinic." If she could go the rest of her life without having to talk to him, that would be a good thing.

"I doubt anything involving those creatures you waste your time on could be considered an emergency." The sneer was in his voice and on his face.

Tess glanced around. Brian Gill, Senior was the only other board member in the room. His mud colored hair appeared to be thinning and going gray and his expensive suit did little to hide his growing paunch.

Her chest tightened. She'd spent the better part of her life making sure she was never alone with him. Senior was the embodiment of the word malevolent.

"Gill, leave her alone." The president of the university

25

walked into the room.

She swallowed. "Where is everyone else?" Thank God her voice didn't sound as small as she felt.

"We delayed the meeting. Someone was supposed to call your office and let you know you didn't have to be here." President Adams looked pointedly at Gill.

He shrugged. "It's been so long since I've seen Dr. Gallagher, I thought we could have a chat."

She wanted no part in any chatting he might want to do. "When is the next meeting?" She tried to ignore Gill.

"Six weeks."

"I'm assuming there's an e-mail explaining the situation." There better be. The sooner she could get out of here, the better.

"Yes, but – " President Adams began.

She held up a hand. The more time she spent with Senior, the more she wanted to throw up. There had been a lot of things she'd grown out of. This feeling wasn't one of them. Before either man could say anything else she bolted out of the room.

Senior wasn't following her. Logically, she knew he wouldn't. He never pulled his garbage in public and hadn't done anything to her that was more than vaguely menacing in years. Still, she needed to leave before he changed his mind and tried something. By the time she got to her car, she'd worked herself up into a state.

Breathe.

She counted to ten as a familiar burning pain spread through her chest. It had been a while since the fiery ache had made itself known. The last time she felt the sensation was probably around the last time she'd been alone in a room with Senior. Funny how that worked out.

Breathe.

It wasn't supposed to be like this anymore. She was a responsible adult. A respected member of the community. He was a bully and a fraud. Unfortunately, he was also good at getting away with it, whatever his "it" of the moment was. Gathering the proof to take him down would take more than a hot second. Other people had been working on it for years.

She braced herself against her car.

Breathe.

"Doc?"

A calming baritone voice washed over her. She turned and saw Cade walking toward her. "Hi." Her voice sounded raspy.

"What are you doing here?" He stopped a few inches away from her.

"I had a meeting on campus." That she was trying to not think about, much less talk about. "Did you see Sonny?"

His green eyes warmed and he pressed his palm to his heart. "Yeah. Charlie took me back to see him for a few minutes. She said I could come back after I'm done here."

"Of course. If someone is in the office, you can spend time with him whenever you want." She blinked as she realized the burning pain was gone and her breathing had returned to normal. It was like he was giving off some kind of vibe that soothed her.

This was new.

He tilted his head. "You okay?"

Better than okay. Now.

She studied him, wondering what this effect he had on her meant. "I'm fine. Thank you."

They stood in silence for a moment. She couldn't tell if he wanted to say something else but didn't mind having a chance to just look at him. His dark hair was cut short, not quite a buzz cut, but close. He had a neatly trimmed beard that made her want to run her hands along his cheeks, and multi-colored tattoos peeking out from the edge of the black T-shirt that stretched taut across his muscles.

It took all her concentration to keep her from letting her gaze drift down to his muscular legs encased in a pair of jeans that had been well washed and clung to his lower body like cling wrap.

She needed to take charge of the conversation. "What are you doing here?"

"I've got a meeting with your grandfather and Ron in a little while."

The football program, right. "I don't want to make you late." She also didn't want to admit she wanted the conversation to continue.

"I'm not. You want to tell me what freaked you out so badly?"

"Not really." More like definitely not.

"But it's something." He looked smug like he already knew all the answers.

Sneaky bastard. "Nothing you need to worry about." It wasn't anything she wanted anyone to worry about. She'd handle the Gills herself, just like she always had.

He stared at her for a moment before nodding and silence stretched between them, filling the air with a weird energy she couldn't identify.

"Did you have any questions about Sonny for me?"

"Not right now. Thank you for everything." He blinked his eyes and looked up. "I was a little out of it."

"Understandable. He clearly means a lot to you." Which

only made Cade more attractive, if that was possible.

"Yeah. I got him and his brother about six months ago, when my discharge came through. We've been together ever since." He rubbed the back of his neck.

"His brother's all right?" Dogs experienced stress because of family injuries, too.

"Sam's good. I stopped home to check on him and change before heading over here."

"Sonny and Sam." She laughed.

"Yeah."

"As in Jurgensen and Huff?"

His eyes widened. "You know them?"

She laughed. "Sonny Jurgensen, quarterback for Philadelphia and Washington. Sam Huff linebacker for New York and Washington, commentators for Washington until Sam Huff retired a while back."

His lips tilted up in a slow smile that made her think he'd made a decision about her. "You know your football."

"I know a lot of things." She couldn't help smiling back at him. Somehow, a few moments talking to Cade centered her.

"I bet you do."

His silky tone sent shivers down her spine and it was like hummingbirds were flitting around her stomach.

I wonder what he tastes like.

The errant thought had her focusing on his lips. His grin grew, making her wonder if he could read her mind.

He cleared his throat. "So, what's next?"

"With what?" She looked from his lips into his green eyes.

"Sonny." His eyes were filled with amusement.

The thought that he was laughing at her was enough turn all her warm thoughts to ice. "He's stable. You can come by and see him later today and we'll go over his chart and prognosis."

She turned to her car, pushing thoughts of him, and her feelings for him, whatever they were, away. Too bad. Getting to know him better might have been fun.

But he had to go and laugh at me.

Chapter 3

What the hell just happened?

Cade watched her drive away and wondered how someone had managed to switch off the sun. One moment he was impressed, and more than a little turned on by the gorgeous vet. It was hot as hell that she knew exactly who Sonny and Sam were named after. The next moment he was getting frostbite from her attitude change.

He checked his watch. Since he was going to be late if he didn't move it, he took off toward the athletic department at a slow run. Between unloading his truck and dealing with Sonny's ordeal, his scars pulled tight. Being on time was worth a little discomfort and a run would help him loosen up his muscles, which helped with the pain from the scarring.

Ten minutes later, Cade strode into Ron Jackson's office. Cormac University's new athletic director stood and greeted him with a smile and a handshake. The older man had a wrestler's build, which made sense, given the four Olympic gold medals displayed in a frame on the wall.

Coach Ed King stepped forward and slapped Cade on the back. He'd wanted to push this meeting off another day. After everything that happened with Sonny, he was fried. Ron had insisted they needed to meet briefly as soon as possible.

So, Cade had left the clinic after spending a few minutes with Sonny. His buddy had still been sedated, but sitting next to him, watching his even breathing had soothed the viper in Cade's gut that had taken up residence there at the sound of the squealing tires.

"Sorry to keep you waiting." He collapsed in a large chair opposite Ron's desk and prayed this meeting would be short.

"Don't worry about it." Ed sat in the chair next to Cade and studied him with shrewd, blue eyes. "Heard about your dog. He's in good hands with my girl."

Cade nodded, not trusting his voice when it came to Sonny. It was different talking about him with Tess. He glanced from Ron to Ed and waited. Since this meeting was scheduled at the last minute, he figured something was up and they would let him know what that was when they were ready. It's not like he was in a hurry to hear more bad news today.

"Guess you're wondering why the urgent call." Ron sat behind his desk then leaned back in his chair. "We thought you'd have a little more time to settle."

"What happened?" Something was up. Ed's teeth were

clamped around the end of a cigar like a vice. It was a wonder he hadn't bitten it off. Ron was grinding his teeth so hard Cade wouldn't be surprised if he started spitting dust any second.

Ron cleared his throat. "We might have an issue."

Ed barked out a short laugh that held no humor. "Issue my wrinkly ass. We've been hit with a grade A cluster fuck with the last name Gill."

"Backup?" Cade hadn't thought of Brian "Backup" Gill in almost fourteen years. He rode the bench as second-string quarterback and spent most of his time gunning for Cade and his starting spot for reasons that remained a mystery. Then and now.

"And his old man. Mostly his old man. Gill, Senior is on the Board and has a lot of influence in this town. Seems he wants to nix our plan."

"If the university wants to go another way, I understand." Cade leaned forward and tried to ignore the sensation that he was about to be set free. "This plan," Cade looked at Ed, "was a little out there."

Ron shook his head. "I'm still behind the plan and the coaches Senior's lined up will take this program in a direction I'm not comfortable with. Not to mention it would give him too much power over the university. I intend to make it clear to the Board that if they go with his plan instead of ours, they'll be doing it without me."

Cade sat back. "I don't understand." He was usually a little quicker on the uptake. All things considered he was lucky to still be relatively coherent.

"The Board is going to hear presentations from us and Junior in six weeks and they're going to vote on them." Ron pinched the bridge of his nose.

"We have six weeks to put together our coaching roster and outline our plan." Ed yanked his still unlit cigar out of his mouth and brandished it like a sword, flecks of tobacco flew from the chewed tip.

"Junior still the same?" Cade hadn't met anyone, before or since, with a bigger chip on his shoulder than Backup Gill. There seemed to be glimmers of another person underneath all the shit talking and attitude, but after all these years they were likely figments of Cade's imagination.

"Yep." Ed practically spat. "He still acts like the world owes him something for breathing."

Cade nodded. "Let me get this straight. In six weeks, the Board hears our two plans and makes a decision." He sat taller when he saw the look that passed between the two men. "What else?" As if he needed there to be something else.

"There will be three plans presented. There's a professor putting together a proposal to eliminate the football program entirely."

"Seriously?"

"Seems to think, given the financial hit we'll take with sanctions, now's a good time to eliminate football and devote the resources to other programs."

"Doesn't this professor know that cutting the football program would basically be the same as cutting all athletics and even some academic scholarships?"

"Well, she's got some juice to her argument." Ron closed his eyes. "My predecessor pretty much let Coach Delano get away with murder. The football program hasn't been supporting much more than the coaching staff and a few pet projects in the last few years."

"I already told Ed I wouldn't be part of a new program unless that changed." Cade had heard of too many programs that didn't use any income they generated to support the other athletic teams that didn't bring in the same kind of money that a successful football program could.

If he was going to stay in one place for any length of time, it was damn well going to be worth his effort.

"I know, and that will be part of our presentation. Should help offset the professor's plan."

"What does this professor want to do with the money?" He couldn't imagine Cormac University without a football team.

Ron shrugged. "No idea. She's new to Cormac. Head of the English Department. She's keeping things pretty close to the vest." He paused, staring at the calendar on his desk like he suddenly found it the most fascinating thing in the room.

"What else?" Cade scrubbed his hand down his face. Given the current conversation, he was glad he'd decided to rent and not buy. Being part of the football program was the only reason he was willing to face the past that lurked in King's Folly.

Is this development a bad thing or a good thing?

Coach shifted in his chair. "My granddaughter's likely going to be the deciding vote."

"Tess? She's on the Board?"

Coach nodded. "The President of the university appointed her a year ago. She's King's Folly born and raised, went to Cormac, both undergrad and vet school. The community loves her, and she has the ear of every generation in town. That girl never says no to anyone in need. Add that she's a genius and it was a no brainer to ask her to serve. There are ten trustees on the Board. We think Tess will be the deciding vote."

"Why?"

"Three of the trustees are chairs of other academic departments. They're probably going to go with the professor. Senior's got two lackeys who will do whatever he wants them to do. That leaves the three longest serving members, who were the only votes against Delano when he forced Ed out, and Tess."

"Why isn't that good news? Doesn't that mean our plan is the favorite?"

"My girl doesn't have a biased bone in her body and everyone knows it. She'll vote for what's best for the university, nothing else."

"And?" Cade was having a hard time following Ed's logic. Granted, he didn't know Tess well, but based on what everyone else had told him it seemed like she would be able to see that their plan was far superior to the other two and in the university's best interests.

"Senior's got to know that Tess would be the deciding vote."

"I'm still not following?"

Ed shifted in his chair. "He isn't going to leave things to chance or in Tess's hands. He's got vendettas on top of vendettas against certain families in this town and mine is at the top of his list."

Cade leaned forward. "Do you think he would try to hurt her?"

"He's not going to do anything obvious." Ron pinched the bridge of his nose.

"Or anything that can be traced back to him." Ed added.

"But he will try something." Cade didn't know much about the man, but Ed and Ron sounded sure he was up to something big.

"Senior definitely won't leave anything to chance." Ed sighed.

"Do we warn Tess? Talk to her about what's going on?" She may be pissed at him for some reason, but the last thing Cade wanted was for something to happen to her.

"You can." Ed responded.

"Me? Why? She's your granddaughter."

"Exactly."

Cade sat and waited for Ed to elaborate. He closed his eyes and rubbed the back of his neck. It felt like someone was poking a thousand tiny needles into his brain.

"My wife isn't crazy about this plan of ours. She liked having me retired, and even though I anticipate being completely retired again in a couple of years, she's pissed."

"You just said Tess would do what's best for the university. She wouldn't go against our plan just to support her grandmother, would she?" This conversation was like playing whack-a-mole. Every time he thought he had a handle on it, another wrinkle came out of nowhere.

"I doubt it. If I'm in the dog house with her gran, then I'm usually in it with Tess. But she's passionate about education and the university. She'll do what she thinks if best for Cormac and King's Folly, no matter whose idea it is."

Coach stood up and went to the window, which overlooked the practice field. "My family founded this town and the university. My grandfather started the football program and a King has led it up until that bastard Delano forced me into retirement. Then he went and fucked everything up. I need to set it right. My grandsons are juniors in high school. They're the next generation of Kings. I want this program to be here for them. Not just that. I want an honorable program to be here for them. One that's about the game, not the money. One we can all take pride in. That's why I suggested this idea." He turned to look back at Cade.

When he met Ed's gaze, something inside him braced. *Here it comes.*

"You were the best player I ever coached. The fact that

you walked away from more money than most people will see in a lifetime to serve your country also makes you one of the most honorable. You know this sport better than just about anyone and you love it as much, if not more. You've been a leader for more than a decade. A few years working with me and you'll know everything you need to about coaching football. You're the kind of man I want to take this program in to the future. You're the man I trust my legacy with."

Something warm and rare spread through Cade at the sound of Ed's faith in him. Undeserved as it was. He took a moment before he spoke to make sure his voice didn't crack. "Still, your granddaughter — "

"Tess will do what's right. That's the way she was raised. We just need to make sure Senior can't make that impossible for her."

"The question is," Cade shifted his gaze from Ed to Ron, "what's he going to try?"

"We'll deal with the Gills and make sure that the only rational option for the university is ours." Ron stood up and approached Cade. "I know you signed a contract, but that was before the Gills picked this fight. I would under-stand if you want to walk away. Six weeks of working for potentially nothing isn't what you signed up for. Ed and I

41

will both understand if you want to explore other options.

Cade stood up then squared his shoulders. "You both know I don't ever walk away from a fight."

Tess walked into her office at the end of the day and embraced the quiet. Sometimes, there was nothing like being alone in the clinic after a long day. Since she spent so much time here, she'd designed her space for comfort. She eyed the couch and thought about sleeping here tonight.

It was the ugliest couch in all creation. The Triplets, her youngest brothers, affectionately known to the rest of the family as the "Trips," had dared her to buy it for her office a few weeks ago. Despite its appearance, she was glad they did. Somehow, it was almost more comfortable than her bed, which made those nights she crashed at the clinic to take care of a seriously sick or injured animal much easier.

She leaned over and let her arms hang down, fingertips brushing the floor. Tess hung there for a few minutes, letting gravity stretch her muscles. Once the knot in her lower back loosened, she stood up, walked to her desk then sat down. Her e-mail inbox was open on the computer and she did a double take. Three hundred? How could she have three hundred new e-mails? Did she even know that many people? Getting even twenty e-mails in a day was a rare occurrence.

Tess scanned through the subject lines of the messages and wondered when everyone had lost their minds. A banging on the front door made her jump and was a welcome distraction from the implications of the world's sudden need to communicate with her. She got up and went to the front door. It was late, and she was alone in the clinic, so she grabbed her cell phone, prepared to dial nine-one-one if she needed to. This was King's Folly, but she wasn't stupid.

The front lights were on and Tess saw Cade through the glass. She stood in the shadows of her office and took a moment to admire him, because, holy smokes, he was worth admiring. She couldn't see his eyes from here, but she remembered his deep green gaze that always seemed to see more than she wanted to reveal. Even years ago, when they were in college.

Since she was almost half the age of the other freshmen, her grandfather's office had been a haven between classes. It wasn't unusual for her grandfather's players to tromp in and out of the office while she was there. Her homework that year hadn't been all that challenging, and the presence of the football players was a nice distraction. Cade was the biggest distraction of them all. He acted like he knew all the best secrets and she'd loved him with all the fervor of a ten-year-old genius with rudimentary social skills that rarely translated well into interactions with anyone but her best friend, Charlie.

Another bang from the door startled her. He was pressed up against the door, hands cupped on either side of his face, and he was looking in her direction. She could feel his gaze focused entirely on her. An unfamiliar warmth began to spread through her body. The shadows weren't as deep as they seemed. There was another bang, jolting her out of thoughts she had no business entertaining, and she jumped forward to unlock the door and let him inside. Once he passed by her, she closed and relocked the door.

"You want to see Sonny." He wasn't the first person to want to make sure his pet was resting comfortably at the end of the day. More insistent than most, but that wasn't surprising.

He nodded. "Yeah. I'm sorry to bother you. Just couldn't get settled at my place without seeing him." His voice was gruff and low.

"I understand. Follow me. He's still resting comfortably." Tess led the way to the back of the clinic where they

kept animals overnight. Since Sonny was their only overnight guest, Tess had him in a bed outside of the kennel. He
was still lightly sedated, so she wasn't worried about him
wandering around and getting into trouble.

Cade brushed past her and went straight to Sonny. He
sat next to him and gently ran his hand through the dog's
fur. That heat she'd felt when he stared at her through the
glass rushed through her like a five-alarm fire.

Oh, Lord. I'm in trouble.

"Hey, boy. I'm here. It's gonna be okay."

Tess's stomach fluttered at the big man's gentle treatment of his injured friend. She'd always been a sucker for a
dog lover and it seemed she was still a sucker for Cade. It
felt intrusive watching him crooning to his dog. Leaving
the door open so he could find her when he was finished
visiting with Sonny, she tiptoed out of the room.

The thought of reading through some of the hundreds
of e-mails waiting for her was more than her exhausted
brain could handle. That many messages in one day
couldn't be a good thing. The aborted board meeting earlier
today, and her run-in with Gill Senior had her on the edge.
All these people wanting to reach her made her want to
jump off it. The messages would have to wait until morning. She would tackle them then.

She pulled her cell phone out of her desk and noted twenty-four voice mails.

What the heck is going on?

She played the first voicemail.

"Tess. It's Gran. Don't listen to this nonsense." Her grandmother's voice soothed her. "You do what you think is right. I trust your judgment."

What I think is right? What does that mean?

"That is the ugliest fucking couch I've ever seen."

His voice drew her attention to the doorway. Cade stood there, all muscle and man. She couldn't keep her eyes off the tattoos on his arms that peaked out from the edge of his sleeves. It would be nice to study them more closely.

Tattoos fascinated her, not the impulsive ones so many students seemed to acquire after a night of drinking, but the ones that symbolized something a person wanted to permanently etch on their skin. She'd given serious consideration to getting a tattoo. So far, she hadn't experienced anything she wanted to permanently commemorate. Maybe one day.

"Problem?" He asked.

"Problem?" She repeated, confused by his ability to disrupt her thoughts.

He nodded at the phone, still in her hand. "You look confused."

46

"I am."

Cade snorted. "I imagine that's a new sensation."

She narrowed her eyes, not sure she liked him making fun of her. "It is unusual. I got more e-mails and voice mails today than I usually get in a month. I don't know what's going on."

"Haven't you read any of the e-mails?" He moved into her office and made himself comfortable on the couch, legs stretched out in front him, hands behind his head.

The sight of him sitting there, clearly comfortable, transformed the butterflies in her stomach to mini-tornadoes. "I decided to temporarily put it off."

"Why?"

"That many people wanting to talk to me can't be a good thing. I'm also exhausted. I can't give them my full attention tonight." She watched him as he watched her, something flickered in his eyes. "What do you know?"

"I can tell you what people are trying to sell you."

"What's that?"

"The Board has called a meeting in six weeks to vote on the competing plans for the football program."

Tess jolted. "I thought the plan was for Grandpa and his staff to train you and your staff to coach a division one football team and then go back to retirement in two to three years."

"That's one of them."

The conversation earlier this afternoon, after the board meeting that never happened, began to make sense. "Since when is there more than one?"

"As of my meeting with your grandfather and Ron there were three. Who knows how many there will be by the time the Board meets to vote on it. I don't know if the Board is going to open the floor to alternate proposals." He raised an eyebrow. "Shouldn't you?"

There was something about his tone that she didn't like. More annoying than his tone was that he was right. Being wrong was not something she handled well. She took her responsibilities seriously and she should have known about this developing situation. Heat rushed up her neck.

If it hadn't been for her tendency to turn into a quivering child when she was forced to deal with Senior on her own, she would have found out everything earlier. The fact that she was caught looking foolish by Cade, of all people, turned the mini-tornadoes in her stomach to rocks. "I can't talk about this with you."

"Why not?" He crossed his ankles, clearly intending to stay awhile.

"Because it's not appropriate." She eyed the couch, and

the large man taking up so much space on it. So much for relaxing for a while before heading home. It was safer for her to sit on the chair, not as comfortable, but definitely safer. Suppressing a sigh, she sat down then tucked her legs underneath her and met his confused green eyes.

"Appropriate? It's not appropriate to have an open discussion about an issue you'll be voting on in six weeks?"

"It's not appropriate for me to have a discussion with you outside the presence of the other Board members and interested parties. I would have to share our conversation with the Board and give the other proponents equal time."

Just the thought of adding all that to her already insane schedule was enough to give her hives. Never mind all the additional meetings would be with people. Face to face. She barely managed to suppress a shiver. It was much harder to say no to someone when you had to look them in the eye while you did it.

"That seems a little strict. After all, you already know about your grandfather's plan."

Tess sighed. "I know the general plan, but I don't really know any specifics. We've both been so busy we've only seen each other at Sunday dinner for the last few weeks, and Gran has forbidden football talk in her presence for the time being."

"Really?" He didn't look like he'd be getting off her couch anytime soon.

"She was planning a world cruise and was going to surprise him with the tickets for his birthday next month."

Cade winced and sank even deeper into the couch.

She ignored the urge to crawl over to the couch and lie down. God, she really wanted to curl up on that couch. "Exactly. She's wrangling with the cruise line now about the deposit, trying to see if she can put it on hold for a couple of years. I'd say the duration of her anger will be in direct proportion to the ability to either get her money back or hold two berths on a future cruise." She couldn't help smiling.

"This is important." He stared at her mouth.

"I'm not going to talk about it with you. Just like I'm not talking to Grampa about it, for the next six weeks apparently." She clenched her fist at her side, not wanting to show weakness in front of Cade, and wishing she could stop obsessing about how comfortable the couch was. How comfortable it might be to share it with him. Exhaustion seeped through her bones. He needed to go soon before she made a fool of herself.

"Do you think the other Board members are going to hold themselves to the same standard?" It was clear he had no intention of moving any time sin the near future.

She laughed, even though there was nothing humorous in the situation. "I know they won't."

"Then why —"

She held up a hand. "I've made my opinions clear to my fellow Board members. I can't control what they do or don't do. I can only conduct myself the way I believe we all should. It's my code and it's important to me."

"But — "

It would be lovely if he would shut his beautiful mouth. "If you keep pushing, you're going to have to leave. As it is, I'm going to have to transfer Sonny's post-operative care to my dad and — "

"Oh hell no." Cade sat forward so quickly he startled Tess into leaning back and almost toppling over the back of her chair.

"My dad is an excellent vet." She gripped the arms of the chair.

He stalked over to her and braced his hands on either side of her, caging her in the chair. "I don't care. Every damn person I talked to since the accident told me not to worry because you were taking care of Sonny. If it means we don't say a word about football for six weeks that's fine, but you're the one treating my dog."

He smelled like Doublemint gum and Old Spice. Heat poured off his body as he surrounded her. A curious sensation slid through her at the thought that this man, who'd known her for less than a day, had more faith in her abilities than people who'd known her for her entire life.

She turned one hand over to take his and gave it a squeeze. "We don't have to go that far. I'll keep treating Sonny, but we can't talk about your plan for the football program unless I can give the other proponents equal time. It's only fair." She squeezed his hand again. "Deal?"

"Deal." Cade leaned in close his lips a whisper from hers and a frisson of excitement slid through her body. Her gaze held his and she thought about those tattoos covering his arms and had a sudden urge to lick them. That would definitely be against her code. Right?

Uh oh.

Chapter 4

Cade sat on his back porch with Sam at his side. The big dog clearly missed his brother and had been all but crawling up Cade's ass since he got home. Not that he blamed the dog. The boys were litter mates, and this was the first time they'd ever been apart. Cade put a hand on Sam's head to calm him and took a swig of the beer in his other hand. Ed had recommended the local beer, Mooneys' IPA, it was a damn good microbrew.

"It's all right, boy. Sonny's going to be fine." Even to himself, his voice sounded raspy and unsure.

Sam whined as if he recognized the hesitation in his master's voice. He wasn't going to be better until his brother was back home. Neither of them would be.

"I know the feeling." Cade ruffled his fur. "We sure got more than we bargained for coming here, didn't we?"

He leaned back and closed his eyes, listening to the sounds of the South Carolina night. King's Folly had always been one of his favorite places despite the memories of his last days here. An hour outside of Charleston along the coast, there were awesome beaches and deep woodsy areas where a man could hear himself think. Tonight, his head was filled with thoughts of a gorgeous veterinarian

53

with intelligent hazel eyes and long brown hair that practically begged him to sink his hands into it.

"Wait 'til you meet the vet, Sam. She's going to be taking care of you, too. Way easier to look at than that old guy near the base. If I was a different kind of man you'd see her more often than once a year."

He wasn't sure where that had come from. It wasn't like he'd ever thought of being anything other than what he was. Sam pressed closer to him, as if he sensed his owner's mood.

"Wonder what she's doing now."

He could picture her on that butt ugly coach, which was pretty comfortable considering the damage it probably did to the retinas of anyone who stared at it too long. If he had her alone on that couch he wouldn't be looking at the hideous fabric. All his attention would be on Tess and finding out what she looked like underneath those surprisingly sexy scrubs.

Cade shook his head. He had no business thinking of her as anything but his dog's vet and his boss's granddaughter. She was a woman who had the word "forever" bursting around her like a fireworks display on New Year's Eve, and Maguires weren't built for forever, especially him. Hell, he still wasn't sure he was built to put down roots.

He didn't know of a single marriage that had lasted in his family. His father and grandfather had been silent about the history of the Maguire relationships, while his mother had spent her days drinking and lecturing him on what horrible husbands Maguires make and telling him he'd never be good for a woman.

Hell of a thing to tell a six-year old.

Then his mother had left and only strolled back into his life when she had nowhere else to go. She'd bleed him dry and take off after firing a new round of comments at him about how terrible he would be at commitment. He hadn't seen her since right before he'd enlisted, after he'd learned about her final betrayal. Right here, on the beach in King's Folly.

He shook his head. "We're not going there, Sam."

As much as he wanted to see what the intriguing vet's taste was in lingerie, he couldn't do anything about it. She was Ed's granddaughter for one, and Sonny's heroine for another. Add to that her amazing way with animals and her strong sense of right and wrong. Hell, he just plain liked her and the number of people on that list was limited.

If he and Ed pulled this off, he was going to be in King's Folly permanently, which was something he'd never done. Starting something with Tess would be self-destructive in the extreme. When it ended, and it would end, there would be no escape from the bullshit that came with a breakup. Or the pain he'd inevitably cause her.

Fucking Maguire curse.

His morbid thoughts were broken by the sound of "Born To Rise" by Redlight King, the ringtone for his oldest friend. He pulled his phone out of his back pocket.

"Boomer."

"Hoss." There was a pause. "What's up?"

"Just sitting here on my back porch with Sam."

"Where's Sonny?"

"He's at the vet. Got hit by a car today." Cade could still hear the sound of the truck's squealing tires and Sonny's yelp.

"Shit. Sorry. How's…" Boomer's voice trailed off.

Cade cleared his throat, wishing he could wipe the memory out of his mind. "He's gonna be okay. Got him to a kickass vet in time. She fixed him up."

"She? Hot or snot?" His friend's voice was raspy but filled with humor.

Cade laughed. That had been their code for whether a woman was fair game, courtesy of their buddy Van Helsing.

56

"Hot, but it's a bad idea." It was a monumentally cata-strophic idea.

"Sounds…like a story." Boomer's voice sounded halt-ing.

"All you need to know is she's Coach King's grand-daughter."

"The kid?" There was a beat of silence. "She did it? Be-came a vet?"

How the hell did Boomer know Tess and why did it irri-tate Cade that he did?

"You remember her?"

"Couldn't forget her. Smartest person…I ever met." Boomer stopped talking for a moment. "The only reason I finished school."

That was news to Cade. Boomer was the golden boy in college. "What are you talking about?" There was another pause. It lasted so long Cade wasn't sure Boomer was going to answer.

He sighed. "School was rough for me."

"Really?"

"Yeah. Tess spent…her free time in Coach's office. Got called in one day because of grades. Coach had to take off and she offered to help. Figured…what the fuck? Nothing to lose. She saved my ass."

There was something in Boomer's tone that was bugging Cade, but he couldn't identify it and didn't want to stick his nose into his friend's business. "I had no clue."

"Not like I was going to tell the team." It got quiet on the other end of the line again. Boomer's speech was slower than it had ever been, which was saying something, since the man was a laid back southern boy from Louisiana. "So, other than having the hots for the local vet...how's division one football?" There was something in Boomer's tone that put Cade on alert.

"A challenge. What's going on with you?" Cade braced for his answer.

"Laid up. Got the word today. Medical discharge."

"Shit man, I'm sorry. I know what a bitch that is." He still remembered the day he'd been told his Navy career was over. He'd busted his ass to make the teams. Losing that had cut him, deep. "How bad is it?"

It took a while for Boomer to answer. "Got another...six months of rehab ahead of me. Should be okay by the end of it...more or less."

"What the fuck happened?" Whatever it was, it didn't sound good. He tried to remember the last time he talked to his buddy. It had been awhile.

"Off-duty snafu. Not going to...talk about it...ever."

The finality in Boomer's tone, not to mention his halting speech, set alarm bells off in Cade's brain. Something bad had gone down with his friend. But he'd said he didn't want to talk about it, and Cade wasn't going to push him. If Boomer needed to talk about it, he would.

Maybe there was something he could give the other man to look forward to. "So, here's the deal. The plan I told you about hit a snag."

"What's happened?" Boomer sounded concerned.

"You remember Backup?"

"Gill? Yeah. What's that fucknut doing?" There was a hint of something in Boomer's voice that sounded almost like he liked the guy.

Cade decided he must be hearing things. "His old man is trying to submarine our plan, hire a bunch of bottom tier coaches he can keep under his thumb to take over, using Junior as the front for the plan."

"Seriously? What Senior…knows about football couldn't fill up a postage stamp."

"You're telling me. Now we've got to put together a plan and present it to the Board in six weeks."

"Guess it's the wrong time to ask for a job."

Boomer was one of his oldest friends and Cade could hear the defeat in the man's voice.

"You're already on my shortlist, man. If we push this through, you've got a spot. Pretty sure Ed feels the same way."

Boomer snorted. "Don't know if I'll get used to hearing you call Coach, Ed. How can I help?"

"You focus on finishing your rehab and let Ed and me focus on getting the Board to vote our way."

"Appreciate it, Hoss."

The two men talked for a few more minutes about nothing in particular. He didn't push, and Boomer didn't volunteer any more information about what had caused the injury that led to his discharge. Or what the deal was with his slower speech. If things went their way he'd have to talk to Tess about finding Boomer a dog. God knows Sonny and Sam had helped Cade get his shit together. And keep it together.

Sam pressed against Cade and whined. He wrapped an arm around him and pulled him closer. They were both missing Sonny. Cade finished his beer in three swallows. After another moment, he got up and opened the sliding glass door. Sam was on his heels as he moved into the bedroom. He stripped down to his boxer briefs and crawled into bed, suddenly exhausted. The minute his head hit the pillow he started to drift off to sleep, thoughts of a sexy vet drifted with him into his dreams until he had one last conscious thought.

Shit, I'm in deep trouble.

Tess tried to power through opening the hundreds of e-mails when her phone rang. She recognized her friend Olivia's number and went ahead and answered it. Olivia was a genius like her, and too new to King's Folly and Cormac to be involved in the latest round of drama. Thank God.

"Hey, Liv. What's up?"

"Well, I, um…that is…I…"

Olivia's stuttering was nothing new. Smarter than Tess, and far more introverted, it sometimes took a minute for her to warm up to a conversation, even when she knew the person she was talking to.

"Everything all right?" Her friend hadn't stammered this much since their first conversation.

"I wanted you to hear it from me."

This didn't sound good. "What?"

"I'm putting together a presentation for the Board about what to do with the football program."

Tess glanced around to make sure her office hadn't

shifted into an alternate reality. "Olivia, you don't know a punt from a field goal. How are you going to put together a new football program?"

"I'm not. My proposal is going to be about an alternate use for the funds. You see —"

The sensation of needles pricking the back of her eyes built. The odds were good that she was going to have a perpetual stress headache for the next six weeks. Stress headaches and ulcers. It was enough to produce flashbacks to being a nine-year old senior in high school.

Tess sighed as she tried to remember where she'd stashed the extra strength aspirin. "I'm going to have to stop you, Liv. I just heard about the Board meeting a little while ago and until I get the lay of the land I'm not going to be talking to any of the parties about their proposals."

"But —"

"I don't mean to cut you off, but I've always been adamant about how I handle the Board's business." She tried to be gentle but wasn't in the mood to hold her friend's hand.

"Oh." Olivia sounded disappointed. "I was hoping you could help me."

"Help you, how?"

"Well, you know so much about the university and what we could do with the funds, I just…"

The world really had flipped upside down. "You know it wouldn't be right for me to help you put together your proposal. I'm voting on them. It wouldn't be fair to the other presenters."

"You're right. It's just that I don't really know what I'm doing." She huffed out a breath.

"Then why are you doing it?"

"I was talking to someone who thought it would be a good idea to offer an alternative to the football program. It made so much sense, and with the schedule constraints there didn't seem to be time to see if someone else would take it on."

Something else was up, but Tess was in no shape to dig into it right now. She also couldn't tell Olivia what to do about this ridiculous idea. "The only thing I can tell you is that if you feel passionately about it, follow your instincts. You're brilliant. You've made presentations to university boards before."

"I guess. I'm not sure I'm doing the right thing." Her voice was halting and nervous.

Tess pinched the bridge of her nose. "You know I really want to be here for you, but it's just not right for me to advise you about the proposal."

"Of course, you're absolutely right. My friend thought

you'd be a perfect sounding board, but he wasn't thinking." Olivia's voice got stronger. "I should let you go. I have a date to get ready for."

"A date?" As far as she knew, the other woman hadn't had a date since moving to town. Tess glanced at the clock. "It's kind of late isn't it?"

"We're meeting for drinks." She cleared her throat. "We're not serious, not yet. It's complicated, I guess."

Relationships usually were. "Well, that is something I can talk about."

"Maybe, but I really should be going. I'm sorry if I put you in an awkward position. You're my only real friend. I wouldn't want to jeopardize that."

Tess remembered that feeling of isolation and promised herself she'd spend more time with Olivia once this whole board debacle was over. "You didn't."

"Oh, good." The relief in her friend's voice practically echoed through the phone.

Tess could relate to realizing you hadn't messed up a relationship. "Go have fun on your date."

They said their goodbyes and Tess hung up. She stared at the phone for a minute before glancing at her watch. It was late, and she should get home, but she still had all these e-mails to wade through, and she didn't want to leave

Sonny alone his first night in the clinic.

Her father told her she shouldn't take her cases so personally, but she hated the thought of leaving the big dog in an unfamiliar place without anyone to calm him if he got upset. Then again, she had her own menagerie of cats and dogs at home.

After thinking about it for a few more minutes she decided to text the Trips and ask one of them to go take care of her animals. That way she could stay at the clinic. Tyler and Trip might have dates, but Theo wasn't seeing anyone right now.

She shot them a group text, which was answered by Theo a few seconds later. A few texts back and forth and the care and feeding of her animals was arranged for the evening. It didn't take long to make the rounds of the clinic, confirm all the doors were locked, and turn on the alarm. All she needed to do was check Sonny's vitals one more time. He was doing well and still sleeping soundly.

A quick trip to the breakroom refrigerator and she had her dinner sorted out. Left over Caesar salad from Bella Luna's was probably better than whatever was left in her fridge at home right now. She couldn't avoid the barrage of communications that waited for her anymore. It was time to go back to her office and sift through the rest of the e-mails.

Ice slid down her spine when she noticed that she had several e-mails from both Gills, Junior and Senior. In the twenty-two years she'd known them, nothing good ever came from their communications. Especially when they both wanted to talk to her at the same time.

She reluctantly opened the first e-mail from Junior. He'd always been easier to deal with, obnoxious but not threatening. His message was surprisingly professional. Junior was presenting one of the competing proposals to the Board and he wanted the opportunity to discuss it with her in person. The request was more than reasonable.

Dammit.

So much for her plan to have dinner with each of the proponents before the vote. It had seemed like the fairest thing, giving them each a shot to make their pitch to her before the formal presentation. But that would mean dinner alone with Brian. She'd rather spend an evening with Delilah and Mrs. Milton listening to them snipe at each other.

Her decision was reinforced when she scanned the two e-mails from Senior. Where Junior was professional and up front. Senior's e-mails were vaguely threatening. She closed her eyes and took a deep breath to keep her Caesar salad from making a reappearance. There was only one person she could to talk to about this. Delilah. Lyin' Brian was her no-good-soon-to-be-ex and she would know what he was up to now. Her future hinged on keeping an eye on her almost ex-husband and ex-father-in-law.

She chewed her bottom lip. Given Delilah's painful history with both men, especially Senior, it might not be the best idea to drag her into whatever this was.

Tess rubbed her forehead, wanting desperately to turn off her computer and go to sleep. But, the e-mails would be waiting for her in the morning. Her whole life was built on doing what was expected and accepting more responsibility, not shirking the ones she had. With a sigh she went through the rest of her inbox. She wasn't afraid of the Gills. Much. Memories threatened to re-surface and she slammed the door shut on them. It wasn't the time or the place to get caught up in the past, especially not that part of it.

Three hours later, she dragged herself away from the desk. Exhaustion weighed her down and it felt like she was carrying a sack of rocks on her back. Fortunately, the ugliest couch on the planet was also a great cure for insomnia. Within moments she drifted off to sleep. It was a pleasant surprise to find Cade waiting for her in her dreams.

Chapter 5

The next morning, Cade walked into Ed's office with Sam at his side. It was bare except for a large mahogany desk and a couple of chairs. Back in the day the walls had been covered with pictures of Ed with his players and his family, a trophy case was reserved for all the plaques and awards in the team's honor. Ron probably couldn't let Ed move in until he was officially back on staff.

"Couldn't leave him alone?" The old man got up and gave Sam a pat on the head before shaking Cade's hand.

"He was pretty fried when I got home last night. Thought he would do better with me today." Cade wasn't sure who was more wiped, him or Sam. He wasn't going to admit to anyone that he probably needed Sam more than his dog needed him right now.

"You checked on Sonny, yet?"

Cade nodded. "Talked to Tess this morning. She's going to bring him off the sedation later today. He's stable. No signs of complications. If it keeps up, she'll send him home in a week or so."

"You want to set up to work from your place?"

Cade turned to his mentor. "Really?" His voice sounded scratchy. He was going to have to get used to civilian life, where people could accommodate special circumstances.

68

"My daughter runs the local animal shelter, I have a son-in-law, grandson, and granddaughter who are vets, I know a thing or two about what injured animals need. Besides, with everything up in the air, this isn't officially my office. Ron could catch some heat if we do our planning here."

That made sense. The last thing they wanted was to get on anyone's bad side before they even had a chance to present their plan. "I'd appreciate it. Tess said Sonny needs to take it easy until his cast comes off."

"You two talk about the Board vote or Senior?" Ed, as usual, had an unlit cigar in his hand, which he waved at Cade.

"Nope, and when I tried to push she threatened to transfer Sonny's care to her dad. So, we made a deal, no talk about our plan or the Board vote. I'll bring up Senior if I can."

Ed sighed, then turned and sat in the chair behind his desk. "That girl. Don't get me wrong. She makes me proud every day. Has more strength of character than just about anyone I know. Does the work of ten people. Always has." He rubbed his forehead. "Still, wouldn't mind her being a little less stubborn."

Cade refrained from making a comment about pots and

kettles. "She did mention your wife isn't too happy with you right now."

Ed shrugged. "Been married for sixty years. There's been a time or two my wife wasn't happy with me. We'll survive this one, too."

"You sure?"

"You ever been married?"

"No, I haven't." Marriage hadn't been on his radar at all before coming to King's Folly and it freaked him out a little that it kept coming up now.

"If I recall, your parents split when you were young."

"I was six, my brother was four." The break up was bad enough, but his mother drifting in and out of his life with a promise of finally giving him the relationship with her he wanted was worse. She always yanked the rug out from under him with another nasty comment about how no sane woman would have him.

"Take it from me. You find the right woman, you're gonna piss her off. It's as inevitable as a blitz on fourth down. Just got to work through it."

"I'll have to take your word for it. I don't think I'll have any personal experience to judge by."

Ed didn't say anything more about Cade's completely fictional marriage and he was grateful. It was making him twitch that the topic seemed to be springing up a lot. The fact that whenever it did he thought of Tess was downright surreal.

"I'll make it up to my wife." Ed crossed his arms and leaned back in his chair.

"How?" Cade couldn't keep himself from asking. He usually didn't involve himself in other people's personal lives, but he couldn't contain his curiosity.

"She's got this bucket list."

"Really?" Cade's eyes widened.

Ed looked over his glasses. "Yeah, we old timers can get in on the new fads too."

"I didn't mean…" There was no way he was going to finish that sentence without making it worse.

"I'm sure you didn't mean to call my wife old." Ed smirked.

Heat rushing up Cade's neck. He didn't know how to respond. It had been fourteen years since he'd seen Ed. Back in the day they had one thing to talk about and one thing only. Football. Now, with this crazy plan and the new relationship they were building, it was clear they were going to be talking about other things, but this was new ground. Experience had taught him to tread carefully in unfamiliar territory.

71

"I'm just busting your balls, kid. I didn't handle retirement too well and, after the triplets brought up the idea, she thought putting together a bucket list for the two of us would help."

"Did it?"

Ed shrugged. "Stuck in my craw the way Delano and his crew forced me out. He didn't even have the balls to face me. Got the Board to vote while I was on vacation. I wasn't ready to hang it up yet. Have to admit I was close, but I needed to make sure the program would be safe in his hands before I called it a day."

"Maybe he knew if that was your criteria for retiring, you never would with him as your replacement." Cade leaned against the wall. He was afraid if he sat down he might fall asleep.

Ed leaned back in his chair. "You've got a point. The bastard always struck me as a little shifty."

"Why'd you hire him?" It had shocked the hell out of Cade when he read the article announcing Delano was joining the coaching staff at Cormac.

"Bob wanted to retire. His wife got sick, cancer, and he needed to leave the field and help her with her fight."

Both men grew silent. Cade remembered Coach Moore's wife. She was one of the sweetest women he'd ever met.

Every season she'd knitted hats and gloves for the entire team. He still had the last set she'd made him somewhere.

"He up for this?" Cade thought of how much Coach Moore seemed to rely on his wife for moral support.

"Yes. They put up a hell of a fight. He's had six years to spend time with the family and figure out the road ahead without her. Truth is, Bob and all my guys are looking forward to one more shot at the game."

"I get that." The thought of standing on a field again, listening to the crowd, being part of the sport he'd always loved, had been the push he'd needed to try settling down in one place. It was a plus that his job would involve a fair amount of travel if they got the program off the ground and made it through the first year.

"That's why I knew you were the man for this job."

Cade cocked his head. In all their discussions in the past few weeks, they'd talked about things other than football. But they'd never really talked about why Ed was so adamant that Cade was the only one that could take over as head coach. "Why?"

"You coach this sport long enough, you see all kinds of players. But kids that make it to college level ball play for one of three reasons." He held up a finger. "Their parents, or usually their dad, pushed them." Another finger went up. "They've got some talent and they see a free ride to college and maybe dollar signs waiting for them in the pros." The third finger raised. "They love the game so damn much they can't do anything but play. Doesn't matter where, doesn't matter when. They just want to be able to play."

Cade nodded. He knew guys that fit every one of those descriptions.

"Bet you had lots of pick-up games in the service. Wherever you were stationed."

"You can always find a game when there's down time."

"You gave up the career. You never gave up the game."

Cade shrugged. There didn't seem a point in saying anything. Ed had him pegged. He always had.

"That's what we need to rebuild the program. We need to find coaches that love this game and understand the meaning of the words pride and honor. These sanctions didn't just set the program back because of a cancelled season and fewer scholarships. The reputation of this program is shit now. It's going to take a lot more than winning to rebuild it. We need men who will walk the walk."

"Do they have to be men? A lot of women out there love the sport and know it. Two pro teams have hired female coaches in the last year."

"You have someone in mind?"

"Frankie O'Connell for one."

Ed jolted slightly. "Bull O'Connell's daughter?"

Cade nodded. "She enlisted in the Marines right out of high school, had a full ride to UT but wanted to get out of her dad's shadow. Served four years, two tours. Got out to finish her education. Been playing in a woman's league for six years while she got her degrees. Last couple of months she's been taking care of her old man. Leads her league in rushing. She's a fucking bruiser, runs right through the defensive line, reminds me of Jim Brown. She's an encyclopedia of football and knows every stat from the first game in 1869."

Cade watched Ed as he thought about the suggestion. Truth was, Frankie's was one of the first names that came to mind when this plan had come up. Cade let out a breath he didn't know he'd been holding when he saw Ed add her name to their list. He was even more pleased when they added Boomer's name a few minutes later. Turns out he was on the top of Ed's list too.

They spent the next couple of hours going through the rest of the names they'd come up with and putting together the group that would be his coaching staff when the old timers retired, for good this time. They still had a few names they didn't agree on, but they had a pretty good roster of coaches started. Once they cleared it with Ron, they'd have to get it by the Board.

Tess reached the top of the climbing wall to the sounds of her brothers cheering her on from the ground. Once she made it to the platform she flopped onto her back and extended her arm over the edge to give them a thumbs up. It was still hard to believe she'd let them talk her into this. A while ago, they had asked if they could use some of her land to build a training course for their new obsession. American Ninja Warrior. They knew it would be years before they could audition, but they wanted to be ready.

She had made the mistake of telling them that completing the course was as much about physics and geometry as it was strength and endurance. That had prompted a debate and series of wagers that had led to her being shanghaied into training with them.

The sound of another set of hands clapping startled her and almost made her fall off her perch. She sat up, swinging her legs over the edge of the wall and turned in the direction the new sound had come from. Cade stood there, arms now crossed, watching her. He was wearing dark sunglasses, but, inexplicably, she could tell his gaze was fixed on her and a shiver ran through her body.

Tess stood up and moved to the pole they'd installed at the side of the wall. Tyler had insisted on it, since it was "way cooler" than the stairs she'd designed at the back of the structure. She had to admit, even though they'd installed both, she rarely used the stairs. Her brother was right. As she slid down, she was completely aware of the man watching her intently. At the bottom she turned and ran straight into a muscled chest. When she tilted her head up she noticed his lips were on the verge of a smile. It was a challenge, but she managed to throttle back the urge to lick the corner of his mouth because…well there had to be a reason.

"Earth to Tess." Tyler snickered.

Oh, right, her brothers.

The last thing she wanted to do was fall on her ass in front of anyone, so she stepped back carefully. The level of humiliation she'd experienced in her life was high enough.

"What are you doing here, Cade?" She didn't know he knew where she lived. Of course, King's Folly was a small town and he was a legend to a lot of locals, which meant all he had to do was ask the right person and her entire life story would be spilled like sweet tea.

"Looking for you."

"Well, you would hardly be here looking for Mr. Good-bar."

The blank expression in his face made it clear her joke had fallen flat, which was typical. The Trips had frequently told her funny just wasn't her thing. It was her theory that they didn't understand her references because of their age, but she now had conclusive proof that references to movies from the seventies weren't going to have a wide audience. Or any audience at all.

She cleared her throat. "Why are you looking for me?"

"I went by the clinic to see Sonny and talk to you and you weren't there." There was an accusing tone in his voice.

"It's my afternoon off. Sonny was doing well when I left, and my dad is a great vet." It's not like she lived at the clinic.

"But he's not Sonny's vet."

"When I'm not there, he is."

"That wasn't our deal." His expression seemed like it was carved out of marble.

"Yes, it was."

"No, it wasn't."

"Yes. It was."

"No. It —"

Tess held up her hand, not wanting to spend the rest of the afternoon going back and forth with him like toddlers on a playground.

"I don't work seven days a week. I have other things to do." So many other things to do. "I am the primary vet for Sonny, but my dad is perfectly capable of overseeing his care when I'm not there."

He had a mulish expression on his face, but there was something in his eyes, an expression she'd seen before. Fear. She ran her hand down his bicep, trying to ignore the feel of his warm smooth skin, rock-hard muscle and the tingly sensation rocketing through her body because of them. "He's fine. I promise."

Cade exhaled. "He and Sam are all I have."

"Are they litter mates?"

Cade nodded.

Litter mates who ended up being raised together didn't usually deal well with being apart. "How's he handling the separation?"

"Not great. He's been up my ass since it happened."

Tess chuckled and glanced around. "Is he in your truck?"

"Yeah. Wasn't sure what I was walking into, and I

didn't want him to get into trouble."

"Go get him. He'll be safe on my property. My animals are in the house right now and they're pretty social anyway." A split second later, she watched Cade amble towards the truck to let his dog out. His love for his dogs amped up his sex appeal by at least a million points.

"What's going on between you and Cade?" Tyler asked.

"Nothing."

"He's not just here because you're his dog's vet." Tyler turned to his brothers. The Trips always seemed to communicate with each other without saying a word.

Tess was used to the "trip-speak," as it was called in the family. Ignoring them when they got like this was usually the best option, so she focused on the Bernese Mountain Dog, the mirror image of Sonny, heading straight for her. She smiled at his exuberance and braced for impact. A sharp whistle from Cade had Sam skidding to a halt inches from crashing into her. She dropped to her knees and ran her hands through Sam's fur.

"Who's a good boy?"

Clearly sensing a sucker, Sam dropped and rolled exposing his belly, his tongue lolling out to the side. His actions were rewarded when Tess laughed and reached out to rub his belly. She peered up at Cade who had an odd expression on his face she couldn't identify. When he shifted slightly, her brothers started laughing and she glared at them.

Cade cleared his throat. "You never answered my question. What's all this?" Cade waved his hand at the course they'd been building over the past few years.

Warmth spread up her neck and into her cheeks.

"It's our training course," Trip said.

"Your what?" He studied the course again before resting his gaze on her.

The dark lenses of his glasses didn't block the sensations rolling through her body at the thought of him focusing his attention on her.

She gave Sam one last belly rub then stood up. "You can't tell anyone about this."

"I don't know what this is."

His smile made her insides go wobbly.

"It's an American Ninja Warrior course. The Trips got me into it and we train together. It's kind of our thing." She absently twirled a curl around her finger as she studied the course, trying to imagine what he saw when he looked at it.

"You going to audition for the show?"

She hadn't expected that question. The truth was she

wanted to compete but didn't think she could fit it into anyone else's expectations of her. "Probably not. I don't have the time. I do this mostly to be able to spend time with my little brothers."

Trip started coughing. Tess narrowed her eyes. When Tyler smacked him in the back of the head she knew they were up to something.

"What did you do?"

The three young men gave each other a look then turned back to Tess with the same expression. It was what she called their 'we're sorry, but we're so cute you have to forgive us' face. "We sort of already sent in an application for you for next season."

"You sort of what?" She took a deep breath, then another one.

One, two, three…screw it.

She reached out to grab Tyler, but he danced out of her graspled as did his brothers. She knew she couldn't chase them all and she was so tired she probably wouldn't be able to catch even one of them. "Stop." She held up a hand. "Tell me exactly what you did."

Tyler stepped behind Cade, like that would stop her. "Remember that video you helped us make for our school project?"

82

They'd told her they were recreating an introduction package from the show. She closed her eyes.

I am a sucker.

"Yes."

"We kind of filled out an application for you and the producers requested a video, which we sent."

She took deep breath.

One, two, three, four, five, six, seven, eight, nine, ten.

"Fine. The odds of me being picked are enormous." She saw the look that passed between the three of them. "I got picked?"

Tyler nodded. "We were waiting to find out which qualifying location you were scheduled for. Then we were going to tell you."

"I...you..." She was not used to being at a loss for words. In fact, she couldn't count on one hand the number of times it had happened to her, because it never had. She looked away from her brothers to find Cade still staring at her. He'd raised his sunglasses and they rested on top of his head. His intense green gaze was zeroed in on her.

Her heart beat sped up and there was a tightness in her chest. She couldn't seem to catch her breath.

Oh my God. I'm having a heart attack.

They were going to have to take her to the hospital and

she was wearing a pair of laundry day panties. The ones that lurked at the back of her drawer and only saw the light of day when the rest were in the hamper.

It was difficult to say what would be more humiliating, having to go to the hospital in ancient underwear or going on national television and plummeting into a pool of water on the first obstacle.

Cade was staring at her and his green eyes made her skin feel like she was standing too close to a plasma globe and Mexican jumping beans were going insane in her stomach. In a flash, he was by her side gently pushing her head down between her legs. "Breathe. In. One, two. Out. One, two. Again."

She tried to focus on her breathing, but his strong hand was gently kneading the muscles of her neck and the Mexican jumping beans in her stomach had been joined by a zinging sensation in all kinds of other places she couldn't let herself think about now. Especially not while she was wearing laundry day panties.

"You're okay." He kept rubbing her muscles.

If he kept that up she'd be more than okay. Sam sat up and butted her with his head. She ran her hand through his fur and her breathing started to ease. People might freak her out, but animals always centered her. After a few moments, she calmed. Finally, she straightened up and glared at her brothers.

"Tell me everything."

They filled her in on all the details of 'her' application and the qualifying rounds.

"So, you're telling me I only have eight weeks to prepare for the qualifying rounds of American Ninja Warrior."

"Yeah." Tyler had the grace to look a little contrite, but Theo and Trip were grinning like idiots.

Trip ambled over to her and threw his arm around her shoulders. "Come on, sis. It's going to be two years before we can tryout. Pave the way. Be the first Gallagher to go where no Gallagher has gone before."

"Seriously? You're trying to convince me with a Star Trek reference."

"If the geek fits," Theo mumbled.

Tess gave him what she knew the Trips called 'the stare.' At least Theo had the sense to look apologetic.

"You do realize I won't be ready. I won't qualify for Vegas. I'll get frustrated and never want to do this again. Which will likely lead to me destroying this entire course in a fit of anger. And you won't be able to keep training. You won't make the show, you'll blame me for all your future failures and before you know it, Mom and Dad will have to have separate family Thanksgivings, everyone else will pick your side, so my Thanksgiving will be me, Mom, Dad, Grandma and Grandpa and everyone will blame me for the 'Great Ninja Warrior schism.'" The end of her rant was met with total silence. Sam huffed like he was laughing at her.

"I don't know." Trip cleared his throat. "I'm pretty sure Aunt Ina would pick your side. She thinks we're hooligans."

God, she wanted to be mad at them. "I can't do it."

"You sure as hell won't qualify with that attitude." Cade crossed his arms.

She turned on him, irritation outweighing tingles. "I haven't been training seriously. It's something I can do with my brothers, and the work out beats those stripper aerobics classes Delilah keeps trying to drag me to."

"I saw you go up that wall and I've seen the show. You've got what it takes. All you have to do is focus your training for the next two months and you'll be ready to compete."

"See." Trip high fived his brothers. "We were totally right. You're going to kick ninja warrior ass."

She held up her hand to stop her brothers before their celebration got out of hand. Recent impulsiveness aside, she always needed a plan to move forward and wouldn't agree to anything until she knew what Cade had in mind.

"Focus my training?"

He nodded toward the course. "The ninja warrior courses are almost all grip and upper body strength."

"I disagree."

"How?"

"The courses are a combination of grip and upper body strength, dexterity, endurance, physics, and geometry."

He blinked and looked like she'd just spoken a foreign language. "Physics and geometry?"

It was beyond annoying that people ignored the importance of science to everything. "Have you seen the wedge?"

"Yes."

"You need to maintain a certain angle and apply the right amount of force when you move the bar. All the obstacles involve some level of mathematical calculations relating to force, velocity —"

Cade held up a hand and laughed. "I get it. You can make even American Ninja Warrior boring."

He's laughing at me again.

She gave Sam one last pat and stepped away. "I'll check on Sonny later. You can leave now." She turned and walked off the course, ignoring Cade's shout behind her as she made her way to her house. Once inside, she slid to the floor and rested her head on her knees.

Why can't he be different?

Chapter 6

Cade watched Tess storm into her house. The door slammed a second after she crossed the threshold. He turned to her brothers. "What the hell just happened?"

"You made fun of the brain. You never make fun of the brain." Tyler shook his head.

"I wasn't making fun of her, I was making a joke."

"Yeah, no." Tyler pinched the bridge of his nose. "You can't joke about how boring she can be."

"What?" Cade watched Tess's brothers. "She has to know —"

"No." Tyler crossed his arms.

"American Ninja Warrior isn't about physics —"

"No." Theo crossed his arms.

Cade ran a hand through his hair. "But —"

"No." Trip crossed his arms.

Watching the three young men say and do the exact same thing at almost one second intervals made him grit his teeth.

He gave them his most intimidating stare. "Someone explain this to me."

All three brothers opened their mouths.

Cade held up his hand. "Nope." That got a chuckle from them. "I don't need an explanation in triplicate. One of you

89

tell me why your sister is pissed."

For a moment it seemed like the brothers were communicating without making any sound. Then Tyler, he was pretty sure it was Tyler, nodded at Cade.

"She's not pissed. She's hurt." Tyler rubbed his chest.

Shame burned in his gut. "I didn't mean to hurt her. I was making a joke."

"Yeah, but you have to remember that she's always the smartest person in the room."

Cade rubbed the bridge of his nose. It was moments like this he missed the Navy the most. Getting a straight answer out of an eighteen-year-old recruit was as easy as giving an order. Trying to get the Trips to answer his question was like trying to decipher an alien language.

"I could do without the extra commentary. Why were her feelings hurt and how do I fix it?" That was all he cared about.

"She graduated from college when she was thirteen."

He had a sudden urge to order the three of them to drop and give him one hundred push-ups. "Fuck me. I know that already. Can you three stop with the riddles and answer my question?"

Tyler stepped in front of his brothers. "She has almost no social skills. She's not good with sarcasm and got used to being teased. She thinks if you are making a joke involving her, you're making fun of her."

This he understood. "Ok. That I can work with."

"What do you mean?" Tyler tilted his head.

"I mean I can talk to your sister and work this out."

"Like now?" Theo choked.

Cade regarded the three young men. Tyler had really stepped up when Cade needed him. Their relationship with their sister was admirable, the way they stuck up for her was impressive and it was amusing that his willingness to face their sister so clearly dumbfounded them.

"You can't just go talk to her while she's still pissed. That's nuts." Tyler scoffed.

"I don't let things go and I don't let them fester. You deal with things head on when they come your way. Putting them off doesn't help." If anyone had learned that the hard way, he had. He turned and faced the direction she'd stormed off in.

"It's your funeral," Tyler mumbled from behind him.

Cade ignored the snickers from Tess's brothers and moved toward the house. It was awesome, a typical southern farmhouse with a wrap-around porch. Somehow it looked lived in and untouched at the same time. He walked up the front steps and to the bright red door. After another appreciative look around, he knocked. When there was no answer after a minute or two he knocked again. After waiting a little while, with still no answer, he tried the door. The knob turned in his hand. Unlocked.

He thought about the wisdom of walking into the home of a single woman without an invitation and decided he needed to make this right. The door opened with a creak. Tess didn't seem like the type to come at him with a weapon. But, he'd been wrong about women before, so he stepped inside with caution.

"Tess?" He glanced around the front hall and was again struck by the combination of lived in and ultraclean. "Tess? Your door was open. Can we talk?" He heard a rustling and a thump from upstairs. He'd pushed his luck enough by coming into her house uninvited. Going upstairs was definitely a step too far.

Cade peered up the stairs and did a double take. Sitting at the top, taking up the entire width of the stairs, was the biggest St. Bernard he'd ever seen. He could have guessed that a vet would have at least one pet, but the dog sitting at the top of the stairs, eerily silent, was unexpected. Was there a reason the dog hadn't barked at his intrusion? Testing a theory, he put one foot on the first step.

A low growl rumbled from the top of the stairs, shaking

the pictures on the wall. The beast curled its upper lip, baring a single large tooth. Since it reminded Cade of a tusk, he took a careful step back and the gigantic dog resumed its silent vigil.

"Can you come downstairs? Please?" He called.

With one last glance at Tess's guardian, which he was starting to doubt was a dog, Cade decided to check out the rest of the downstairs while he waited for her. He turned and wondered if he'd stepped into an animal twilight zone. At least six cats and dogs lolled around the downstairs without making a sound.

It was weird enough to walk into a house and have one dog not bark at the intrusion, but there were two more to his right that just stared at him. Well, the little black one, terrier maybe, whose hind legs rested in some kind of cart, stared at him. The beagle was clearly blind.

The cats weren't in much better shape. There was a gray one hanging off the armrest of a couch, literally. Its hind legs rested on top of the armrest and its front paws rested on the floor. It wasn't moving. There was an orange cat missing a paw and a white cat missing an ear. A black and white cat was asleep on the couch one second, freaked out the next like it had been zapped with a jolt of electricity, and then went back to sleep.

It felt like he was back in the sandpit waiting for his next move to trigger an IED. One false step and boom. He had no idea what these animals would take as a sign of aggression. The next time he saw Tess's brothers he was going to give the little bastards hell for not warning him about their sister's pets.

"They won't hurt you." Her lilting voice came from the top of the stairs.

Cade turned toward her. She stood next to the big dog, absently patting his head, like a queen deciding the fate of a minion. He noticed another cat sitting on the St. Bernard's back like a jockey riding a horse.

"I wasn't laughing at you."

"All evidence to the contrary." Tess started down the stairs the behemoth and its companion a step behind her.

"I was making a joke. A bad one it turns out. I wasn't making fun of you. I wouldn't do that." He hoped she believed him.

Tess reached the bottom of the stairs and was quickly surrounded by her menagerie of animals. "You wouldn't be the first person to make fun of me." There was a quiver in her voice.

The obvious pain she'd experienced made him want go back in time and fight all her battles for her. "Give me a list."

Her brows drew together. "A list of what?"

"A list of the people who made fun of you. I'll kick their asses."

The corners of her mouth tilted slightly. "It's an exceptionally long list."

"Really?" He couldn't imagine anyone hurting her, let alone enough people to fill an 'exceptionally long list.'

"I graduated college at the same time I started puberty. What do you think?"

It was not secret that some people mocked what they didn't understand. "I think, collectively, people are assholes. Give me the list. I better start on those ass kickings."

"You can't beat up everyone that has ever made fun of me." She sounded breathless.

"Why not?" The rage that slid through him at the thought of anyone causing her pain dictated he do just that.

"Most of them are women. You wouldn't hit a woman."

"You're right. But I have a couple female friends who owe me some favors." They didn't like bullies any more than he did.

Her grin lit her face, brightening the whole room. It struck him again that being with her was like being bathed in the warmth of the sun.

He tried to ignore the way the sight of her smile made him feel like a conquering hero. That combined with the fact that he was the one who made it happen could lead him into dangerous territory. It's not like he was magically relationship material, and she deserved exactly that.

"Do you want something to drink?" She petted the St. Bernard.

Her sudden change of topic threw him, but he'd come inside with a mission. "Are you going to forgive me?"

"According to you there's nothing to forgive."

"I hurt you. Intentionally or not, that means I said something I shouldn't have. I'm sorry." He wasn't a big fan of bullshit, 'if I upset you' apologies. If you hurt someone you took responsibility for it. All his mother's apologies had been couched in similar non-apology language and he wasn't ever going to play those games.

"You're forgiven. Now, do you want something to drink?"

"Should we get your brothers, tell them it's all clear?"

She looked out the window. "They're playing with Sam right now. I think the four of them will be all right for the moment."

Tess turned and walked to the kitchen, her collection of animals and Cade on her heels.

96

"You have interesting pets." He reached for a safe conversation topic.

"They're freaks, like me."

He didn't want anyone calling her that, even herself. "Don't use that word."

She shrugged. "The definition is one who is markedly unusual or abnormal. Average IQs range from 90 to 109. The last time my IQ was tested I scored 190. By definition, that makes me a freak."

"Definition or no definition. I don't want to hear you call yourself that, because that's not you, and I want you to tell me if anyone else calls you that."

Tess ignored him, opened the refrigerator door and grabbed a pitcher. "Sweet tea?"

"Sure."

She took down two glasses from a cupboard then opened the freezer. When both glasses were filled with ice, she poured the tea and returned the pitcher to the refrigerator. She motioned for Cade to follow her when she went out to the back porch.

The Trips and Sam barely glanced up to watch Cade and Tess take a seat. Her brothers smiled and resumed their game.

Tess stared at the training course. Somehow sensing that

she needed a moment, grateful that she had forgiven him so easily, Cade waited for her to figure out what she wanted to say.

"I'm not sure it's obvious, but I am hyper competitive."

"Really? I wouldn't have guessed." He tried to keep the sarcasm out of his voice.

She glared at him, which only made him want to push her buttons. Somehow, he restrained himself.

"I enjoyed building this course with my brothers, mimicking the obstacles we saw on television, trying to be as accurate as possible. Creating obstacles of our own. Training together has let me get to know them better. I've been taking it seriously, but not competition seriously." She continued to stare at the course.

"You're good. I know it's hard to get past the qualifiers and from watching the show it's clear sometimes a split second can change everything no matter how much you've prepared." He'd always thought the competition could be of fun. Not football fun, but fun.

"Still, there's training so that I can stay in shape and keep up with my little brothers and there's training to be the first woman to finish stage four." She sounded thoughtful and a little scared.

Cade nodded. He understood completely. Whenever he

did something, he wanted to be the best. "So, you train to finish stage four. You've got time."

"I don't know if I can. My schedule is already over loaded. Besides that, the only person in my life who understands that kind of commitment is Grandpa, and I can't ask him to help."

"Because of the vote?"

She shook her head. "No. The problem is that he has his hands full with the football program for the next few weeks. Not only that, Gran finally calmed down about the cruise and picked some new things from her bucket list that are local. If I ask Grampa for help that's going to put a wrench in her new plans. I won't do that to her."

"So, I'll help you." Cade wasn't sure where that offer came from. He'd all but convinced himself to stay away from Tess if it wasn't related to Sonny. The less time he spent with her the less risk of him hurting her. Finding a way to put down roots was one thing. Adding a relationship to the mix was asking for a miracle. Miracles weren't for men like him. But he couldn't seem to stay away from her, and it would let him keep a close eye on her in case the Gills tried something.

"You?"

The disbelief in her voice irritated him. "Don't sound so

incredulous. I do know a thing or two about competition and training."

"I know that." She shrugged. "I just got the sense that you didn't like me very much."

"Why would you think that?" If anything, it was the exact opposite. He liked her too much, which made his offer an eleven on a one to ten scale of stupid things to do.

Tess stared at the Trips and Sam for a moment. "I think we've already established my deficiency in picking up social cues."

"Right. So, here's the deal. We coordinate schedules. Whenever we're not working, you're training. We'll get you ready for competition." And that's all he was going to do. Get her ready to compete.

She turned to face him. "Are you sure?"

Absolutely not.

Looking into her hazel eyes, filled with hope, he wasn't going to say anything like that to her. "Absolutely."

Tess stared at her schedule for the next eight weeks. She wanted to bang her head against the desk, except she knew from experimenting as a little girl that it was ultimately a futile and painful way to vent frustration. Between the clinic and training, her schedule was already full. With the board presentation about the football program coming up, and everyone clamoring for her attention to discuss it, she was overloaded with people requesting 'a few minutes of her time.'

In her experience, having someone take a 'few minutes of her time' usually meant boring her stupid for at least an hour. She chuckled.

"What's got you laughing?" Her heart jumped at the sound of her father's voice. He stood in the doorway, smiling at her. Warmth lit his hazel eyes, so like hers. Technically, hers were like his given that she'd inherited his genetic code for eye color.

"I was thinking about all these people who want to talk to me about the proposals for the football program."

"That made you laugh?" He looked skeptical.

"No. The fact that everyone tells me how quick and easy the meeting will be made me laugh. What's up?" She knew he probably hadn't come to see her for no reason. He rarely did.

That wasn't fair.

Sometimes, he sat with her to enjoy a few minutes of quiet. Since everyone still came to him first, her office was usually the only place he could find that.

"That cruise your grandmother was going to surprise your grandfather with…" Her father wasn't looking her in the eye.

Her stomach did a small flip. "What about it?"

"Your mother and I bought the tickets from her." Finally, he looked directly at her.

Did I hear that right?

"What?"

"She wasn't going to be able to get her deposit back and the cruise line wouldn't bump the reservations to a future date. Your mom told her we'd buy the tickets from her." He sounded excited.

"The cruise is in four weeks." She knew the dates because she'd been with her grandmother when she'd made the arrangements.

"Yes."

"Your planning on leaving the Trips on their own for three months? Over the summer?" They were good kids, but the amount of trouble they could get into, harmless or nor, in a weekend was mindboggling to her.

"About that." He shrugged his shoulders.

"There's also the practice. I mean, I know I handle more of it than you do, but that's so you can teach. Your summer schedule is full." She knew his calendar as well as she knew her own since she handled all the scheduling for the practice and she usually juggled calendar to help him cover his when something came up.

"We know there's a lot to manage. Hopefully we can count on you to help."

"What are we talking about?" She had a sinking feeling that helping her parents would mean cutting back on her training. Letting go of the dream of competing that she'd just let herself acknowledge was important to her.

"We thought the boys could stay with you while we're gone. You have plenty of room at your house, and you've been spending a lot of time with them."

"And?"

"Well, you already manage the practice. My teaching assistant can grade my finals for my spring classes, and I was able to get other professors to cover most of my courses for the summer. You'd only need to cover one seminar. Hopefully, with a little extra effort you can handle that."

"What about the shelter?" Her mom had responsibilities that would need to be covered, too.

"Your mother just hired a full-time assistant. All you'd need to do is check in there from time to time."

"So basically, I am supposed to be you and mom while you're gone, while still being myself at the same time." This was ridiculous. "Last time I checked, you had six other adult children." It was long past time for one of them to step up.

"Well —"

Tess held up her hand. She knew what he was going to say and didn't want to hear it again. Your siblings live so far away, they have such busy lives. Blah, blah, blah. She'd never regret her decision to stay local. It would be nice if she didn't always feel like she was punished for it.

She sighed, wishing she had time for a nap. "We'll figure it out. I'm sure gran is happier knowing that the tickets aren't going to waste, and you and mom haven't taken a vacation without any kids tagging along in a few decades." She'd handle the added workload. Like she always did.

"Thank you, darlin'. We knew we could count on you." He kissed her on the cheek then turned and left her office.

Her schedule taunted her. The phrase 'I feel like my head might explode' had always baffled her. Until now. She moved to her office door and closed it. There was no time for a complete meltdown since she had surgery in fifteen minutes. The pillow on her couch beckoned her to grab it, press her face into it and scream. So, she did. And kept on screaming until a knock on the door interrupted her.

With the pillow still grasped in her hand, she opened

the door to find Cade waiting there.

"What was that noise?" He looked from her face to the pillow in her hand.

"Me losing what was left of my mind." Tess stepped back and waved him inside.

Cade moved into the office and closed the door behind him. He glanced at the pillow in her hand. "I came by to see Sonny and talk about your training."

Tess shook her head. "No point. I'm pulling out of the competition."

He blinked. "Why?"

"My schedule is already unmanageable. In a month it will be impossible."

"What happens in a month?"

"My parents are taking the bucket list cruise. Which means the Trips will be living with me, I'll be running the practice solo, teaching my dad's summer seminar and keeping an eye on my mom's animal shelter. I won't have time for training. It was a silly idea anyway." It didn't matter that she really wanted to do it. Pulling out of the competition was the responsible thing to do.

"I don't suppose you can tell your dad no."

Punching him might be an adrenaline rush. But it was

wrong. Instead she grunted. He didn't understand the dynamics in her family and she didn't have all day to explain them. She checked her watch. Ten minutes until surgery.

"I'll take that as a no. Don't you have six other brothers and sisters?"

"Yes, but none of them are local and we can't ask them for help." It wasn't that complicated. Her siblings got to live their lives secure in the knowledge that Tess would handle the family stuff at home because she was the one who'd stayed.

"Why not?"

Tess got up. "I don't have time to explain."

"How about telling your dad about —"

She shook her head. "No. That won't work."

"What about —"

"No."

Cade held up a hand. "You're not quitting."

"You can't tell me what to do." She'd been making her own decisions since she was a little girl.

"True. You're still not quitting." He crossed his arms.

Why was he being so difficult? "I have to."

"No. You don't. I don't know why you can't tell your parents about the competition, or why you can't ask your other siblings for help. I do know how excited you and your younger brothers are about this competition. So, we'll figure it out. Tonight, Sam and I are coming to your house tonight. I'll bring dinner and we'll figure it out. Between the two of us and the Trips, we can make it work."

With that he left, leaving Tess wondering if this is what it was like to have someone completely on her side.

Chapter 7

Cade got off the phone and smiled at Ed. "Deke's in. He was ready to put in his papers. He has a couple of months before his discharge comes through and he says he might have some personal stuff to resolve after that, but he'll be here before the end of the year."

Ed nodded and went to the board they'd set up to track their progress.

"We still need to get confirmation from Frankie and we need a strength coach."

"I'm waiting to hear back from her. There are a lot of moving parts for her and she's making sure she can put them all in place. As for strength coach, I was thinking about Nick Jacobs."

"Really?"

Cade had expected the skepticism. He knew of all his suggestions, Nick would be the toughest sell. It didn't take long for Ed to voice his concerns.

"We're trying to clean up the program. Not sure how the board is going to react to a felon being on our shortlist."

"Technically, he's not a felon. He was a minor and his record was expunged when he completed the terms of his deal." Cade wished Nick would tell people the whole story.

"He drove drunk and killed a kid."

"Nick wasn't drunk that night. Tests showed no alcohol in his blood stream. There's more to the story, which is his to tell. For a lot of reasons that had nothing to do with the actual accident, Nick was facing serious time. The judge gave him a choice, military or juvie then prison. He chose military. I served with him. There's no one I'd rather have at my back in a fight and not many who love this sport more than he does. Hell, you recruited him before he chose 'Bama. I guarantee, you give him this shot he's going to do us all proud."

He watched Ed expectantly. This was the last position they needed to fill, and Cade wanted Nick. His friend wouldn't just do a great job, he would be able to lead by example. No one deserved a second chance more than him.

"Set up a call. If I like what he has to say, we'll bring him in, but we won't mention it before the Board meeting. I don't want to give the Gills any ammunition. Jacobs would be a controversial choice. I also need to run it by Ron since Nick would eventually be running the strength and conditioning programs for all the university's sports programs."

"But —"

Ed held up a hand. "We are pushing some boundaries here and I am all for pushing them for the right people. But we need to be careful how much we present to the Board.

We don't want to give them any reason to vote against us."

"He's one of the most honorable men I know."

"I get that. I'm leaning towards bringing him in, but we have to watch out for the Gills. They've only gotten worse in the last fifteen years. Especially Senior. We give him anything to target before the vote, he'll use it, and he'll play dirty while he does."

"What the hell is their problem?" He'd been going over all his memories of Backup in the last couple of days and hadn't come up with any encounters that would explain the man's apparent hostility for Cade.

"How much time you got?" Ed looked exhausted.

"Probably not enough, so why don't you give me the highlights?"

Ed was silent for a moment, which only made Cade nervous. His mentor wasn't a man who chose his words with care. The fact that he was doing it now didn't bode well.

"What don't you want to tell me?"

"There's a lot you hold back from your players. The top priority you have as a coach is to get a bunch of individuals to think and play as a team. You let too much show and you can destroy that dynamic."

"Meaning?"

110

"Meaning I never told you that I had no choice about putting Gill on the team and his father tried to have me fired when I recruited you and gave you the starting spot at quarterback."

Cade shifted in his seat. It felt like a piece of lead had taken up residence in his gut.

"Gill was a good player, but he had issues we couldn't help him with. Those issues made him a loose cannon. Unreliable on the field."

Cade blinked. He'd never had any clue his signing with the Knights had caused Ed any problems.

"I'm sorry —"

Ed stood and paced the room. "Nothing to be sorry for. I recruited you because you were the best high school quarterback on any team that year. Cormac needed you. That's also the reason I kept my job. The Board wasn't going to fire me because I brought in one of the most talented players in the country. They were used to Senior's bullshit."

"Why didn't he send Backup somewhere else?"

"Nowhere else to send him. Kid was a problem from the day the doctor smacked his ass in the delivery room. With his record and grades, he only made it into Cormac because of his daddy's money and position in the community. Senior started lobbying for his seat on the Board of Trustees

111

about a minute after they voted to let me keep my job after recruiting you."

Cade almost felt sorry for Backup. "I had no idea."

"You weren't supposed to. Point is that Senior got used to being able to use his money and position to make Junior top dog, wherever he was. The only place that didn't work was this team. He's had a hard on for me ever since."

"Add Backup's hard on for me and —"

"We've got a pair of Gills gunning for us. Senior's meaner than Junior, but that's not saying much. What they've really got going for them is that neither of them has ever seen a line they wouldn't at least think of crossing. That makes them unpredictable and dangerous."

"Gotta say, I'm not loving this part of the job." He'd never been a fan of playing politics and he wasn't a fan of fighting dirty.

"Neither do I. But it's a necessary evil. You're dealing with a multi-million-dollar program, everyone's going to have something to say. Best advice I can give you is to always keep a finger on the pulse. That'll help you stay ahead of the worst of it. Truth is, once the vote is done, Tess will be our best friend on the Board."

Cade smiled. "Yeah, she's a no bullshit kind of girl."

"Something you want to tell me?" Ed crossed his arms

112

and studied Cade.

A prickle of alarm tingled at the back of Cade's neck. It was the feeling he got in combat when he knew his next step could go very, very wrong. He had zero experience dealing with the families of women he was interested in, but even he knew you didn't admit to a woman's grandfather that you wanted to bang her.

"We've spent some time together because of Sonny. Strikes me as a straight shooter. Her wanting to make sure all the plans are treated fairly says a lot about her, too."

"Yeah." Ed seemed to accept that explanation for Cade's admiration.

"Seems to me we've got two fronts were dealing with in this war." The more he found out about their opposition, the more grateful he was for his combat experience.

"Guess we are at that."

Cade held up a finger. "First, we've got to plan the kind of program that every university dreams of, make it irresistible to anyone not in Gill's pocket."

"I think we're on the way." Ed studied their board.

Cade agreed. He held up second finger. "Next, we need to stay a step ahead of the Gills the whole way."

"Senior considers himself a king in this town. This vote goes our way, we're going to have to stay a step ahead of him for the duration."

So much for their troubles ending with the vote. Cade couldn't disagree with his mentor. Backup had nipped at his ankles the whole four years they'd been at the university together. Sounds like he would keep that up for the foreseeable future.

Cade couldn't say he relished the idea of having to deal with the man or his father long term, but he wasn't going to let them get away with anything. If his second chance at football meant having to deal with Backup, he'd do it. After all, he'd bested him all through college. Nothing he'd seen or heard could convince him he wouldn't do it again.

A few days later, Tess stared into the open refrigerator. The Trips and Cade had left a little while ago. After one of the most grueling workouts of her life, all she'd wanted was a shower. She'd stood under the steaming spray for what felt like hours, hoping to ease the aches in her muscles. Instead, the sting of the water let her know that more aches and pains were on the horizon.

Now dressed in gray sweat shorts and an old flannel shirt she'd stolen from her grandfather years ago, she knew she needed to eat. She couldn't afford another ulcer, especially not now.

Unfortunately, she hadn't put grocery shopping anywhere on her list of things to do when she had worked out a schedule with Cade. The contents of her refrigerator included a can of diet soda, six grapes and a...well she doubted whatever it was had been that shade of green when she bought it.

She jumped at the sound of a knock on the front door. The pathetic display on her refrigerator shelves mocked her as she checked the clock on the wall. Time for another epic Chinese versus pizza debate.

She opened the front door and saw Cade standing there with a large pizza box balanced in one hand and a six pack of beer in the other. Sam by his side.

"Pepperoni, half mushroom, half sausage."

Pizza it is.

"Pepperoni and mushroom is my favorite." Her brain felt like it was on a five second time delay.

"Your brothers told me. That half is for you. The other one is mine." He held up the beer. "Pale ale from Mooney's."

"My brothers are getting chatty." The Trips weren't known for their ability to open up to anyone but each other.

Their oversharing with Cade probably meant something, but right now all Tess could focus on was the smell of the pizza.

She stepped back, indicating he should come in. Sam immediately took her up on the offer and dashed off to visit with her animal crew. Cade followed her into the kitchen and set the pizza box on the counter while she got plates and napkins. Tess took the six pack from him. Before putting it in the refrigerator, she grabbed a beer for each of them.

"I admit I peeked inside your fridge earlier. Pretty bare, Gallagher."

Was she supposed to be embarrassed? "I forgot to put grocery shopping on the list." These days, if it wasn't on the list, it didn't get done. "God knows when I'll have time to add it."

"Give your list to me. I'll get your groceries tomorrow before we work out and bring them to you." He piled three pieces of pizza on a plate and went to the table.

"You don't have to do that." She stood at the counter, trying to keep some distance between them while her brain caught up with the situation. Was it his offer or just his presence that made her nervous?

He shrugged. "I promised I'd help you, so let me help."

"You promised to help me with training. I'm a grown woman with an above average IQ. I can take care of myself." She always had.

"No doubt. Problem is you can't say no to anything. I know this board vote —" he held up a hand when she opened her mouth to interrupt him. "We're not talking about it. I've seen that monstrosity you call a schedule. It's clear you need help and you won't ask anyone for it. So, consider me your trainer and occasional assistant for the next seven weeks."

"I can't possibly —"

"Yes, you can. My schedule has some flexibility until the Board vote." He put his hands up as if in surrender. "Still not talking about it. Ed and I have some work to do, but we meet in the mornings mostly. Other than that, I'm a man of leisure for the first time in my life."

"How's that going for you?" She smirked.

"I hate it. If you think about it, you'll be the one doing me a favor. Helping you with your insane schedule will give me something to do for the next few weeks. Hopefully, by the time we're done with your training, I'll have an insane schedule of my own."

She watched him, unsure what to do or say next. Offers to help her were few and far between. They always had

been. Everyone usually mistook her high IQ for self-suffi-
ciency. Even Charlie, her staunchest defender, had somehow decided that Tess only needed help with social interactions. Taking care of herself, and helping to take care of
everyone else, had become such a part of her routine that
she had stopped asking for help years ago.

Cade bounced his knee, his boot tapped on the hardwood floor. "You're being too quiet."

"I'm not used to people helping me." It was a heady
feeling. Having someone openly want to take care of her.

"I wouldn't have guessed."

She knew that tone. "That's sarcasm, right? I assume my
talkative little brothers told you I'm not always good with
that."

"You seem to be getting a handle on it." He smiled.

A fluttery sensation began in her belly at the sight of his
grin. "You've met the Trips. Understanding sarcasm is a
matter of survival around them."

Cade chuckled. "They are a trio of smart asses."

She nodded. "I've enjoyed getting closer to them in the
last few years, but sometimes it seems like they're aliens
sent here to drive me insane."

His chuckle turned to a full-throated laugh. The flutters
erupted into a windstorm and a warmth that spread

through her body. She cleared her throat.

"The pizza smells good." She put a couple of pizza slices on her own plate. "Do you want to eat in here?"

He blinked. "What are my options? You've never given me the tour of your house."

"We can eat in here, in the dining room or on the porch." The porch was her favorite part of the house.

"Kind of muggy out tonight."

"It's enclosed."

"Porch it is. Lead the way." He stood up from the table.

Tess led him through the archway to the most peaceful place she knew. It was the back half of the wrap around porch, which she had enclosed after she inherited the farmhouse from her paternal grandparents. She'd had floor to ceiling windows and sliding glass doors built so that the back porch could be usable year-round. It could be completely open to the elements on a beautiful spring day or closed off and toasty during a frigid winter snow. She could watch nature in perfect comfort, no matter what the weather.

They settled in and ate their pizza looking out over the view. Once they'd finished, Cade set down his plate and took a swig of his beer.

"So, how do you feel after your first full workout?"

"Ask me tomorrow." The full effect of the workout was probably still a few hours away.

"I'm asking now."

His tone made her sit up a little straighter. She was already starting to recognize his 'coach voice.' "I'm sore, tired. It's like I've never completed the course before today."

Cade nodded. "That's good. The whole point of pushing yourself harder is to build your endurance. I've watched that show. Half the competitors gas out way before they make it to the last obstacle and they don't have anything left to help them to the finish."

She knew he was right. Competitors frequently lost their grip in the late stages of the course due to fatigue. "That makes sense."

"And we're not just training you to qualify for Vegas, we're training you to make it to stage four in Vegas. That means you're going to have to be ready for longer, timed courses."

"When are you going to start timing me?" It was hard to focus on the conversation when he was this close to her.

"When I think you're ready." His tone was full of confidence.

Her hands clenched and unclenched. "When will that

be?"

"When I say so."

She was too tired for a conversation that seemed better suited for a firing range. "I'm not sure you understand. I am asking you for your plan."

"I understood perfectly." His gaze flicked upward. "My IQ may not be in the stratosphere like yours, but it's in the triple digits."

Tess shifted in her seat. "That's not what I meant."

"That's how it sounded." He clenched his jaw and the muscles in his throat clenched.

She rubbed her forehead. This back and forth was giving her a headache and she was suddenly more exhausted than she'd ever been before. "Maybe this won't work." Maybe she just wasn't strong enough for this. For him.

"Didn't take you for a quitter."

"I don't think our personalities are compatible." The flutters in her belly had turned to rocks, even as her skin tingled because of his nearness.

"Bullshit." He crossed his arms.

She crossed her arms, deliberately mirroring his action. "I beg your pardon?"

"Beg all you want. It's still bullshit."

"You have no idea what you're talking about." As difficult as it was to follow his logic, she could still tell when he was trying to push her buttons.

"You're scared."

Tess looked down at her clenched hands. "I don't think so." This wasn't what fear usually felt like.

"I do. You don't want to do anything that will put you in the spotlight. It's like the years you spent as the odd one out because of your giant brain have pushed you completely in the other direction, trying to disappear. You've trained yourself to not go after what you want most."

"Thank you, Dr. Freud."

"Is this where I'm supposed to make a dick joke?"

Tess sat back. She hated when conversations were so non-linear. It made it hard to for her to respond and that frustrated her. She stood up and paced toward the window, looking out into the night.

"I don't know what you want from me."

She heard a rustling noise behind her, which she supposed was him. After a few moments of silence, she could sense him behind her. His body was almost touching hers and the blast of warmth from him was almost enough to ease her aching muscles. An answering heat rose in her own body and she was tempted to turn around to see what would happen. Her legs were weak. Whether it was from his closeness or her workout, she couldn't tell.

"I'm trying to help you. I'm training you like I would any other athlete."

"I'm a veterinarian not an athlete." Her monotone was an attempt to make the conversation less personal.

He snorted. "Sure thing, Jules."

She whipped around, not caring, much, that her quick movements brought her chest in contact with his. His taut muscles rippled at the contact. Her heart pounded so loud she was sure that he could hear it.

"Jules?"

"Well, Bones would have been too obvious. You're not an anthropologist and since the 'I'm a doctor not a what-ever' thing actually started in Twenty Thousand Leagues Under the Sea, Jules seems appropriate."

She laughed. The heat remained but it was joined by a warmth in her heart that she'd never experienced before Cade.

"You know Star Trek and Jules Verne?" It was a lethally sexy combination.

"Television's not so easy to come by in the sandbox, so reading kills some time. As for Star Trek, I've been known to watch an episode or two."

"Are you a fan of just the prime universe or the alternate too?"

"What the hell's the prime universe?"

"So, a trek fan, not a trekker." The geek speak came out of her mouth and she couldn't seem to stop it.

"Again, what's the prime universe?"

"It's the original timeline from the original series. The alternate universe originated with the JJ Abrams reboot."

"I think I understood what you just said, but I don't know if I want to be sure." He smiled, pressing closer to her.

"Well —" Before she could launch into a soliloquy on the pros and cons of the prime versus the alternate universe he leaned down and kissed her.

Her mind went blank as his warm lips pressed against hers, firm and demanding. His tongue brushed along the seam of her mouth seeking entry. Her lips parted, as she pressed closer to his body, needing something she couldn't identify.

Strong arms closed around her, gentle and secure. He pulled her even tighter to him, pressing every inch of her front against his. She'd never felt this consumed, this wanted.

She pressed closer to him, lost in the embrace. It felt like they were both learning each other's taste and feel. Her hands ran up his arms and she was entranced by the steely strength of his muscles and the velvety warmth of his skin. Could she stay here forever? In this moment where there were no plans, no votes, no demands. Only strength and safety and feeling.

Reality returned when his hand slid under her shirt and moved up. Reluctantly, she broke away, surprised she could as fused as she'd felt to him seconds before.

"What was that?" She'd never, until this moment had her mind go blank.

"You're the one with the IQ in the stratosphere. Don't tell me you can't recognize a kiss when you feel it." His cocky grin was equal parts appealing and annoying.

"That was more than a kiss." She'd been kissed before. This was definitely something else. Was she ready for something else? With him?

"Doesn't have to be." He peered over her shoulder.

"Everything has to be what it is." She wasn't sure she would be able to 'just kiss' him.

He focused on her and cleared his throat. "Let's not say what it is right now."

"I don't think —"

He brushed a curl behind her ear. "You think too

much."

"That shouldn't be a bad thing." It helped to be prepared. To be aware of what was happening.

"Talking too much can be."

"But that's not what you said."

Cade stepped back running a hand through his hair. "I think we've gotten way off track and should call it a night. I'll see you tomorrow."

With that, Cade whistled for Sam and was out the door like he'd been zapped with a cattle prod, leaving Tess to wonder what had happened and what was she going to do about it.

Better yet. When was it going to happen again?

Chapter 8

Cade berated himself the entire way home. Sam occasionally whined as if to try and let his master off the hook, but Cade knew he'd really stepped in it. He had no business going *there* with anyone, much less Tess. She was Ed's granddaughter, one of the votes they needed for their plan and a well-respected member of the community.

Add to that the fact that he just plain liked her, and he needed to keep his distance. The problem was that he couldn't.

Setting aside his promise that he'd help her with her training and her life in general for the next seven weeks, he didn't think he would be able to stay away from her. In his entire life he'd never met anyone who took so much on for so many people without a single thought for themselves.

How was he supposed to keep his distance from someone who was funny, smart, sexy, and gorgeous, and who so obviously needed someone to have her back?

Everything he'd ever heard any of his buddies say they were looking for in a woman rolled up into an unbelievable package. When she had so earnestly started to explain the differences in the trek universes to him, he had been compelled to kiss her. Having her in his arms was fucking paradise.

Now he was left with nothing but the memory of the feel and taste of her, and a hard on that could last forever. His rational side said he needed to go to the nearest bar and find a jersey chaser to scratch the itch. Except Tess wasn't an itch, and he had a feeling that no one else could really help him with his current problem.

Besides, King's Folly was still a small town, the odds of a story getting back to Tess were high. Even worse, it would go through a round of telephone or two. By the time Tess heard it there would likely be a threesome or a gang bang.

He may not be a forever after kind of guy, but he wasn't a total dick either. There was no way he could live with himself if his actions hurt her.

More disturbing than the fact that he wouldn't go to a bar just to get laid because it might get back to her, was that he didn't really want to. Right now, he would rather use his hand and think of Tess than fuck some random woman to take the edge off. He was so screwed.

The next morning, Cade and Ed were going through their plans for the team.

"We still have to deal with the problem of workouts. The sanctions say we can't use university training facilities until after next football season, not if the coaching staff is going to be there. The strength coach can work around other team schedules and run them through their conditioning in the weight room, but we can't have a full workout with the coaches and the team on university property until after the National Championship."

"So, January. Why so harsh? The last time they brought down the hammer, the team could still use all the facilities and run practices. They just cancelled a season and limited scholarships."

"Delano was more of an asshole than most." Ed looked embarrassed.

"Why the hell did you hire him?" Cade had known Delano briefly back in college. They'd played against each other and were billed as one of the great rivalries at quarterback. Delano hadn't taken it well when he'd lost the Heisman to Cade.

"He makes a good first impression."

"And a shitty one every time after." Cade had a scar on his right arm from their second encounter, which had taken place after the Cormac Knights had beaten Delano's team.

"You ever meet him off the field?" Ed must have heard something in Cade's tone.

"Couple of times. Once was too much." The bastard wasn't a good opponent in any capacity.

"He was a top quarterback. Could have gone pro if he hadn't blown out his knee." Ed stuck the ever-present cigar in his mouth.

Cade shook his head. "Even if he'd been drafted he would have been cut from the roster. Probably, before the regular season. If he was lucky he would have been on a practice squad."

"He had a hell of an arm. Accurate too." Ed scoffed. "Not record setting. But solid."

If anyone knew that wasn't all it took to be a quarterback, it was Cade. "He was a selfish player. Hung in the pocket forcing his line to work overtime. Played his own game to pump up his stats and screwed the running game. That last play, where he blew his knee, if he'd thrown to the wide receiver that was open just past the line of scrimmage, instead of waiting for the running back to get open in the end zone, he'd never have taken the hit. He blew his knee because he wanted the touchdown pass in his stats."

"And you think he wouldn't have played pro even if he hadn't blown his knee." Ed chewed on the cigar.

"Coaches don't mind prima donnas if they have the talent to back the flash. Delano was all attitude no gratitude. He wouldn't have fit in any of the pro programs looking for a quarterback that year. He might have made it to training camp, but I doubt he would have gotten the kind of offer he was looking for."

Ed leaned back and smiled. "This is the smartest thing I've ever done."

"What?" Tess must have gotten her ability to make random comments from her grandfather.

"Bringing you on board. It took me years to figure out what kind of player, what kind of man Delano was. You had him pegged just by watching him play."

"You can figure out everything you need to know about a person by watching them train or compete for something." Cade thought of Tess. She was a bruiser on the course, hyper-focused, relentless. Throw in her giant brain, and she was a force of nature.

"Earth to Cade."

Cade shook his head. "Sorry, drifted for a while."

"Must have been some minute."

Heat rose up his neck. He needed to change the subject. It was a bad idea for Ed to find out how distracting his granddaughter was. "Tess's place."

"What about it?"

"She's got a pretty amazing obstacle course out back, plus the field behind her house. We could use it for workouts."

131

"When were you over at her house?" Ed's tone was part curiosity part over-protective

"I went by to talk about Sonny. She had the afternoon off and wasn't at the clinic. I kind of freaked."

Ed chuckled. "You and those dogs. Can't say I blame you. Our pets have always been part of the family."

"Yeah." Cade cleared his throat. "So, anyway. She's got a hell of an obstacle course behind her house and lots of room for —"

"Why does she have an obstacle course behind her house?"

The minute he heard Ed's question, Cade realized his mistake. Only the Trips knew about her hobby and training. Since she didn't want to share with the rest of her family yet, Cade had to think fast.

"Well, she's been spending more time with the triplets, trying to get to know them better. I think she built it with them as something to do that would interest them."

"Must have bored her silly. Tess isn't really the athletic type."

Cade wanted to correct Ed but couldn't without breaking Tess's confidence completely. He wished she would come out and let her family know about her training and the competition, but it wasn't his secret to tell, so he played dumb.

"I'm going by the clinic later to see Sonny. I could see if she would be willing to let us use her back field and obstacle course for some training next season. We won't have as many players as we usually do, so —"

"I want to check it out before we firm up the plan. I'll give her a call, see if I can go by her house later today to check it out."

Cade nodded. He would have to make sure he talked to Tess before her grandfather did, so he could explain how he let the cat out of the bag.

And to try and keep her from kicking my ass.

Tess eased herself down into the chair in her office. Every muscle in her body ached and she wondered, for what felt like the billionth time, if this was really a good idea. She'd thought she was in shape. One training session with Cade had her doubting if she understood what being in shape truly meant.

Before last night she would have been confident in her ability to identify every muscle in the human body. Now, she was wondering if there were muscles she had never learned about. The aches in her body suggested she'd discovered some new ones.

She closed her eyes and focused on her breathing, that helped. Of course, it didn't help with the memories of that kiss. It made no logical sense, but she swore she could still feel his lips against hers. Why did it feel like she had been waiting all her life for Cade Maguire to kiss her? Now that he had, she had no idea what to do next. It couldn't go anywhere.

Could it?

Her reverie was interrupted by the sound of her office door banging open. She slowly turned her head and saw Delilah and Charlie standing there, shoulder to shoulder, clearly united for some purpose. The thought of them being united for anything was more than a little frightening.

"All right. What the hell is going on with you?"

"What she means to say…" Charlie gave Delilah a side-eye.

"What I mean to say," Delilah side-eyed Charlie right back, "is what the hell is going on with you?"

Charlie sat down across from Tess. "The queen of tact is worried. You're acting weird."

"She's acting like a spaz." Delilah flopped down next to Charlie, who sneered in return at getting jostled.

"Can you not, for one second of your life, act like an ass-hole? Please? My friend is clearly going through something and she needs me." Charlie tried to push Delilah off the couch.

"Our friend needs us." Delilah made it clear she wasn't going anywhere.

Tess tuned out their bickering, opting to focus on her breathing and trying to forget the kiss. The way Cade ran out made it clear he wasn't interested in anything more, and the last thing she should do right now was add a relationship with him to the insanity that was her life. The relationships she already had were more than she could handle most days.

Charlie snapped her fingers. "Earth to Tess."

"Seriously, what the hell is going on?" Delilah wasn't going to be put off.

"Nothing."

"Tell me another one."

"Delilah…" Tess searched for the words to head this conversation off before it went somewhere she didn't want it to go.

"Don't try to spin it. Something is going on with you. The rest of these yahoos may let you get away with this solo genius doesn't need anyone act you've got going, but I won't."

"Who are you calling a yahoo?" Charlie jumped into the conversation.

Delilah pointed at her. "You. I'm calling you a yahoo."

"I've been her friend since we were babies."

"Good for you. If you're such good friends, tell me what's going on with her."

"Well —"

"You can't. You can't tell me what's going on with her, because you and everyone else let her live in her safe bubble of responsibility."

"Hey, when you were torturing her in front of the entire town, I was the one standing by her side."

"Well let's give you a medal. You stuck up for your friend against a bully. What else?"

"What do you mean what else?"

"I mean, Tess and I got over our past and have been friends for a year now and near as I can tell everyone goes to her with all their problems, including me, and she helps. She gave me a job when I needed the extra money. She picks up the slack for her father every day of the week and twice on Sundays. She hangs out with her brothers at their convenience. She's there for you to cry to when the loser of the week steals your latest set of Walmart pillows. And there's a whole other list of things she does, which I can't go into because it's so freaking boring I might die. Who, including me, has been there for her?"

Tess sat there thinking of Delilah's accurate, if somewhat obnoxious, speech. Cade had said something similar when she had been talking about quitting the competition.

Do I take on too much?

"Tess." The sound of Charlie's voice snapped her back to the present.

"What?" She pressed her lips together and leaned her head back on the couch.

"What is going on with you?"

Tess checked her watch. There was definitely not enough time for this conversation. "I have an appointment in five minutes."

They exchanged a look before glancing back at her.

"You guys want to come over for dinner tonight?" Tess wasn't sure where the impulsive decision had come from, but the minute she said it she knew she was moving in the right direction.

"At your house?"

The way Charlie stressed the word house made Tess cringe. Had she really been such a scrooge with herself?

"Yes, my house. I'll be done with training around 7:00

137

so you can come by around 7:30. We can order —"

"Hold on." Delilah held up her hand. "Training?"

"That's one of the things I need to tell you about."

Delilah and Charlie stared at each other. When Charlie finally spoke, she sounded hurt. "Why haven't you talked to me before now?"

"I haven't talked to anyone but Cade and the Trips until now."

"Why them and not me? Your very best friend in the entire world?"

"Or me?" Delilah chimed in. "Your other very best friend in the world." She gave Charlie a pointed look.

"You can't force yourself into her life and call yourself her best friend after you spent years being a total bitch to her. That's not how best friends work."

"Really? How do best friends work oh wise one who doesn't know diddly squat about her best friend's life." Delilah made air quotes when she said the words 'best friend's.'

"Enough." Tess sat forward and instantly regretted the speed of the motion. "We can talk about this later." She rose slowly, trying to stretch a little as she did. She left her office listening to the sounds of her friends' bickering, again.

Why am I friends with such total pains in my ass?

138

Chapter 9

Cade pulled up to Tess's house later that afternoon. He'd tried to let her know he was bringing company, but she had been impossible to reach all day. She stood on the front porch, dressed for a workout. Even from a distance he could see her eyes widen in surprise when she saw her grandfather's truck pull up in her driveway.

As Cade got out of his truck, before he could close the door and go around to the other side, Sam wiggled his way out of the driver's side door and bounded towards the front porch and Tess. He tried his best to hide that he was probably as excited as his dog was to see her.

Ed and the Trips were right behind him as he walked toward Tess.

"I've been trying to get a hold of you all day."

"I know. I had some issues today. I thought I'd see you when you came in to see Sonny, but I had an emergency surgery."

Cade nodded. "I kind of suggested that the team could use your back field and obstacle course for training next fall, since we can't use university facilities for practice or team events."

"Kind of?"

"Where's this course I've heard so much about today?"

Ed interrupted the conversation.

"What have you heard?" Tess gave Cade the side-eye. He usually hated it when people did that to him, but in this case, he deserved it. Not to mention, from her it kind of turned him on.

"That you have a huge obstacle course in your back field that you let the Trips build to do their ninja thing," Ed huffed.

Tess smiled. "American Ninja Warrior."

"Sure. That. Let's take a look at this." It was clear from the tone of Ed's voice that he didn't hold out much hope for the usefulness of the course.

Tess led them around the back of the house. Ed stopped so abruptly, Tyler almost ran into his back.

"What the hell?" Ed stared at the course.

The Trips started talking at once, trying to explain each obstacle to their grandfather. Cade held up a hand. Tess was standing there, perfectly still. He hoped she'd forgive him for what he was about to do, but she needed to let more people see her. All of her.

"Tess can run the course and show you."

"Tess can?" Ed took a cigar out of his pocket, shoved the end into his mouth and crossed his arms.

Shit, he was pissed.

"I can?" Tess stared at Cade. Her stance mimicked her grandfather's, minus the cigar.

Shit, she was pissed.

"Yes, you can." It probably wasn't the best idea to throw her into the deep end without her permission, but she was going to have to go public sooner or later considering the competition was televised nationally.

Cade let her stare at him for a moment before he gently took her hand and led her to the beginning of the course.

"You can do this."

She rolled her eyes. "I know I can. I don't know if I want to."

"You have to start letting people see you." It baffled him that she didn't know how spectacular she was.

"I actually understand that, but I kind of thought I would be able to choose who and when." Her irritation was almost a living thing.

"Sometimes choices are made for you and you have to roll with it."

"That may be, but I'm making it clear that I don't appreciate you making the choice for me. Especially because this is my family." She emphasized the last two words.

He thought about what she was saying. Was his slip really an innocent mistake? It wasn't as if he understood her

141

need for secrecy, but she'd trusted him. Inadvertently or not, he'd betrayed that trust, and her. His gut burned.

"You're right. I'm sorry. I should have been more careful about keeping your secret. It wasn't up to me to tell your grandfather."

She gave him a look he couldn't interpret before giving him a brief nod and facing the first obstacle.

He doubted all was forgiven. Once a trust was broken, it had to be rebuilt. Now that he'd damaged it, he realized how important her faith in him was. His work was cut out for him.

"You going to time me?" She barely spared him a glance as she focused on the course in front of her.

Her voice pulled him out of his disturbing thoughts. He nodded and moved to join Ed and the Trips. Ed looked at the stopwatch when Cade pulled it out of his pocket.

"Why are you timing her?"

"She's training for the competition. Her qualifying round is in about seven weeks."

Ed's gaze snapped from the stopwatch in Cade's hand to his granddaughter.

"Go," Cade yelled. He smiled when she took off. Watching Tess fly through the course was a thing of beauty. It was almost like the calculations she made danced above her head as she approached a new obstacle.

It was obvious she was getting gassed about halfway through the course. Her pace slowed, and her actions became less deliberate as her strength visibly waned. She finally made it to the warped wall and barely pulled herself up to the top. All twelve obstacles took her almost ten minutes, the were really going to have to work on her conditioning, especially if she was going to reach stage four in Las Vegas.

"What the ever-loving hell?" A feminine voice called from behind. The tone and attitude could only be Delilah's.

Cade turned to see her and Charlie standing at the side of the house. He turned back to Tess who was…was she actually…yep, she was flipping off her friends.

"Tess is flipping us the bird," Delilah said.

Charlie shook her head. "She's flipping you the bird."

Cade stopped watching the show the newcomers were putting on and turned to Ed who had an expression on his face like he was seeing his granddaughter for the first time.

"Was that really Tess?" There was no missing the hint of awe in the man's voice.

"She's a hell of an athlete."

"Since when?"

"We've been doing this with her for a while now,

143

Grandpa. She was in pretty good shape before we started." Tyler volunteered.

Theo and Trip made their way over to the warped wall and disappeared behind it. They reappeared less than a minute later on top of the wall and dropped down on either side of their sister. Cade couldn't hear the hushed conversation from where he stood, but he was confident her brothers would make sure she got down off the wall safely.

"So, what do you think of the training opportunities here now?" He clapped Ed on the back.

"I still can't believe she finished all of those obstacles in one go. You and I both know football players who couldn't make it through in a single pass."

Cade wasn't entirely sure he would have been able to before his time in the Navy. "She's pretty impressive."

"And you say she's actually competing in this show?"

"We signed her up." Tyler kept his focus on his brothers and sister, as Tess slowly stood.

"You signed her up?" Ed pointed at Tyler. "She didn't want to do this?"

"She wants it so bad she can taste it. It's that she doesn't think she should do it."

"Why not?" Ed focused on Tess who was stretching, still at the top of the wall.

"She's too busy trying to do what everyone expects her to do. We hardly ever see her do what she wants to do. We figured she'd never go for it without a push." Tyler shrugged. "So, we pushed."

"That's what I was saying this morning." Delilah smacked Charlie on the shoulder.

The brunette rubbed her shoulder but stayed silent. Cade didn't know what was going on with Tess's friends, but he had a bad feeling this afternoon was about to go off the rails. They were still supposed to train for a few hours. So, he turned to all the newcomers who were watching Tess with unreadable expressions on their faces.

"Clearly you have questions for Tess, but we've got a limited amount of time to get her ready for competition. She's on the clock with me until seven. You can hang out and watch, but no talking to her until we're done."

He ignored Delilah's smart-ass salute as he turned to head back to the obstacle course. Tess was sitting on top of the warped wall, a triplet on either side of her. One of them said something to her and she threw her head back and laughed.

The moment of obvious joy stopped him in his tracks. A bolt of desire hit him like a blitzing player from the defensive line. Whether it was desire just for her or something more, he didn't know, and he wasn't sure he would ever be ready to figure it out.

Three hours later, Cade waited for her at the bottom of the wall. If he hadn't been there to brace her when she slid down the pole she would have crumpled at the bottom like a house of cards in a stiff breeze.

"Hell of a job, Jules."

"Is it wrong that I have a strong desire rip out your larynx right now?" She let herself relish the thought of working out in total silence.

"My larynx?"

"So I don't have to hear you say 'five more minutes, Jules' ever again."

He laughed. "I'm sure I'll be saying more annoying things to you over the next seven weeks."

They stopped, and she took in the group that had made themselves comfortable watching her train. The Trips were sprawled out on the ground. Sam lying across their legs. Charlie and Delilah were huddled together. Their conversation stopped as she and Cade approached. Her grandfather had no doubt dissected every move she made on the course, pinpointing everything she did wrong.

"Sorry I didn't get a chance to warn you about Ed. I tried."

"It's okay. I guess it was stupid of me to think I could keep this all a secret from everyone."

"I wouldn't use stupid to describe anything about you."

"I would, when it comes to dealing with people." She was tired of feeling inadequate in that area. Especially since she suspected that her issues with people were less about her IQ and more about her desire to keep her head down and focus on everything she needed to do instead of everything she wanted to do.

As they approached the observers, her grandfather stood from the chair someone, probably one of the Trips, had found for him. He walked up to Tess and pulled her into his arms. Her throat closed as his arms came around her.

"You are amazing." His voice sounded scratchy.

She couldn't speak. Of all her family, his opinion about her athletic endeavor meant the most.

He cleared his throat. "I wish you'd said something sooner."

Speechless, she tilted her head back. His eyes gleamed and there was a satisfied smile on his face.

"Your brothers talked to me while we watched you."

Her grandfather glanced at the Trips. "A lot."

She smiled. "They have a lot to say when they're on a roll."

"Something else I learned today." The corner of his mouth tilted in a rueful expression. He turned to Cade. "Call Nick. See if he wants the job."

"I thought you wanted to hold off on hiring him."

"I've been reconsidering. If we're going to do this, we need to go for it from the start. Watching you put her through the workout, I see how helpful he could be with Tess's training. Make sure he knows that if he's on board we need him right away."

"Who's Nick?" She wasn't sure she needed her grandfather and Cade making plans without her.

"He's a friend of mine. We're looking at him for the strength coach for the university," Cade said.

"Why do I need his help?"

"Strength is going to be your weak spot. That course needs a lot of upper body strength. You're gassing out because you don't have the endurance that comes from more strength training." Her grandfather crossed his arms as he studied the course and the back field.

"Grandpa. I barely have enough time to train. You want me to add more to my schedule."

"What's going on that you can't make a little time?"

"Mom and Dad are going on the round the world cruise you couldn't take. The triplets are coming to stay with me, I'm covering the whole practice and teaching a seminar for Dad."

"What the hell? Why are you taking up *all* the slack for your parents?"

She didn't have a response for him. Looking back, she'd been taking on more and more since graduating vet school. The rest of her siblings were finishing school and finding their own way. Everyone seemed to assume she was settled, despite her age, and kept pouring more responsibility on to her shoulders.

"Because everyone is used to her doing it," Tyler said.

"When did you get to be so smart?" Grandpa studied his grandson.

Tyler shrugged. "We're the youngest. Everyone is so busy with their own lives, they don't notice us much. We spend a lot of time watching."

Tess smiled. She really enjoyed this new relationship with the Trips. It made things much more interesting. She turned to her grandfather. "Do you want to see the course up close?"

He nodded.

"We want to look too." Delilah chimed in.

Tess rolled her eyes. She had decided to share this part of her life with her friends, but she wasn't prepared for them to watch. The last thing she wanted to do was make a fool of herself in front of anyone.

"Come on. We're prying all your deep dark secrets out of you tonight anyway, might as well get it over with."

"She could use some extra training." Cade stepped toward the group. "I'm going to run her through some of the obstacles and I'll explain everything."

"Just a minute big guy." Charlie stepped forward at Cade's pronouncement.

Cade held up a hand. "She has less than seven weeks to prepare for this competition. I know you all have questions, but she has a lot of work to do if she's going to qualify for finals and reach stage four in Vegas."

"Vegas." Delilah started jumping up and down.

Tess bit the inside of her cheek. It figured that would be the detail that caught her friend's attention.

She stretched her back, knowing Cade had plans. "What's next?"

"Suicide sprints in the field. Start on my mark and stop when I call time."

It was a tempting thought to go full toddler and throw a

tantrum. But it wouldn't change his mind. They had mapped out a spot the size of a basketball court in the field and she got started running full court and back, three quarter court and back, half court and back and quarter court and back. She knew Cade was going to keep her doing them for a while. If she was honest with herself, this was preferable to the inquisition that would come afterward.

Chapter 10

Cade did his best to split his focus between Tess and Ed. He owed the Trips big time because they were keeping Charlie and Delilah occupied while he and Ed focused on the course and Tess.

They were getting ready to wrap up. She was hanging from the circuit board. He had told her to stay there for the last fifteen minutes of their training session to work on her grip and upper body strength.

"Gotta admit, when you mentioned this, I thought you were nuts. I've only seen that show a couple of times. Didn't know what to expect from a training course."

Cade nodded. "If our guys can run this full course a couple of times without losing steam, we'll have the toughest team in the division. The area behind the obstacle course is big enough for a practice field. If everything works out, we can get some basic blocking equipment. It'll be rough, but our guys will be ready when the sanctions ease."

Ed tilted his chin towards Tess. "She done, yet?"

The words were barely out of the older man's mouth when the alarm on Cade's watch beeped. The second the tone went off, Tess dropped. It was obvious she'd been listening for the beep. She shook out her arms as she approached them.

"Good job." Cade gave her a thumbs up.

"Baby girl, that was amazing." Ed drew her into a hug. "I didn't know you had that in you. I couldn't be prouder."

"Thanks Grandpa."

He slapped Cade on the back. "Call Nick tonight. Make him the offer. Let him know that we need him right away to help with her strength training."

"Grandpa —"

He held up a hand. "I'm calling your brother. He's got a partner in that fancy ass practice of his, not to mention he always has time to jet set off on his ritzy vacations. He can come help you out and cover your dad's seminar."

"I don't want to bother anyone." She chewed on her lip.

"Bull puckeys. You've been not bothering us your whole life and we've let you get away with it because it was easier than looking past our own damn noses to see if you needed more than you were letting on. Your parents are going on that cruise. Can't change that, or your gran will kick my ass. But you can let the rest of us help cover for them so you don't have to give up on what you want."

Tess started to speak when Ed took her hand.

"The boys and I are going to get out of your hair. Looks like you have a girls' night planned."

Ed hustled Cade and the Trips away and left the girls

153

alone. Cade peered over his shoulder. Charlie and Delilah were waiting for Tess on the porch, their arms crossed and their feet tapping. Tess looked back at the course like she might prefer hanging on the circuit board to hanging out with her friends.

Later that night, Cade took a swig of his beer. He had arranged the living room for Sonny, who was coming home tomorrow. There was a large dog bed in the corner next to a huge leather sofa, which he'd had delivered today. The walls seemed bare. Maybe he should put some pictures up. There were probably some in the boxes his grandfather had just shipped to him. The ones he'd stuck in a closet.

He picked up his phone and dialed Nick. After two rings he heard his friend's voice for the first time in a couple of years.

"How's it, brother?"

Cade laughed. "Hanging in. How's it with you?"

"Same shit, different day."

"What are you doing these days?" The last time he'd heard anything, Nick had moved back to Alabama after his discharge.

"Building bikes."

Cade smiled. Nick hadn't changed. Never use four words when two would do.

"Still playing in the shit kicker league?"

Nick laughed. "Leading it."

"Want to get back in the real game?"

There was a pause on the other end of the line. "What?"

"You remember Coach King."

"Yeah."

"Still chatty as always aren't you?" Having a conversation with Nick was always a challenge.

"Yeah."

"So, you heard about what happened at Cormac, with the Knights?" It burned in Cade's gut, the depths his alma mater had sunk to.

"Total cluster fuck."

"That about sums it up."

"What's it got to do with you?"

"Ed is building a new program. His crew is coming out of retirement to spend the next two to three years training their replacements. I'm going to work with him, take over as head coach when I'm ready."

Nick whistled. Cade smiled. A whistle from Nick was a sign of interest.

"We need someone to work with Bob Moore and take over as strength and conditioning coach."

There was another pause. "You want names?"

"We've got one. You."

Silence. Cade waited. He knew Nick well enough to know that he wouldn't say anything until he was ready. Cade took another swig of beer.

"Why me?"

"You're disciplined, focused, talented and you know more about what it takes to get a body ready to play sports than anyone I know."

Another round of silence.

"Still pretty well known in those circles. Not for football." Nick's voice was raspy.

"Time for a second chance."

"Don't deserve one."

"I disagree." Second chances were created for guys like Nick.

"She's dead." The guilt in his voice was almost a living thing.

Cade closed his eyes. "Not your fault."

"I could've stopped it. Didn't."

"You've taken the weight long enough. Time to move forward."

"Don't know if I can."

"Bullshit."

Nick chuckled. "Bullshit?"

"You heard me. You're a good man. You fucked up, not the way everyone thinks you did, but you still fucked up. Your friend ended up dead and the person responsible went on to live a pretty good life. Meanwhile, you've been doing penance for a crime you didn't commit."

"Matter of opinion."

"I need you." Cade played his ace.

"Plenty of guys can do that job."

"True. To them it would be a job, a good job. It would be something more to you."

Cade could hear Nick clear his throat and decided to keep going.

"Ed's crew is all on board to come out of retirement. He and I are putting together mine."

"And you want me?"

"Your perfect for my crew. All vets. All people who know this game backwards and forwards." He didn't understand why Nick was resisting this chance.

"People?"

"We're getting Frankie Connell to coach the wide receivers.

Another whistle. "Saw her play last year. She's a bruiser. Hell of a Marine, too. Saved my ass more than once."

157

"Saved mine, too."

"Ed's on board with Frankie?"

"He's on board with you, too. We still need to present the plan to the Board in about five weeks. The vote might not go our way."

Nick made a choking noise. "Call me back when it does."

"We need you here double time for a special project."

"What?"

"Training Ed's granddaughter."

"To play football?" Nick sounded shocked.

"No. She's competing in American Ninja Warrior in about seven weeks. We need help getting her strength and endurance up."

Another whistle. "So, you want me to quit my job, move there now to train Ed's granddaughter and maybe have a job after that?"

"I know it's a risk." It was a risk for him too. He had a year lease on this cabin and might be out of a job in five weeks. He still wasn't sure about putting down roots, but he wasn't all that sure about not putting them down.

"More than that. Got a good job. Worked hard to build my reputation."

Cade knew what he was asking his friend. "You should

go out on your own."

"What?"

"Bet between you and your brother you've got enough saved to open your own place. You won't be training Tess twenty-four seven. You'll have time to open your own shop. First year of the program we're all on light duty. Hell, my whole crew won't even be here until next spring. You'll have plenty of time to get things up and running before we hit the weeds. If the program doesn't go, you'll have your own shop in a good place that doesn't have the same memories as your home town. If it does, you'll have football and your brother can run the auto shop."

Cade waited while Nick thought about it.

"Not sure I deserve this shot," he whispered.

"If we all got what we deserved in life it would be a pretty shitty place. We get what we get, run with the good stuff, play through the bad. Say yes. I want you on my team."

"What the hell. Gotta' talk to Simon. He's going to have a say too."

"Call me when you know. You two can stay with me as long as you need."

"I'll be in touch." Nick hung up.

Cade tossed his phone on the coffee table and sank his

fingers into Sam's fur. He leaned his head back and slumped in his chair. He knew his friend still had a long road ahead of him, but he was hoping that bringing him on board would help him start down the right one. After a moment, he stood. He gave Sam a quick whistle and went to the back door. Time for a walk to clear his head. A certain brunette had taken up residence there.

I never knew a woman could look so sexy hanging from a circuit board.

Tess sat back and took a sip of wine. Drinking probably wasn't the best idea, since she could barely keep her eyes open. She didn't know if the exhaustion was from the workout or the conversation she'd just had with Charlie and Delilah. Either way, all she wanted was to finish dinner and go to sleep.

"So, you're a secret jock." Delilah pointed at Tess with a chopstick.

"I'm not a jock."

"We saw you on that course today. You totally are."

Tess was too tired to argue. She raised her voice. "Fine. While other little geniuses were dreaming about science and Nobel prizes, I was longing for a baseball mitt."

Charlie snickered. "Leave her alone, Delilah. She hasn't had some secret dream to be an athlete all these years."

"How would you know? You're the one who's always talking about how you've been friends since infancy and I've only known her for a minute. Did you see this coming?"

Charlie's silence made Tess's stomach turn. She hadn't meant to hurt her. Tess flopped onto her back and sighed. "I'm not good with people." It sounded like a lame excuse, even to her.

"Bullshit." Charlie turned to her. "You've always been a good friend to me. You've listened to every problem I've ever had and always had my back. We may not have gone to school together, but no matter how busy you were with college and vet school, you always had time for me. You almost missed your graduation from veterinary school because of me. It's not about you being a bad friend to me. It's about me being a bad friend to you."

"You were a great friend to me." No one else had taken the time to put up with her idiosyncrasies.

"How? As Delilah's pointed out, I've never been there for you. You've needed me and didn't feel like you could turn to me."

Tess sat up. "That's not true. You stood up for me

whenever Delilah or anyone else said something nasty."

Delilah had the grace to blush.

"Charlie. You came to all my birthday parties. You were the only one outside my family that did. You invited me to all yours. Whenever you got together with your friends from school you invited me, even when you knew I couldn't go. I'm a freak. There's no denying it. You gave me the only normal in my childhood. I just got so used to handling my stuff by myself and I didn't know how to ask anyone for help."

When Tess stopped talking both Charlie and Delilah were in tears.

"I am such a bitch," Delilah wailed.

Charlie rolled her eyes. "You are —"

"Charlie," Tess admonished her.

"But you're our bitch. You are now using your incredibly bad attitude to fight the forces of evil."

"Really?" Delilah sniffled.

Charlie sighed. "Really."

Delilah smiled. "Cool. Now I want to talk about what it's like to be trained by the incredibly hot Cade Maguire."

It took Tess a moment to catch up to Delilah's rapid change of topic. Warmth spread up her neck.

"Oh…my…God, you're blushing," Delilah crowed.

"You are." Charlie joined in. "What happened?"

"Nothing." She tugged on her ear.

"You're lying." Charlie pointed at her. "You always tug on your ear when you're lying."

"I do not." Tess tugged on her ear again.

Charlie and Delilah broke into peals of laughter. Tess flopped onto her back again, waiting for their laughter to fade, willing herself to remember it was her friends' laughing and it was harmless. She couldn't stop the tears that slid from her eyes.

Delilah poked her arm. "You're crying? Why are you crying?"

"Crap, crap, crap." Charlie took her hand. "I'm sorry." She looked at Delilah. "We're sorry."

"Why are we sorry?" Delilah seemed perplexed.

"Because Tess, our friend," Charlie emphasized the word, "has a thing about people laughing at her."

"I'm used to it." Tess brushed a tear off her cheek with the back of her hand.

"You're not. It's happened a lot, so you expect it, but you're not used to it, and it hurts, which puts one more point in the Charlie and Delilah are crappy friends column." Charlie squeezed her hand.

"You're not crappy friends. I'm —"

"You're awesome." Delilah interrupted her. "I know I bulldozed my way into your life. I was a flaming bitch to you when we were growing up."

"And the award for understatement of the year goes to —" Charlie mumbled.

"Shut it, Charlianne."

Tess gasped. No one ever called Charlie by her real name. Ever. It was probably one of the reasons that Charlie resisted making friends with Delilah. Her 'don't mess with me' attitude was aimed at everyone in her life, including people she called friend.

"Before you two turn this into a brawl, please stop. I'm too damn tired to break up a fight right now. Besides, I could totally kick both your asses if you make me."

They stopped mid-bicker and stared at her. Tess wasn't sure what they saw, but they both burst out laughing.

"What's so funny?"

"The thought of you kicking our asses," Delilah said.

"The thought of you kicking anyone's ass," Charlie added.

Tess got up, feeling every inch of movement from head to toe. "You guys can crash here if you want. I'm going to bed."

Ignoring the protests from her friends, she made her

way upstairs. She was done right now. Everything was pressing in on her and being scrambled at the same time. It was terrifying and exhausting to think about what her life would look like when it finally stopped spinning out of control.

Chapter 11

Cade sat in the lobby of the clinic, his left ankle propped on his right knee to keep it from twitching. Sonny was coming home today. Tess had said he was healing well and she was pleased with his progress. Sam would be relieved to have his brother home. The last couple of days had been tense at the cabin. He'd slept for shit, which was likely a combination of Sonny's absence and Sam's pacing the floors.

I need a distraction. I can't lose it a few minutes before I bring Sonny home.

He looked around the waiting room. Sheila finished up with the client with the…animal that looked like it had stepped through some kind of demonic portal. He watched the woman and her minion leave.

"What the hell was that?" He nodded towards the closed door.

Sheila gave him a knowing smile. "That was a Sphinx cat."

He stood and paced toward the reception desk. "That was not a cat."

"That was a very expensive cat."

"Someone paid good money for that thing?"

Sheila laughed. "Indeed, she did."

166

"Why?" He understood paying for service dogs but there were so many homeless dogs and cats, he thought people should adopt them before shelling out cash for some fancy breed.

"Some people like show cats."

"Some people like tofu, too. Doesn't make it right."

Their conversation was interrupted by Tess who came up to the front desk dressed in dark green scrubs. He'd never thought much of the utilitarian clothing. The nurses who treated him after he was injured were good people, some of them were even good looking, but none of them filled out a pair of scrubs like Tess did. Fantasies about playing doctor with the sexy vet rolled through his head.

Someone cleared their throat, forcing him to let go of the image he'd been building in his mind and focus on Tess and the dark circles under her eyes.

"What's wrong?" All he cared about was fixing it for her.

"Nothing." She tugged her ear. "Sonny's fine."

He could tell something was wrong and wasn't all that comfortable that he knew her well enough to spot something she was trying to hide. "I wasn't asking about Sonny."

She closed her eyes. "Long night."

"I thought you were having a girls' night with Charlie and Delilah." Sheila inserted herself into the conversation. "Oh." A look of understanding crossed her face.

"What, oh?" When he'd left them last night, the three women were planning on ordering dinner and talking.

"I don't want to talk about it." Her chin trembled. "Sonny's ready to go. He's in exam room three. Let's go back and go over his home care instructions."

Tess led him to the exam room and his excitement over taking Sonny home was mixed with concern for her. She was moving slowly, which he would expect from her hard workouts for the last two days, but there was something else. Her shoulders were slumped, and she wouldn't look him in the eyes. He'd never seen her appear defeated. Seeing her like this made him want to slay dragons for her. If only it were that easy.

He walked into the small room, the scent of antiseptic stinging his nostrils. His eyes were drawn to Sonny, lying in the corner wearing some kind of shirt. The dog's ears perked up, his tail thumped, and he gave a quick bark. Cade walked over then knelt by Sonny.

"Hey buddy. You're coming home today. Sam's looking forward to it."

Cade ran his hand gently over Sonny's head. His shoulders dropped at the sight of the shirt and the cast on the dog's hind leg when Tess knelt next to him.

"He's doing really well. I know you wanted to bring him home earlier, but the extra few days have really helped his healing. There's no sign of infection, but we're going to send you home with some antibiotics to finish the cycle we started him on after his surgery. We're also going to send you home with some pain medication and valium for him." She smiled at the dog who continued thumping his tail.

"What's with the shirt?"

"It's a modified thunder shirt to keep him calm and stop him from licking his bandages. It doesn't constrict his breathing, but it's tight enough him from bending to chew on his cast."

"I was worried he would need one of those cones."

She smiled. "We try to avoid those if we can. It's easier on everyone."

He nodded. "Good."

"You should give him the pain meds as prescribed. The instructions will have you taper them off over the next few weeks. He might experience some anxiousness being home after such a serious injury. So, the valium is as needed. If you see him displaying any unusual behaviors or anxiety,

169

you should give him one to calm him, to keep him from tearing his sutures or reinjuring his leg. You also need to keep him off that leg as much as possible while it's still healing."

"He'll be okay with Sam, right?" As much as Cade wanted Sonny home, he didn't want to set his recovery back.

Tess nodded. "Since Sonny and Sam are litter mates, you should see Sam caring for Sonny and taking it easy with him. Hopefully, he'll be a calming presence and you won't need the valium." She turned her attention from Sonny. "All dogs are different. You know them better than anyone else, so let your knowledge be your guide."

"Okay. Before I take Sonny home you need to tell me what's wrong."

"I need to help you put your dog into your truck so that I can return to work." She pursed her lips.

He wasn't going anywhere until he knew what was wrong with her. "Tess."

"Cade."

"Tess."

She leaned back, sitting on her heels. "We know each other's names, which is good because otherwise I would be worried one or both of us had suffered a traumatic brain injury overnight."

"How about we cut the bullshit and you tell me what's wrong?" He leaned toward her. She was clearly evasive when it came to letting people help her, but he thought they were past that. Her avoiding the issue, whatever the issue was, with him made him want to put his fist through a wall.

She wouldn't look in his eyes. "Why would anything be wrong?"

"Why are you avoiding the issue?" He wanted to get Sonny home, but every instinct he had told him Tess needed him right now.

She sighed and rubbed her hand down her face. "They laughed at me," she mumbled.

"What?"

Her eyes met his, and her lower lip quivered as tears slid down her cheeks. "They laughed at me."

There was nothing to think about. He pulled her into his arms and held her as the tears fell. The sobs racking her body made him want to wrap her in cotton and protect her from the world.

When had he become the guy that pulled a crying

woman into his arms? He didn't stick around for the emotional stuff. It wasn't fair to let women believe he could be something he wasn't. But, in this moment, he wanted to be. For her.

The smartest thing he could do for her, for both of them, would be to get up, find Sheila and leave her to handle Tess's tears. That wasn't going to happen. Comforting a crying woman wasn't something he'd ever done or wanted to do. But he couldn't walk away from her. He tightened his arms.

"What happened to the spitfire that got pissed at me when you thought I was laughing at you?"

"That was different." She hiccupped.

"Why?"

"I didn't know you very well. I didn't expect more from you."

"And you expected more from them?" It hurt, but it made sense. They were her friends, not a guy she'd met a little over a week ago.

"Everyone told me I need to rely on people more, open up. I thought it would be safe to open up to them and they laughed at me."

She leaned back, her hazel eyes, glittered with moisture. His chest tightened. Her tears made him feel something he'd never felt before. Helpless.

"Jules." His voice sounded hoarse.

"Why does everyone always laugh at me?"

His mouth was dry. What could he say? "They don't. Not really."

"It seems like it."

"It's not that they're laughing at you to be mean. Sometimes you say and do things that make people laugh. You're pretty fucking funny sometimes."

She ducked her head. "No. I'm not."

"Yeah. You are. You and your brothers sometimes get going and its hilarious." He'd lost track of the number of times he'd thought about getting some popcorn and sitting down to watch the siblings.

"No, we're not."

"You are. You four go all geek while you're training. It's awesome."

"Really?"

The desperate note of hope that rang in her voice almost broke his heart.

He pulled her close. The feeling of being able to hold and comfort her created an unfamiliar sensation in his stomach. One he wasn't going to examine now. If ever. "Really. I don't know what happened with you and your girls last night, but I'm sure they didn't mean to hurt you."

The moment was interrupted by a wet nose pressing between them. Tess laughed. "Looks like someone feels left out."

Cade loosened his hold on her to pet Sonny. He knew the dog was responding to Tess's pain and doing what he did best. Offering comfort. "You're sure he's going to be all right at home?"

She nodded. "He'll be fine. He shouldn't move around too much. He's going to be slow when he does, and he'll know his own tolerance levels. You know them, too. Trust him and trust yourself."

Cade nodded as he brushed the tears from her face. *God, I want to kiss her.*

Instead, he got up then helped Tess to her feet. In no time at all they had Sonny curled up in the back of his truck.

"I'll see you later for training."

"I can train without you, so you can watch Sonny today."

Cade shook his head. "I've made arrangements to have someone watch them while we're training."

"You're sure?"

"I made a promise to you. I don't break my promises."

174

She smiled and nodded.

Cade got in the truck and drove away before her smile got him to make any other promises to her. If he kept it up, sooner or later they would get attached and he would screw it up. The last words his mother said to him drifted up from the recesses of his memory. He could still see her face, red with anger and hear her voice, laced with bitterness. "You're like every other Maguire man, no good for anyone, not even yourself."

Tess collapsed at the top of the wall. She tried to catch her breath and wondered if she ever would again.

The voice she was coming to loathe called from below. "You're gassing out too quick."

"You're gassing out too quick," she mumbled, trying to mimic his deep voice.

"I heard that." He chuckled.

She leaned over the wall and stared down at the current bane of her existence. He stood there, arms crossed, looking up at her. His expression was serious, but the crinkles in the corners of his eyes told her everything she thought she needed to know. The familiar bile rose in her throat at the thought of someone laughing at her.

"Hey, Jules. Not laughing at you." He seemed to read her mind.

She ignored the fluttery sensation in her chest and nodded. "Not laughing at me, just torturing me."

"Wait until you meet Nick."

"When does he get here?"

"Any day now."

"I still don't understand why he's going to help train me."

"Because I asked him to. Now get your ass down here. You need to do the circuit board two more times before we're finished for the day."

Tess dragged herself up and started for the stairs behind the wall. Instead, she turned to the fireman's pole and slid down. Her feet hit the ground with a thud. Laughter bubbled up inside her. The feeling of flying that came with going down the pole was liberating, even if it only lasted a few seconds.

She trudged over to the circuit board and hoisted herself up to the platform. Even though she'd memorized the intricate pattern of holes and lines designed to look like what it was called, it wouldn't help her at the tail end of her workout. Fatigue rode her hard as she grabbed a handle and inserted it into the first hole.

"I've got the Trips working on a new board."

She moved through the obstacle, every second of it created an intense ache in her upper body and hands.

"Why?" She huffed.

"Because you know this one by heart. Part of the challenge is seeing everything with fresh eyes. You won't know all the obstacles when you're actually competing."

It sounded logical. Intellectually she knew it was a good idea for her training. Right now, as exhausted as she was, she thought it sounded like the dumbest idea since New Coke.

"Tell me about Nick." Maybe he could distract her enough she would forget how tired and sore she was.

"Can't."

"Why not?"

"We'd be too close to talking about our proposal for the team."

Tess focused on pulling the ball out of the hole and moving it toward the next. She twisted her grip to secure it and hung in the air, suspended four feet above the ground. She was really getting irritated with her own policy. She wanted to talk to Cade about more than her training and his dogs. He didn't want to talk about the Navy and his current passion was working with her grandfather to build the new football program for the university. Since she wouldn't talk about it with him that left a lot of conversations hanging. A lot of words left unsaid.

"You going to hang there all day?"

"Thinking about it."

"Come on, Jules. Move your ass."

"Remind me why I asked you to help me with this again." She pulled herself along the board inch by painful inch. Her pace was slower than it usually was, and if she didn't know the layout of the board, she would have dropped by now. She didn't want to talk any more, but he always talked during training. Something about building her lung capacity.

"You need someone who knows how to train for a competition to push you."

"I could probably do this on my own." She dropped to the platform at the end of the obstacle. Her lungs burned as she breathed in and out.

"You'd be lounging on your couch by now with that motley crew of pets surrounding you."

"Watch how you talk about my crew." Each animal in her house was there because no one else would give them a forever home.

"They're awesome, but you got to know they're weird."

She somehow managed to shrug even though her upper body felt like it was made out of concrete. "They're mine."

"Break's over. Go back the other way and we're done."

"I don't want to." She wouldn't admit she didn't think she could.

"Tough shit."

"When the feeling comes back in my arms I'm going to punch you right in the mouth."

"I'd like to see you try."

He smiled that condescending smile that made her want to smack him or kiss him. She could never really decide which in any given moment.

Tess looked back across the obstacle. It was only ten yards, but it might as well have been a thousand. "I don't think I can."

"You can." His tone was gentle and confident.

"Cade."

"No excuses. Winning isn't easy. Winning is hard and it's work. It's looking at the finish line and knowing in your head you can't make it across but digging into your gut to find the strength to go the last mile. Now get your ass up and finish that obstacle."

Her eyes met his. It was moments like this that he let her

see the man underneath the bravado. He showed her everything in that moment. His strength. His heart. His weakness. She gave him a curt nod then broke eye contact.

Tess reached for the first handle and began to work her way back across. Her arms were on fire and felt like overcooked noodles, but she held on to the handle. Slick sweat covered her palm and a burning sensation ripped up her arms.

I'm not letting go of this handle.

Her fingers cramped as she tightened her grip. She pulled deep breaths into lungs, almost as if she would need to hold them forever.

Grip, shift, grip. Grip, shift, grip.

The words became a mantra as she dangled above the ground. Four feet felt like four thousand. In her head, falling from the obstacle now was admitting defeat. Giving up wasn't an option. She looked from the ground to the end of the circuit board. It seemed like it was miles away. With a deep breath and an exhale, she moved forward.

Grip, shift, grip. Grip, shift, grip.

Finally, with the last of her strength she hung inches from the finish. She closed her eyes and forced her legs to swing until she had enough momentum to hurl herself onto the waiting platform where she collapsed in a boneless heap, gasping for breath.

After a few moments warm strong arms slid under her legs and shoulders. Cade lifted her into his arms as if she weighed nothing. She let her head flop onto his shoulder.

"Where're you taking me?" She slurred her words, too tired to even concentrate on forming syllables.

"You need to clean up, rehydrate and relax, not necessarily in that order."

His words drifted away as exhaustion claimed her.

Chapter 12

Cade eyed Tess's menagerie as he carried her up the stairs. He'd never been up here and was curious about her inner sanctum. Family photos covered the walls, and the farther he went up the stairs, the more personal they got. It was weird. The more intimate the photographs became, the less she was in them. If she was the photographer of the more candid moments, it would explain her perpetual outsider status. Always looking at the experience, never being a part of it.

He stopped at the top of the stairs and saw a picture of all her brothers and sisters. At least he hoped that was all of them. They looked relaxed and...connected.

"That's my favorite picture." Her voice whispered across his neck.

"Why?" He studied the picture. It was cool, but it would have been better with her in it.

"Look at them. It was a perfect moment."

"Where were you?" Didn't seem like the moment would be all that great without her.

She lifted her head from his shoulder. "I took the picture."

It wasn't the time, but he couldn't help himself. "The more personal the moments the less you're in the pictures."

She stared at the picture. "I was there."

"Yeah, but you weren't part of it."

"I don't understand." Her head flopped onto his shoulder as if she was too tired to hold it up anymore.

He decided this was a conversation that needed to happen when she was more coherent. Her soft snore told him she was asleep anyway.

Cade went down the hall to what he thought must be her room. His instincts were right. Her room was a surprise. It was what he would have imagined a fairy's room would be like if he had ever imagined something like that. Not a totally girly fairy though, with pink and purple everywhere. It was all blues and greens.

Cormac University colors.

The king size four poster bed gave him ideas. Some kind of filmy material was intertwined with what looked like actual boughs that ran between the posts.

He moved toward the master bath and found himself staring again. She had brought the outdoors inside with furniture and fixtures that looked like they were made from tree branches.

A vanity was set up next to the sink and he set her gently down on the small cushioned bench. He squatted down in front of her and gave her a slight shake.

"Jules."

Her eyes drifted open and she gave him a sleepy smile. "Sleep."

"Not yet. I'm going down to the kitchen to get you a sports drink and maybe something to eat. Can you handle getting cleaned up?"

She nodded. He stood up and made sure she was steady and somewhat alert. When she started to pull her T-shirt over her head he turned quickly and started the shower for her. The size of the shower gave him more ideas and he adjusted his shorts. Her borderline comatose state should make it easier to keep the evidence of his reaction to her secret. With one quick glance at her to make sure she was still upright he made a strategic retreat.

He was in the middle of making a sandwich for her when he heard the pad of her bare footsteps on the hardwood floor followed by the click-clack of what sounded like a herd of animal claws.

Her hair was still damp and piled on top of her head in a messy knot that was held in place by red sticks. A dark green robe was wrapped around her. The shapeless terry cloth should have been a turn off, but it made him think of what she might be wearing underneath. Or not wearing.

"That looks good." She smiled.

184

Her smile did things to him that he didn't want to examine to closely. "You up to eating?"

"Sure. The shower woke me up a little. Thanks for getting me upstairs."

He shrugged. This was unfamiliar territory here and he wasn't sure what to do about it. He'd never considered himself a caretaker. The fact that he liked doing it for Tess was confusing. "You're welcome."

They lapsed into a comfortable silence. He finished making her dinner and nodded toward the kitchen table.

"Sit down. You worked hard today."

Tess shuffled over to the table then dropped into a chair. Cade chuckled as her menagerie of pets slinked further into the room and arranged themselves on the floor around her. He set the food in front of her with a sports drink.

"You need to eat and rehydrate."

She actually grunted as she picked up her sandwich to take a bite. Who knew a grunt could be such a turn on? He sat to eat his own meal and had to focus on eating instead of watching her.

"So, who's Nick again? And why is he training me?"

"Nick is going to be the strength coach." Cade held up a hand. "If our plan is approved. He needs a change. He's going to come early, help train you and look into starting an auto shop with his brother."

"Isn't he taking a risk coming before the Board vote?"

"If the plan doesn't go he'll run the shop with his brother. He needs a fresh start."

She nodded. Her eyes drooped as she took a sip of her drink.

He glanced down, noticing she had eaten most of her sandwich and finished half her drink. "You done?"

Her yawn was accompanied by the sound of her jaw cracking. It startled her and a few of her pets.

"We can talk more tomorrow." He had to leave, or he might forget how exhausted she was. Every damn thing she was doing right now was so cute he wanted to carry her up to that unexpected bed and explore every inch of her.

Her eyes widened. "You want me to work out tomorrow?"

He smiled. "We're going to take it easy, but you need to work out every day to build your strength and endurance."

She rolled her eyes. "I'm going to start charging you for repeating yourself."

"We can't all have giant brains like yours. Some of us only know so many words. Finish that." He nodded toward her glass and grabbed their plates and stood up. He went into the kitchen to do the dishes.

Things were getting too intimate and he wasn't sure he could handle it. When he made his way back to the table, her glass was empty. Tess was face first on the table. He started to speak when he heard her make a snuffling snore. If her grunt was cute her snore was off the charts adorable. He couldn't keep the grin off his face.

Her animals were looking at him expectantly. His skin tingled as he moved to her chair. Cade gently lifted her into his arms, trying to ignore the thought that not only could he get used to this, he would probably enjoy the process.

Trailed by her giant St. Bernard and its cat rider, Cade carried her up to her room then laid her gently on her bed. He covered her with a blanket. She let out one more snore before her cats jumped up on the bed and made themselves comfortable around her. He turned out the light and, with a will power he didn't realized he had, left her alone to sleep.

Tess was asleep at her desk, dreaming of licking Cade's tattoos when a loud bang, accompanied by a slam next to her head woke her up. She reared back and threw a punch in the direction of the sound that woke her and knocked a huge veterinary text off her desk. A snap of pain shot through her knuckles. It was the chuckle that drew her attention and she saw her oldest brother, TJ, standing there with what could only be described as a shit-eating grin on his face.

"Wakey, wakey, Sleeping Beauty."

She wanted to hit him but didn't have the energy. A fantasy smack upside his head would have to do for now.

"What are you doing here?" She hadn't seen him in months, not since his drive by visit last Christmas.

"I'm your reinforcements." He looked annoyed.

"What do you mean?" She'd never had reinforcements before. Not that she remembered anyway.

"Grandpa called. Got me and Dad on the phone and lit into us for the way we've been treating you all these years." He moved to the chair next to her then threw himself into it the way he always did.

Interfering old man.

"He shouldn't have done that." Would he? Without warning her?

"What? Let us know you needed us?" There was an accusatory look on his face.

Warmth crept up her neck and she lowered her gaze to her lap. "No. He shouldn't have yelled at you."

TJ scrubbed his hand down his face. "Yeah. He should

have."

She didn't understand his mood and waited for him to elaborate. He would. Eventually. TJ had never been one to bottle up anything inside.

"We left you holding the bag too much." She started to speak when TJ held up a hand. "You were a tough kid to get to know. I didn't understand you and you seemed content to be in your own world, so we all left you there. It never occurred to us to try again as you got older."

She didn't know what to say so she shrugged.

"I could have at least opened the doors by talking about work. We're both vets, for God's sake. I'm willing to bet you could have helped me through vet school if I'd asked you."

"I didn't know you needed help." He'd always seemed so confident. Almost larger than life to her.

It was TJ's turn to shrug. "I wasn't the most disciplined student. I was smart enough to coast through college, but vet school kicked my ass."

That was news to her. "I'm sorry I didn't help."

"Right there." He pointed at her. "That's what you do."

"What?" His change in topics confused her. What did she always do?

"You take everything on yourself. You would have

helped me with vet school if I'd asked. Hell, you'd been working with dad for years before I even started classes."

"I would have. I wanted to offer, but I've never been very good at making the first move." She'd been saying that a lot lately. It was something to think about, the fact that she was held herself back from doing things she wanted to do.

"Hopefully, we can get to know each other better while I'm here." He sounded happy at the idea.

She smiled. "I'd like that."

"Me too. So, here's the deal. I am taking over your patients today. You're wiped out and it shows. Delilah's driving you home. I'm bringing dinner by your place tonight. After your training's done we'll talk about dividing up all the duties Dad tried to throw on just you."

She started to protest but didn't get very far. Within moments, Delilah appeared and hustled her out to her car.

"How are you getting back?"

"I'm hanging out with you for a little while. You and I are having a come to Jesus moment about this friendship. Charlie too, since I'm her proxy."

"I don't think I understood a word you just said." She'd thought the major friend discussion had happened the other night.

"Yeah. You're the smartest dummy I know. Here's the deal. Charlie and I are your friends. We have your back one hundred and fifty percent. Friends tease each other. It's not meant to be mean or hurtful. It's supposed to be light-hearted, fun even. You need to stop taking yourself so damn seriously and start enjoying your life."

"I enjoy my life." Why did everyone think she wasn't happy?

"In secret. You don't share the important stuff. You pretend it's not a big deal and since we don't know about it, we don't know what's important to you."

"I really don't understand what you're talking about." This was the way it had always been. She did what she needed to do. Sometimes she was happy about it. Sometimes she wasn't.

"Of course, you don't." Delilah rubbed the bridge of her nose. "It took me a while, but I figured it out. Your family worried about you because you were so smart and different. So, they let you do your thing, wanting you to be comfortable. I bet they were doing cartwheels when Charlie latched on to you."

Her parents were pleased with her friendship with Charlie, right from the start. "Why?"

"Because you had a friend your own age who would

help with your socialization, which, by the way, was a hor-rible idea."

"Why?"

"Because you both suck at interacting with normal hu-mans."

"Charlie is very social." She had more friends growing up and was always going out.

"She tries to be, but it's tough to get close to people with a ginormous chip on their shoulder."

"What chip?"

"See, right there. You deflect. This is an analyze Tess session, not Charlie. We'll deal with her issues another time and there will be pitchers of margaritas involved."

Tess understood all the words coming out of Delilah's mouth, but wasn't grasping their meaning. Fatigue rolled through her as she got into the car with Delilah. What little energy she had left was being drained by this conversation.

"I don't think I am alert enough for this." There was a chance she would never be alert enough for it.

"Tough. You are my captive until your training this af-ternoon."

"I thought you were supposed to drop me off so I could nap." She wouldn't be able to follow a discussion if she didn't get some sleep.

"You'll sleep after we've had our conversation."

Did Delilah have any idea how exhausting that sounded? "I could just go to sleep."

"You could try."

Tess got chills up her arms watching the smile that crept across Delilah's face.

"I'm a pretty heavy sleeper and I'm tired."

"How many years did I torment you before we became friends? Do you doubt my powers?"

Tess shivered. No, she didn't doubt Delilah's abilities. She had certainly cried enough over the years because of them. All she wanted to do was sleep before her training session. Clearly, she was going to have to listen to a lecture before that happened. It wouldn't be the first time she had to do something she didn't want to do to make someone she cared about happy.

"Don't worry." Delilah patted her arm. "This won't hurt, much."

It couldn't hurt more than she'd already been hurt. That was something, at least.

Chapter 13

Cade checked his watch. The meeting with the local high school coaches went long. The plan was to set up a few intramural games next season with some of the local varsity teams. It would be good practice for both the high schoolers and whatever members they had on the university squad next season.

Recruiting was going to be an issue. They were going to be behind the eight ball to begin with because they couldn't start recruiting eligible players from high schools or other colleges at all until after the national championship game next January. Other teams would have their rosters almost filled by then. Hell, some programs would have a few high school juniors and sophomores committed for subsequent seasons. It was going to be tough to recruit talent to come to Cormac given the years of sanctions they had ahead of them.

He was so deep in thought he didn't see the man standing by his truck at first. When he noticed him, he worked hard to hide his reaction to the unwelcome sight of Brian Gill, Jr. leaning there. He hadn't changed much except for his clothes. The college uniform of board shorts and T-shirts had given way to khakis and a button-down shirt. His blonde hair was cut short and his eyes were concealed by sunglasses that looked like they cost more than some peoples' cars. They probably did. The Gills liked to show off their money.

"Gill."

"Maguire."

Cade walked past the other man. He didn't have time for him and didn't want to make it.

"We need to talk." As always, Gill ignored the signals.

"Not really." The term need wasn't one he ever associated with his once, and apparently future, rival.

"This plan you've got going with the old-timers is cute, but it's not going to pass the Board. So, I'm here to make you a one-time offer." He sounded smug.

"Make it a no time offer and we're good."

Cade wasn't surprised when Gill didn't pick up on the joke and stepped in front of him.

"We've got Coach Sorenson ready to commit." Gill paused, clearly wanting a reaction from Cade.

Cade gave him one. He laughed. "That's the ace up your sleeve?" Clay Sorenson was a joke. Everyone knew he was all flash and no substance. His drinking problems were the most well-known secret in college sports and he was hopping colleges, trying to stay ahead of the press and the consequences of his own shitty choices. One of these days he was going to implode and take the team he was with at the time with him.

"He's a respected Coach. He took the Cougars from two and ten to nine and three in one season."

"He did do that. Right before he took off to another team and left the Cougars to go down in flames." Cade glanced at his watch. "You want to make your point? I have shit to do today." None of which included dealing with this pain in the ass.

Gill smirked. "Sorenson said he'd be willing to hire you as an assistant. In a few years you'll have the experience you need to actually coach football."

Cade wanted to wipe that smirk off the others man's face. He had ever since he was eighteen and Gill had said he was the starting quarterback and Cade should enjoy riding the bench for four years.

When Cade had out worked him for the starting position Gill had been pissed and had tried to make Cade pay for it ever since.

I guess daddy couldn't hand him everything in life.

Gill rubbed the back of his neck. "Face it, Maguire. This plan of yours is entertaining, but it's not going to fly. The university is never going to risk what's left of its reputation on a longshot like this. I'm throwing you a bone. You should be thinking about your future."

"You worry about your own future, not mine." Cade stepped around Gill. He pulled open the door to his truck then climbed in. Before he drove off he rolled his window down. "You can tell Sorenson that I won't need the job."

Sweat trickled down the side of Gill's face. It seemed off on such a cool spring day. "Your plan will never pass the board. You know that."

"I don't. I know that our plan is the best one, and you're the one who needs an alternative, Backup."

Gill went rigid at the sound of his old nickname and whipped off his glasses to look Cade in the eyes. "I'll be fine." His voice was clipped, and his blue eyes were icy.

"You're scared, and you know it." After fourteen years in the Navy, which included a couple of combat tours, Cade knew fear.

"What would I have to be scared of?" There was something in his voice that was...wrong.

Cade didn't miss Gill's flinch. "We started going head to head almost twenty years ago and you've never beaten me. Not once."

Gill's face turned red and he clenched his fists. "I wouldn't say that. I can think of one time." He smiled.

When the other man didn't elaborate, Cade decided he

was done. "In case you think it's a good idea to come for me again, think again. I don't have time for your shit. I don't have time for your daddy issues. I don't have time for you. Our plan is the best one for the university. If the Board buys the garbage you're selling for some reason, I'll be fine on my own. I wouldn't work for Sorenson if it meant I'd never go near another football again."

Cade didn't even bother to roll up his window as he backed out of his parking spot. He looked in the rearview mirror and watched Gill, who stood in place like a statue. The look on his face made Cade nervous. There was always something about the other man that had bothered him. He was a spoiled prick, but there was a desperation underneath his attitude that never made sense to Cade.

Trusting his instincts had kept Cade alive more times than he could count, and his gut was telling him they were missing something huge when it came to the Gills, particularly Backup.

What's the real deal with this guy? And how is it going to bite me in the ass?

He related his conversation to Ed later when they sat down to go over their latest plans.

"He's got something up his sleeve." The older man absently rubbed Sonny's head.

198

Sonny was settling in at home and was being good about staying off his leg. Sam hovered around his brother and nipped at him when he thought his brother was doing something he shouldn't.

He tore his attention away from his dogs. "Yeah. As far as I can tell, he's always been hiding something."

"It's gotten worse the more he's under Senior's thumb. You want to know what he might be up to, you need to talk to Delilah."

"Tess's friend Delilah? Why?" Why would she know anything about Backup?

"She's married to him. Going through a nasty divorce. If anyone outside of the Gill's inner circle is going to know what's going on with him, it'll be her."

"If they're split she might be out of the loop."

"That girl? She's keeping her eyes and ears on him until the divorce is final. And if she isn't, her grandmother is. The Derringer women see all and know all."

Cade nodded. "I'll talk to her next time I see her." Odds were good he'd see her the next time Tess trained. Those three friends were joined at the hip since Tess's big revelation.

"What's the latest from Nick?"

A knock on the door kept Cade from responding. Sonny

huffed but didn't move. He left it to Sam to handle the potential threat. Sam rose to the challenge and bolted for the front door, barking all the way.

Cade went to answer the door. A glance out the window made him smile. Looks like Ed would be able to ask Nick about the latest himself. He opened the door and held out his hand for his old friend. "Long time no see, buddy."

Nick took his hand and drew him into a brief hug, slapping him on the back before he let him go. "Good to see you, man."

Cade stepped back. His friend was still the biggest bastard he'd ever seen. Six four and all solid muscle. If anything, he'd added more bulk since his discharge. Sam had stopped barking and decided that Nick was a friend. The decision was made obvious with a symbol universally recognized by dog owners everywhere. He stuck his nose in the man's crotch.

Nick reached out and pushed the dog's nose away. "This must be Sam."

"Yeah. Come meet Sonny."

Nick picked up a bag and followed Cade into the cabin.

"You were asking about Nick's status." Cade looked over his shoulder. "Here he is. Ed, I'm sure you remember Nick Jacobs."

Ed stood and shook his hand. "Good to see you again. You're looking good, son."

Nick didn't respond. Cade knew he was a man of few words, so it would be up to him to move the conversation.

"Pull up a chair. We were just going over some of the details for the program."

Nick followed Cade and Ed to the table and started looking over the papers that were spread out. He picked up the list of names for the coaches and nodded.

Cade smirked. "I take it you approve."

"Decent choices."

"High praise." Cade chuckled.

"Don't have much to say do you?" Ed asked.

Nick shrugged. "Only when I've got something worth saying."

"Anyone on the list you disagree with?"

Nick studied it for a moment. "Nope." He turned to Cade. "What's this private training gig?"

"Tess, Ed's granddaughter, is training for American Ninja Warrior."

Nick nodded. "Cool."

"She needs some strength training." It was obvious to Cade from the start that they needed to round out her workouts.

"Got to see her in action."

He glanced at his watch. "We've got a training session this afternoon. You'll see her then. We'll have some dinner after. Talk to her about a schedule."

"You should have TJ there for that." Ed sat down.

"Who's TJ?" Nick took a seat opposite the older man.

"Tess's brother. He's going to help cover the veterinary practice while Tess is training and their dad's out of town."

"When's your brother coming?" Cade studied his friend. As usual, it was impossible to read him.

"A few weeks. Since you needed me to help with Tess right away he's going to wrap everything up on that end while I find us a house here."

Cade sat next to Nick and began shuffling through papers. They spent the next few hours bringing him up to speed on their plans, including the opposition. Like Cade, Nick had never backed away from a fight and Cade liked their odds with him on their side.

Tess felt better after her nap. Sort of. The training was exhausting. She imagined it would be a while before her body really adjusted and she was at one hundred percent. She put on her workout clothes and stood up.

The room started to spin, and her stomach rolled. It was a good thing the wall was close enough for her to brace a hand against. She took a few deep breaths and waited for the dizziness to pass. That's all it was.

I must have stood up too quickly.

Once she felt better, Tess went downstairs to face her training. Of course, Delilah was still there, but at least she'd stayed quiet for a couple of hours so Tess could sleep. She checked the clock. It was ten minutes until her workout. Her stomach growled. No time to eat now. She'd have to make sure to have a big meal when they were done.

When she got to the foot of the stairs, she stopped. And stared. Her kitchen was full of people standing or sitting around the table. There hadn't been this many people in the kitchen since before she'd inherited the house.

The Trips and TJ were at the back window, her younger brothers pointing out the obstacles on the course to the oldest Gallagher. Her parents and grandparents were chatting at the kitchen table. Someone had made coffee.

I can't believe I didn't smell it.

Charlie and Delilah were leaning against the kitchen counter staring at Cade and the biggest man she had ever seen in person, who were listening to the Trips go on about the course. Cade noticed her and checked his watch.

203

"You're here. Time to start."

"Why are you all here?" There were so many people in the room.

Her mother smiled. "We wanted to see what you do. We'll be on the cruise when you compete in the first rounds, so your father and I want to see you live so we can follow it better when your brother Skypes it."

She could hear the hurt in her mother's voice. Her parents had always supported her. Tess couldn't explain, even to herself, why she thought this would be any different. She'd spent so much time hiding her passion and trying to do everything everyone asked her to do. It never occurred to her that people would care about what she was doing in her sparse free time.

Better not go there. She turned to her friends. "Why are you two here?"

"We are here to support you. We've decided that we're not waiting for you to come to us anymore." Charlie smiled.

"Because, clearly, we would be old and gray if we did that." Delilah's eyes were focused on Nick and Cade.

Tess had an idea her friends were intent on taking advantage of a few fringe benefits that came with hanging out with her while she trained, one of which, she couldn't deny, was the view.

Deciding it was better to work than to focus on all the dynamics now swirling around her, Tess turned to Cade. "What's first today?"

"I want you to run the course full out three times. Nick needs to see you in action and we're going to do a few drills after that." Cade crossed to the back door then opened it. "Ladies first."

She took the few moments between the house and the beginning of the course to focus. The thought of all these people watching her had her stomach doing somersaults. An audience wasn't ideal, but she was going to have one anyway when she got to qualifiers. It wouldn't hurt to run the course in front of other people now.

Two hours later she was collapsed on top of the wall trying to catch her breath. She had lost track of how many times she'd run the course. Once he'd gotten a sense of her style and the course, Nick had taken over barking orders and Cade sat back and watched, adding suggestions occasionally.

Two Simon Legrees for the price of one.

There was a soft touch on her arm and she knew before she opened her eyes who it was. Only her mother would be that gentle. It was hard to focus on the woman hovering over her. How could even her eyelids hurt?

"Well, your grandfather wasn't kidding when he said you were probably the most talented athlete in the family. Your brothers are going to be annoyed."

Tess tried to smile as her mother helped her lurch to her feet. Her muscles hurt so much it probably came off more like a grimace. She limped to the edge of the wall and reached for the pole.

"You wouldn't rather use the stairs?" Her mother fidgeted.

A shrug would take too much effort. Instead she reached for the pole and slid effortlessly down. The only problem was her legs were like limp noodles and she didn't have the strength to brace herself. Instead, when her feet hit the ground she kept sliding and ended up in a heap at the foot of the wall.

"Man down," Delilah yelled.

Tess rolled over. She opened her eyes and stared at the sky, which was quickly blocked out by the faces of her workout spectators.

"Shouldn't be that tired," Nick commented.

She really wanted to roll her eyes, but even that was too much effort right now. Cade grabbed her hand and helped her to her feet.

"You, okay?" He put an arm around her waist to steady her.

"Been resting all day, shouldn't be this gassed." Nick glanced down at a notepad. "What's her diet like?"

Tess wanted to say something, but she couldn't make her brain work. She managed to put one foot in front of the other, but without Cade's help she would have planted her face in the ground. There were mumbles around her and she didn't understand why it sounded like they were coming through a tunnel.

Cade turned her to face him, but she couldn't focus on what he was saying.

"Tess? Tess?"

The last thing she heard was someone yelling, "call 911."

Chapter 14

Cade paced the waiting room. Nick had gone back to the cabin to sit with the dogs, once he'd been promised an update on Tess's condition when there was news. After she'd passed out they'd grilled Delilah about how they'd spent the morning and early afternoon and figured out that Tess hadn't had anything to eat or drink at all that day. She hadn't eaten much the night before either.

If he could kick his own ass he would. He'd been so focused on training her for the course, he hadn't thought about going over proper nutrition with her. According to her family she never ate much. There was no way she'd taken in enough calories or electrolytes to keep her body functioning for the rigorous training.

"You can't blame yourself."

Cade turned to Ed. "Who should I blame? The woman who knows nothing about training for an intense competition? The family that didn't even know she was training? I've been training my body for decades, first for football then for the Navy. I should have talked about her calorie intake with her before we started pushing her so hard."

"Cade." Tess's mom interrupted them. "If we've learned anything about my daughter, it's that she's incredibly stubborn and private. She's also a genius. She would have known that she would need to take in more calories and stay hydrated if she was going to train harder. You can't blame yourself."

"Besides, she's clearly as tough as they come." Tess's father joined the conversation. "She'll be fine. She'll take it easy for a few days and be back on her feet with the proper training diet."

"Maybe this is too much for her." Cade didn't want to ask her to quit, but he wanted her to be safe. He'd spent the last fourteen years of his life facing life and death situations, but he didn't remember ever feeling the terror he'd experienced when Tess collapsed in his arms. Not even when Sonny got hit.

"Yeah, she's not going to quit." Tyler joined the conversation. "Once she's in, she's all in."

Cade wanted to argue, but he knew enough about Tess to know her brother was right. His thoughts were interrupted by the arrival of the doctor.

"Tess Gallagher?"

Tess's parents stepped forward and the rest of the group fell behind them. Cade stepped up to her father's side.

"We're her parents." Trevor took his wife's hand. "How is she?"

"I'm Dr. Baccarri. Your daughter is stable. She was dehydrated and slightly malnourished. We've given her some fluids which will help put her body chemistry back in balance. We'd like to keep her overnight. If her labs come back within normal limits in the morning we can discharge her."

Ed stepped forward. "How long will she have to take it easy?"

"A couple of days." The doctor studied the chart in his hand for a moment. " I understand she's training for an athletic event."

"Yes." Tyler leaned around Cade. "She's competing in the qualifying round of American Ninja Warrior in a little over six weeks."

Dr. Baccarri nodded. "She'll have to take it easy for a few days. I'd recommend no exercise for the first two days and then light workouts for the next three. After that, if she's taking in enough calories and staying hydrated, she can resume her normal workouts."

"Can we see her?" Tess's mother asked.

"We're getting her settled in a room. A nurse will be by to take you to see her."

Cade let the Gallaghers and Kings visit Tess first and stepped outside to make a call. Once he updated Nick, Cade made his way to Tess's room.

He was surprised that her family was gone when he got there. She was asleep. Rather than wake her, Cade settled into the chair by the window. Visiting hours were over and a nurse would probably kick him out, but he was going to stay as long as he could. There was no way he'd leave her voluntarily.

Her soft snores were pretty damn cute, but he was too far away from her. Cade slid the chair closer to her bed then settled back, relaxed, and took her hand in his. He closed his eyes and listened to the cadence of her breath and the machines that told him her heart was beating a normal rhythm. The events of the day caught up with him and before he knew it, he was asleep.

Sometime later, Cade jolted awake. The dream dashed back into his conscious mind. More like a nightmare. The words his mother hurled at him as she stormed out of his life the last time spun through his head. He glanced around the dark room and stilled, not recognizing his surroundings.

The sounds of machines brought him back to the moment. He was in Tess's room at the hospital. Her hand was clutched in his. The moonlight gleamed through the window and illuminated her face.

The dim light was enough to see his watch and the dial

told him he'd slept for almost four hours. Cade shifted in the seat.

I wonder why no one kicked me out.

"No one's supposed to disturb me." Her voice drifted through the room like she'd read his mind.

He jumped and tried to ignore the feeling of warmth that spread through him at the sound. "I thought you were asleep."

"I was."

"Did I wake you?"

She shook her head. "Bad dream."

"What happened?" He let go of her hand and reached up to brush his fingers through her hair. She leaned into his touch.

"I was competing in the qualifier and I tripped on the first obstacle. The whole crowd started laughing and …"

"And what?"

She bit her lip, which had him shifting in the chair. All he wanted to do was kiss her.

"What happened next?" He prodded. She needed to tell him so he could fix it.

"The whole crowd started laughing and chanting." Tears pooled in her eyes.

Cade slid his thumb down her face and caught the first

tear before it could trickle down her cheek.

"What did they chant, Jules?"

"Weak-kneed Wylie." Her voice came out as less than a whisper.

If Cade hadn't already been leaning in close, he wouldn't have heard her.

"Where did that come from?"

"It was something Delilah and her groupies used to chant when they thought they got the better of me."

"Why are you friends with her?" Of all the people in Tess's life, Delilah was the one that didn't quite fit.

A small smile lifted the corners of her mouth. "She's definitely an acquired taste."

"She's a grade A smart ass who has to make an effort to think of anyone but herself."

She shook her head slightly. "That's not true. She's got a good heart."

"She tormented you while you were growing up, so much that you have nightmares when you're supposed to be resting."

Tess closed her eyes. "She's been through a lot. Sarcasm and snide comments are her defense mechanism." She took a deep breath. "It's not my story to tell."

Which, he knew, meant she wouldn't say any more

about it.

She amazed him. Constantly. "For someone who says she doesn't understand social cues, you see a lot."

She shrugged.

He ran his hand through her hair the silky strands made his skin tingle. "You should be resting."

Tess yawned. "I've been sleeping for days."

He checked his watch. "Four hours isn't days."

"I slept for most of the afternoon." She protested.

"You collapsed. Scared the shit out of me." He rested his forehead on hers.

She sighed. "I'm much better."

"Not good enough. I should go, let you rest."

"Don't." She gripped his hand.

"Jules."

"I don't like hospitals. I don't want to stay here alone."

He was torn. She needed to rest, but she was clearly wide awake, and he didn't want to leave her alone if she was scared of being here. Still holding her hand, he settled back in his chair. This connection between them was unlike anything he'd ever known, and he was reluctant to let it go, even for a little while.

"If I stay, will you try and go back to sleep?" Bargaining might be his only option.

"I'm not sleepy."

"You're here because the doctor said you need to rest." He tried to sound stern.

"I'm not going to run an obstacle course." She smiled. "Talk to me."

"What do you want to talk about?"

"Anything." She yawned again. "Did you ever regret not going pro?"

He didn't answer right away. It was a question he'd been asked a lot over the last fourteen years. Talking about it meant talking about the reason he'd made his choice. It was easy to avoid any real discussions with sarcastic comments or deflection. How did you talk about your mother betraying you and destroying your dreams?

"I didn't mean to get too personal. I'm sorry."

He squeezed her hand. "Don't be. It's not a new question."

"But you don't like answering it."

"Haven't ever really done that." Not even his father or brother knew the whole story.

"People let you get away with not answering a question?"

Cade laughed. "Sometimes I think you know more about human interaction than you let on, and other times I wonder how you get along with people at all."

He saw her face fall and wanted to kick his own ass. She wasn't as sensitive lately, but she still didn't like it when she thought people she trusted were laughing at her. The fact that she trusted him enough to be hurt by him was secondary to the knowledge that he could cause her pain.

All he wanted to do was fix it. He took her face in his hands. "Hey. I'm not laughing at you. I won't ever laugh at you. I promise."

Tears pooled in her hazel eyes. Her chin trembled as she blinked them away. "I don't like it."

"What?"

"That people can't say what they mean."

"Honey, if I could explain human nature to you, I would." Needing some space, he sat back in his chair. For some reason he couldn't bring himself to lose contact with her entirely, so he held on to her hand.

She sighed. "I don't understand why people make things so difficult."

He shrugged. Philosophical discussions weren't his thing. There was no point in them. You dealt with the road in front of you. Everything else was usually a waste of time and a distraction. In football, distractions could cost you the game, in the military they could cost you your life.

"Even I can tell when someone's thinking deep thoughts."

He heard the smile in her voice. "You bring it out in me."

"You didn't answer my question."

"Which one was that?"

She gave him a look he couldn't decipher. He wondered if there would be a time that he knew every one of her looks, and he wondered why he was thinking like that. That kind of knowledge came from spending years with someone. His own mother had told him he was only good at short term. Nothing that had happened since she'd walked out on her family had shown him anything different.

"Do you ever regret not going pro? Joining the Navy?"

"No."

"If you don't want to talk about it, you don't have to."

"I guess I don't know how to explain it."

"It's all right."

He squeezed her hand. "I never regretted not going pro. I missed the game, and didn't have enough chances to play, but I had a new team in the Navy, and I was doing something important. I come from a long line of sailors. Since there's been a U.S. Navy there's been a Maguire serving in it."

Cade looked away from her and stared out the window into the night. "Truthfully, my dad was a little pissed I was going to play football at Cormac. He'd already secured me a spot at the Naval Academy. I figured Cormac would be my big rebellion. I didn't think I would end up in the pros. I always planned to enlist after I graduated college."

"Really? You had to know how talented you were. I was only ten when you started with the team. Even I could tell how amazing you were."

"Every player that makes it to college has talent. You know how many of them make it to the pros?"

"Less than two percent."

He laughed. Of course, she knew the statistic. "I had colleges start recruiting me my sophomore year in high school. They were trying to lock me down when I was sixteen and didn't know shit. One of the reasons I chose Cormac was because the first time I met your grandfather he told me I would be a jackass if I committed myself anywhere before my senior year."

The memory of that first conversation with Ed played over in his mind. "When I got here I heard all about Gill. Everyone said he would be the starter. He was connected and I was just some asshole kid with a good arm and a chip on his shoulder. Figured I'd ride the bench, play a little ball and earn my degree. Then I'd do what every generation of Maguire did before me, join the Navy. I was as surprised as anyone else when I got the starting spot. Played four years and loved every minute of it. Still didn't think had a shot at the pros."

"You were the best quarterback in the country. You won a Heisman. How could you not think you'd get drafted?"

"I just didn't." It was impossible to explain this to her without talking about his mother, and he wasn't going there.

"Empirically you had to know —"

He held up a hand. "We could go back and forth on this. You know my stats. I know how many players with stats as good as or better than mine never played pro, in more sports than football."

"You were so good."

He didn't know why her insistence on his talent made him feel so warm and cold at the same time and thought it was a bad idea to try and analyze it right then.

"Anyway, we won the championship my senior year, and everyone started speculating that I'd go number one in the draft. I figured what the hell." He tapped his foot. "Why not declare?"

"Then why did you withdraw?"

Could he tell the story without leaving out his mother? "I was dating someone. Thought we were serious. The night before the draft, I found out that she'd betrayed me. All she wanted was to be hooked to a professional athlete."

She gasped and tears pooled in her eyes. He couldn't resist and leaned in to kiss her gently. No one had ever cried for him.

"Don't cry for me. It's not like she ripped my heart out."

"But —"

"I was young and stupid. She was young and hot. It wasn't a fairy tale romance. We had all these plans, but they were based on lies."

He leaned back. The words were coming easier. For a second, he wondered if it was just the fact that he'd started the story but discarded that thought. He was finding the right words because he was giving them to her.

"The next morning I enlisted."

"Did your father ask you to?"

"No. Funny thing. Once he understood I was serious about going to Cormac, he was glad I hadn't caved to him. Proud I'd followed my own path."

"What did he say when you told him?"

"I didn't. I enlisted and pulled my name from the draft.

Then I went dark. Showed up to boot camp. The old man didn't know what happened until I was almost through with my training."

"How did he take it?"

"He was confused and proud. Came to my graduation." It had been hard not sharing everything with his dad, but he didn't want his old man blaming himself for the shitty excuse for a mother he gave his sons.

"Where is he now?"

"He's got his own command, a nuclear sub. They're deployed. Don't know where. He'll tag me when he's got leave."

"Have you talked to him since you got discharged?"

"No. He got deployed right after my injury. Hadn't gotten my medical yet."

"How will he take it?"

Cade shrugged. He hadn't given a lot of thought to his father's reaction to his current situation. If the Board vote went their way he'd have his life settled, which would go a long way to easing that conversation. His father was all about having a plan.

"How did you take it?"

This was the longest non-training conversation they'd ever had. "You sure are chatty tonight."

"I'm sorry." She didn't sound at all sleepy.

He let out a mildly frustrated sigh. "Don't be sorry. I'm being an ass. I've just never been big on talking about stuff. Especially this shit."

"I should probably talk about things more than I do." She admitted.

"Why?"

"Because I still have problems figuring out social cues, unless they'd be obvious to a blind person. I need to ask people what they're thinking so I don't do something insulting or misunderstand their behavior towards me. You may have noticed I can be a little sensitive."

He saw the insecurity in her face and his stomach knotted because he'd put it there.

"How about we make a deal?"

She watched him with suspicion. "What kind of deal?"

"You can ask me whatever you want. But, you can't get pissed or hurt if I say I can't talk about it."

"Will you just tell me you can't talk about it?"

"That's all?"

She nodded. "I just want people to be honest with me. I don't want to push you or make you uncomfortable. So, if I get too personal or ask you about something you don't want to talk about, tell me. You don't even have to explain it. I just need you to be clear."

"It'll be that easy?"

"I'm sure you've figured out by now that I'm not like most women. I have my own ridiculous boundaries. I can respect yours."

Cade sat back and stared. This battle he waged against his attraction to Tess was a losing one. Before he could think of what to do about it, he noticed her eyelids were starting to droop. "You need some more sleep."

Her eyes popped open before her lids drooped again. "Don't leave me alone."

"I'll stay on one condition."

"What?"

"You'll tell me why you're afraid of hospitals when you're better."

"Okay." Her voice dropped and a moment later he heard that cute little snort, which was part of her snore. He loved her snore. Who knew a snore would turn him on so much? Everything about her was either intriguing, adorable, or just plain hot. He was in deep.

How am I supposed to fight this? Fight her?

She was going to lose her mind. It had been a pleasant

surprise to see Cade asleep in the chair when she woke up in the hospital. For a split second she thought her recovery wouldn't be that bad. Two days later she knew she couldn't have been more wrong. Once she made it clear she still intended to compete, Nick and Cade had come up with her new training program, which included a new diet.

Cade brought her home and she was immediately surrounded by family and ordered to stay in bed for the rest of the day. Nick showed up with Sonny and Sam, and suddenly her living room turned into the office for putting together a plan she wasn't supposed to know anything about yet.

Nick turned into her own personal chef. He was a talented cook and the food tasted delicious. But it was Delilah's chocolate jalapeno cupcakes that turned out to be Tess's addiction.

The problem with having a personal chef who was also your strength trainer was that he watched every bite she took and made notes. Notes. Like she was a lab rat.

Since she was finally cleared for light activity, she had gotten dressed, planning to go into the office to check on things. At the foot of the stairs, she was met with a wall of muscles when Nick put himself between her and the door.

"Nope."

"I can go to my own office. I don't have any patients scheduled, I'm just going to check in." It's not like she was going to walk to town.

"Nope."

She was a grown woman. "I'm not going to do anything but sit at my desk."

"Nope."

"Do you have anything else to say?" This was ridiculous.

"Nope."

She threw her hands up and went back into the kitchen to find her tablet. If she couldn't go to the office, she would bring the office to her. A large hand reached in and took it from her.

"Nope."

She stared at her hands, which no longer held her own damn tablet. "What nope? I can't read now?"

"Can't check your e-mail. Plenty of books in the other room if you want to sit and read until Cade and Ed get here."

"What happens then?" Was someone going to tuck her and give her a blanky?

"You'll see."

"Is it a state secret?"

"Nope." Nick sat down at the kitchen table across from her and watched her.

"Why are you watching me so closely?"

"Cade told me to keep an eye on you."

She doubted Cade meant it so literally. "That's not all."

"Feel bad."

"Why?"

"I made Cade push you past your limits the other day. You ended up in the hospital."

Lord save her from overprotective martyrs. "Because I hadn't been eating properly or taking in enough fluids to keep up with my training."

"Saw you were done. Pushed you too hard."

"If you'd eased up I would have collapsed anyway. My body was running on empty." She reached across the table to take Nick's hand. He stared down at her hand like it was a foreign object. "It wasn't your fault."

"Could've —"

Tess squeezed his hand. "You're not God. You're not even a god, all appearances to the contrary." She smiled when the corners of his lips tilted slightly. "I have news for you. You're not responsible for everything that happens around you. The adults around you are going to make our own stupid choices without your help. I have an exceptional IQ. I should have adapted my diet for my workouts. I was spread too thin and I just didn't think about it. This is on me."

He didn't look like he was convinced, which made her wonder why he saw the need to take this on. A knock at the door interrupted their conversation.

"I'll answer it." Nick got up and left the room. He returned a few moments later followed by Tess's friend Olivia.

"Olivia." Tess moved to stand up.

Olivia waived her back. "Don't get up." She moved to Tess and hugged her. "I heard what happened." She shifted, obviously uncomfortable.

"I'm fine. It's nice of you to stop by." A little surprising, but nice.

"I don't want to intrude." She fidgeted as she tried not to look at Nick.

"Olivia Valenti, this is my friend Nick Jacobs. Nick this is Olivia Valenti."

Nick nodded at the pretty brunette and Olivia smiled at him as she wrung her hands.

"You didn't have to come by."

Olivia closed her eyes and took a quick breath. "I just —

"Have a seat. Tell me what's going on."

"I can't stay long. I've been busy with work and everything. I just wanted to stop by and see you. You've been so nice to me since I came to town, and after I heard about your collapse —"

"It's sweet of you to come by. I'm sorry I haven't been available to talk lately. There's a lot going on."

Tess's statement was punctuated by the sound of the front door opening, followed by the clack of paws in the front hall as Sonny and Sam made their way in to greet their friends. A few moments later, Cade and her grandfather appeared in the kitchen. They both moved to Tess, giving her assessing gazes before turning to Olivia. Tess made the introductions, which were followed by an uncomfortable silence.

"Well, I guess everyone knows that the architects of two of the three proposals for the Board are in the room." Tess pointed directly at the elephant in the room.

When no one responded, Tess turned to her friend. "Olivia, I want you to know that Cade and my grandfather are helping me train for a competition. I'm not favoring their plan."

"Well, he's your grandfather. Of course, you're going to

vote for his proposal." Her words were little more than a whisper.

"There's no of course about it. He's my grandfather and you're my friend. I didn't even tell them I know the professor who was making the pitch to the Board." Tess stiffened her spine. "I have made it perfectly clear to all the men in this room that I don't want any information on their proposal. Just like I told you that we couldn't talk about yours. I am going to give everyone a fair shot and I will vote for the plan I think is best for the university."

"I've insulted you, now. I should go." Olivia rushed from the room before anyone could stop her.

Tess made a note to call her later. Something else was clearly going on that her friend probably didn't want to talk about in front of strangers.

"She's a skittish little thing." Her grandfather sat next to her at the table and patted her knee. "How you doin' this morning?"

"I was trying to decide what my sentence would be if I stabbed Nick in the eye before Olivia got here and distracted me." She turned to Nick. "You should thank her for saving your life next time you see her."

Nick laughed. Both Cade and her grandfather stared at him. She noted their looks of surprise and made a note to ask them about it later.

Tess stood up. "How are we tormenting me today?"

"You eat all your breakfast?"

Tess crossed her arms. This was getting ridiculous. When the silence stretched out, Cade turned to Nick.

"She eat all her breakfast?"

"Yep."

"She's standing right here and she's not a child." Tess tapped her toe.

Cade narrowed his eyes. "Probably shouldn't act like one then."

"I shouldn't..." She couldn't find any words. Tess marched out of the kitchen, slamming the back door behind her when she left the house. All she wanted was a little time alone. The obstacle course was as good a place as any to find a little peace."

"Tess." He stormed after her. "You make a run through that fucking course and you and I are going to have a problem."

She'd had no intention of do anything of the kind, but something about his tone made her want to push his buttons. So, she walked over to the floating steps then stepped onto the platform.

"I'm warning you." Cade's voice was barely more than

a growl.

A shiver ran through her and, for a moment she thought this might not be a good idea.

"I mean it, Tess. Don't put one foot on that thing."

Something perverse took hold of her. She knew she wasn't up to running the course, or even tackling one obstacle. There was no way she was going to do anything stupid. But she did extend her leg and rested her foot on the first of the stepping stones and held it there.

There was no time to process that it was a bad idea to challenge him. The moment her foot touched the obstacle, Cade roared and exploded into action. He rushed her and snatched her from the platform. A second later he was carrying her towards the house. It occurred to her that, angry as he was, he was holding her like she was made of spun sugar. His jaw looked like it was carved in stone and he was focused on the house. She heard a truck driving away.

"Cade..." His name was barely a whisper.

He tightened his grip on her. "Don't."

"I wasn't..." Wasn't what? Going to run the course? Trying to piss him off? She didn't know what she was doing anymore.

"I said don't."

Moments later she found herself somewhat unceremoniously dumped on her bed. She started to rise when he followed her down. He caged her with his body. The momentary frisson of fear gave way to anticipation.

"Cade?"

"What am I going to do with you?"

She shrugged, not brave enough to tell him what she'd like him to do. His eyes were molten as his gaze locked on hers.

How could his eyes be greener?

Before her thoughts could wander too far he lowered his head and claimed her with a kiss.

Chapter 15

Cade felt her move beneath him and his last ounce of control vanished. He needed her. She tasted like chocolate laced with jalapeno. Her flavor rolled through his system imprinting there. In the back of his mind he knew he'd always crave the zing that shot through his blood because of her. He let his weight settle, pinning her down as he deepened the kiss. His elbows rested on the mattress as he sank his fingers into her thick brown hair. He wanted to touch her, everywhere, but his entire focus was on her lips beneath his, and he wasn't ready to move on from them, yet.

Her busy fingers yanked his T-shirt from the waist band of his jeans and she ran her palms up his back. Her slightly calloused hands moved along his skin, sending a charge zipping up his spine. She paused along his right side as she explored the scar tissue. The feel of her hand on his damaged skin shot straight to his heart.

Her hair slipped through his fingers as he reached over his back and pulled away long enough to yank his T-shirt over his head. She stared at him and studied the scarring along his right side. It should have made him feel small, her fascination with the part of him that was less. Instead, her tender gaze made him feel larger than life.

He lowered himself back down and trailed kisses down her jawline and discovered another intriguing flavor that was all her – kettle corn, that salty, sweet flavor that made him think of carnivals and wild summer nights. He needed to taste more of her. Hell, he craved all of her.

While he continued to sample her, she ran her hands up his sides. Her left hand skimmed along his scars, lavishing them with a gentle touch. He leaned back to look at her. She stunned him. Hazel eyes were clouded with passion and a small smile played across her lips.

God, she's gorgeous.

He'd never seen anything so beautiful in his entire life. He wanted to hold on to this moment forever.

In one swift move, he rolled, settling her on top of him, which set off a whole new round of zaps to his system. He reached up and tore her T-shirt from her body. Some part of his mind knew he should regret destroying her top. The part in charge didn't care. He was desperate to be closer to her.

Her dark blue sports bra was a contrast to her lightly tanned skin and was sexier than any lacy concoction he'd seen on other women. Her eyes were wide, like she'd been drugged. He liked the idea that he was the one making her high. He traced the edges of her collar bone with his hands before sliding them down underneath the blue spandex that separated him from finally seeing her breasts. A moment later her upper body was bared to him. He lightly rubbed his thumbs along her nipples, the sight of the dusky pink points going taut under his touch made him harder than he'd ever been.

She rubbed her hands along his chest. And he was harder still. Her tentative touch was a bigger turn on than any of the practiced gropes he'd experienced before this moment. He let that thought go. There was no room in the moment for anyone but Tess and him. When she leaned in and hesitantly licked his neck he shot up like a jack in the box. As much as he wanted to take his time, if he didn't move this along, she was going to make him go off like a teenager having his first wet dream.

Cade yanked his jeans off and made sure to grab one of the packets he kept in his wallet before returning to her. He grabbed the waist band of her shorts and slipped them off her in one move. When he made sure she was protected he crawled up her body savoring the spicy vanilla scent that would always make him think of her.

Within moments skin touched skin everywhere. He worshipped her with his body, trying to show her everything he was feeling. She was so responsive. Everywhere he touched she shivered and her shivers ran through him like they were his. Everywhere she touched there was power building inside of him. When he finally slid inside her he felt something he'd never known before. He was home.

After the most amazing experience of his life Cade pulled a trembling Tess closer, grateful he'd managed to keep his own release at bay until she'd found hers. Neither of them spoke as they recovered from what they'd just shared. He didn't know what to say. He'd never been good with words. For the first time in his life he wanted to be.

"God, I hope Grandpa and Nick aren't downstairs."

He laughed. He wasn't sure what he expected her to say, but it wasn't that.

"They took off when I went after you. Said something about looking at the campus gym."

"That's good. You're kind of loud."

"Me? Jules. I wasn't the one screaming."

Her skin, already flushed and slick with sweat, turned pinker. It was adorable. He couldn't resist running a trail of kisses along her neck. She giggled. A long dark curl danced along her cheek and he brushed it out of her face. Cuddling and post-sex conversation had never been his thing but somehow, with Tess, he didn't want or need to leave.

"Do you think they know what happened?"

She bit her lip, a gesture which made him want to lick where her teeth pressed. He gave in to the impulse and licked along the edge of her lip. They should probably talk, but he couldn't stop kissing and touching her.

"They figured we were going to have a huge fight."

"I'm a lover not a fighter."

Her voice was so serious it took him a second to see she was joking. He rolled over onto his back, pulling her with him and burst out laughing.

She smiled at him. "I like your laugh."

It sounded rusty to him. "Don't think anyone's ever told me that."

"They should."

"Most of the people I hang out with don't talk about stuff like this."

"What do you talk about?"

"Work. Football. More work." There really wasn't much else to talk about.

"Sounds like my conversations not too long ago. Not necessarily the football, but the work definitely." She rested her head on his shoulder and snuggled into him.

"What changed?" It was surprising, this need to know everything about her.

"The Trips. Then Delilah. They're all kind of hard to resist."

He laughed. That was an understatement. The four of them were the damn Borg. "I understand the Trips, they're your brothers. What's the deal with Delilah?"

"About a year ago, I had a kind of meltdown."

"What happened?" His nerves went on alert. He didn't care about the story with her friend. Whatever had sent her into a spiral a year ago was more important than anything else.

She rubbed a hand down his chest, petting him to calm him like she would one of her pets. "It's nothing now. But I went to The Dive one night."

"The Dive?" He couldn't picture here there. It had been the place the athletes went to let loose and stay off their coaches' radars.

"Delilah was there. She was a mess and drunk enough to tell me some of what happened. It was bad."

Cade waited. She wasn't going to give him details. He knew that, but just the little she shared with him told him everything he needed to know. For now. "I'm glad you have such good friends."

Tess nodded. She was quiet for a moment. "So you really think Grandpa and Nick thought we were going to fight?"

He smiled back. "I wasn't looking for a fight."

"I wasn't going to run the course. I just needed some space."

"Jules, you've only been out of the hospital for two days."

"I know. I think we can all agree I'm not stupid. I know my limits, now more than ever. You need to let me get back to my routine. I can't train for the competition if you coddle me."

He gritted his teeth. "I know. I just..." He gently gripped the back of her neck and pulled her closer so their foreheads touched. "You scared the shit out of me." For the rest of his life he would remember the moment when she collapsed in his arms. His entire body had seized with panic. The sight of her limp and unresponsive had made him think about a world without her and made him want to collapse too.

He'd been frozen, unable to do anything, unable to react in an instant. Other than when Sonny got hurt, that didn't happen to him. Since the day his mother had walked out, telling him how useless he was, he'd been the man with the plan. His need for order had come directly from that moment when his life had turned to chaos. Being unable to help Tess had made him feel like that six-year old boy who couldn't make his mother stay.

"I didn't mean to."

"I know. You're just going to have to give me a minute to come back from that." A minute, a month, a lifetime. He wasn't sure he'd ever come back from it.

"I understand."

"I don't think you do. I've been in combat. I've watched my men die around me. I've never been as scared as I was when you collapsed. It's not something I can do again."

"Not my favorite moment either." She burrowed closer in to him.

He tightened his grip on her neck a little. "I mean it. I'm not an easy man. Words are sometimes hard for me to find, and I'm all about control. Seeing you like that, not being able to do anything…you need to know if we're going to do this, whatever this is, I'm going to probably cross some of your boundaries."

She was quiet for a moment. "Well, since we are doing this, whatever this is, you should probably know that I'm going to push your buttons."

"No shit. You really weren't going to run the course?" He still couldn't explain the torrent of emotions that coursed through him when he saw her walk to the course.

240

"No, I really wasn't."

"So you just put your foot on the stone — "

"Because you told me not to."

He rolled them over again in one swift move. He rested his weight on her, loving the feel of her slim body beneath his. "I really shouldn't find that hot. But I do." With that he proceeded to show her exactly how hot he found it.

The sound of weights clanking to a rest filled the air. Tess wrinkled her nose at the scent of sweat. Her training team had decided she needed to add weightlifting to the program. They'd gotten three month passes for the local gym, since Cade and Nick couldn't get access to the university gym until they were on staff.

She finished her last set of reps and let the barbell fall back into place. Nick stood behind her spotting her. He was so close to her she was surprised she hadn't hit him in the face. Cade usually gave her a few more inches of space. She'd tried to help him relax, thinking he still blamed himself for her collapse the week before. But he stuck to her like a red-billed oxpecker cleaning an impala whenever Cade wasn't there.

She sat up and stretched her shoulders. "You can relax a

little."

He shook his head. "You're Cade's. Nothing's happening to you on my watch."

While the description of her as Cade's sent all kinds of unexpected tingles zinging through her body, she wished it didn't come with an apparent bodyguard, when the man himself couldn't be with her. She also wished it didn't come with the feeling that she was waiting for the other shoe to drop. It didn't take a relationship genius to know Cade was holding something back.

"Your form is pretty good." Nick handed her a towel.

High praise coming from him. He picked up her bag and waited for her to finish wiping down the weight bench.

"I need to hit the shower."

He nodded and looked at his watch. "Cade's meeting us for lunch by your office in forty-five minutes."

She shrugged. "I only need fifteen." She sauntered off, hearing him chuckle as he followed behind her.

True to her word, fifteen minutes later she exited the women's locker room. Nick was waiting for her at the end of the hall. He stood there, rigid like he'd been fossilized a million years ago. When she saw who he was talking to, or rather who was talking at him, she understood.

To say Brian Gill, Jr. was not her favorite person, was an

understatement of epic proportions. She'd met him for the first time when she was six and he was fourteen. They were both at a guidance counselor's office. Her family had just discovered she was gifted. His family had discovered he was not. They'd been alone in the waiting room while their parents met with their respective counselors. He'd been sullen and withdrawn and, in her innocence, she'd tried to be kind. He'd snidely dubbed her "Wylie Coyote, super genius." A nickname Delilah had latched onto.

But it was his father's comments when he'd come out of the meeting that had terrified her. Since that day, Junior had gone out of his way to be annoying and sarcastic whenever they ran into each other. At every opportunity, Senior had chosen to be impossibly cruel.

The truth behind her friendship with Delilah rested less in Delilah's contrition and more in what Senior had done to her, and Junior had allowed during her marriage to the younger Gill. Delilah didn't remember divulging the worst of it to Tess when they had run into each other at The Dive. But hearing what Delilah had suffered at both the Gills' hands made it easier for Tess to forgive her for Delilah's own mean girl antics, which, looking back were more juvenile and petty than cruel.

Whenever Tess saw Brian she usually made sure to

move in the other direction, but seeing him harangue Nick, who wouldn't retaliate, gave her the strength she needed to finally stand up to him.

She squared her shoulders and marched toward them. Brian was too busy laying into Nick to notice her approach and didn't stop his diatribe because of it.

"How's it feel to kill someone, Jacobs?" Brian sneered.

Tess didn't miss the tightening of Nick's entire body. A minute ago, she didn't think he could have gone any more rigid than he already was. She didn't know Nick's entire story, but she knew something terrible had happened his senior year in high school, ending his college football career before it had even begun. It didn't matter to her what it was. Nick was her friend and Brian was a bully.

"I'd be careful throwing around accusations, Brian." She stood next to Nick, arms crossed, eyes narrowed. It might take her another minute to build up the courage to stand up to Senior, but Junior, she could handle.

He jumped, and his glance darted from Nick to her. She was sure she must have misinterpreted the momentary expression of regret in his eyes but decided to give that some thought later. After they got rid of him.

"You've adopted him too? You have a taste for losers lately." He sneered.

"The only loser I see is you, lyin' Brian." His face turned red at her use of Delilah's nickname for her soon to be ex-husband.

"You tell that gold-digger to stop talking about me."

"You call my friend a gold-digger again, and I'll put your "Tiny Dancer" video on You Tube."

He opened and closed his mouth like a fish out of water.

"Yes. I have a copy. I have a copy of everything you've sent Delilah over the years. She might be afraid to use it since you're stalling the divorce, but I'm not."

Sweat beaded on his forehead. "You don't know what you're messing with."

She stepped up to Brian. He had five inches and at least sixty pounds on her, but she was done with his garbage.

"I know exactly who I'm dealing with. I've known since I was six years old, you pathetic douche nozzle. You started picking on me then and haven't stopped since."

With that pronouncement the air in the room changed. She could actually sense the danger emanating from Nick.

"I have no idea what you are talking about."

"Yes, you do. You're almost too lazy to bother with, except you're trying to hurt my friends. So, before you take this game any further, you need to remember that I know where all your skeletons are buried, and I do mean all of them."

Brian stiffened. "You don't know what you're doing, Wylie."

"I know exactly what I'm doing." She stepped closer to her nemesis. "I won't let you hurt her again."

Something flared in Brian's eyes. "I didn't hurt her."

"You didn't stop it." She poked him in the chest.

He closed his eyes. When he opened them again she had to step back at the pain that flashed there for a moment before it was gone. Brian spun on his heel and left.

What was that about?

Tess pressed her palms to her eyes for a moment, then turned to Nick. "You okay?"

"What were you talking about?" He stared at her like he'd developed x-ray vision.

"When?"

"When you said you'd been dealing with him since you were six." His feet were planted in a wide stance and the muscles on his neck were corded. "What were you talking about?"

"I'd like the answer to that question, too." Cade's quiet voice startled her and Nick.

Tess turned to face him. "I thought we were meeting you at lunch."

"Ed and I finished early. Thought I'd see if I could catch you here. What did you mean about Gill?"

"It's not important."

"The hell it isn't, Jules. If you were six when he went after you the first time that means he was fourteen. A fourteen-year-old boy going after a six-year-old girl is all kinds of wrong." He cracked his knuckles.

"He didn't go after me. Not the way you think." It wasn't as bad but at the same time infinitely worse than what they must be thinking.

"So, put our minds at ease. Tell us what happened."

"I'm not going to talk about this right now." She walked away, hoping they would follow her and drop the subject, even if it meant she'd only have a temporary reprieve.

Chapter 16

Cade walked into his cabin after leaving Tess at the clinic. He had a few hours with Ed and Nick to work on the program before she went home. Tess had been completely close mouthed about Gill. Despite his best efforts, and Nick's, they hadn't been able to get her to talk during lunch. The more they'd pushed the quieter she'd become. It was clear he would have to wait until she was ready to talk to him about it. That burned.

I can't fix it if I don't know what it is.

His body tensed and sweat trickled down his back. The thought of Gill at fourteen and Tess at six made him want to put his fist through something, preferably through Gill's face.

"What's up your ass?" Ed asked from the recliner he'd had delivered to the cabin after they'd started working on the program. He wouldn't let Cade pay him back for it. Said it was a gift to his old bones just as much as it was a housewarming present for Cade.

"Nothing." The last thing he wanted to do was tell Ed about what little Tess had said earlier. That's all they needed. A pissed off grandfather on a rampage.

"Bullshit."

Cade looked at Nick who shook his head slightly.

Ed caught the look. "What are you two hiding?"

"Nothing to do with work."

"Something to with Tess." It was a statement not a question.

"Didn't say that."

"Son, I didn't just fall off the turnip truck. Saw you this morning. You were fine. Had lunch with this one and my girl and your pissed as hell. So, what's wrong? She have any health issues with her workout?"

"No. We ran into Gill at the gym. He got in Nick's face, pissed us both off."

"That it?"

Cade didn't want to lie to Ed, but Nick had made a good point earlier. With everything that had happened with Tess recently, if her family got wind of something going on with Gill, they would be all over her, and she would be even more angry at him than she was right now, after he hounded her about it at lunch. Since he really liked spending time with her, he didn't want to give her a reason to stop.

"Gill is the reason I'm pissed."

And whatever he did to Tess.

"He's always been a broody little shit. You can't let him get to you. He moves around trying to play head games with everyone. He's mostly harmless. It's Senior that swoops in for the kill."

"Yeah. Nothing's changed." Cade didn't have much experience with Senior. He was going to have to ask Delilah about him.

"He just go after Nick or did he get in Tess's face, too?"

"Tess got in his face." Nick sat down.

"Really?" Ed jerked his head back.

"Yeah. He made his bullshit comment, and she was on him like white on rice. Told him she knew where his bodies were buried and to watch his ass."

"Yeah. Delilah probably had some dirt for her." Ed didn't seem concerned.

Cade shrugged. "If we spend the afternoon talking about Gill instead of working on our program, he's going to get what he wanted by trying to get into Nick's head."

"You're right." Ed pulled out some paperwork. "Here's where we are and what we still need in the next four weeks."

A few hours later, Cade pulled up in front of Tess's house. He let Sam out, who joined her menagerie lazing around on the porch and waited for Cade to carry Sonny up to join them. Tess and Delilah were already down by the obstacle course. It was a relief to see she was stretching and

250

hadn't started a heavy workout without him to watch out for her.

The protective instincts that Tess aroused in him made him a little queasy. He was used to standing with a team and being prepared to stand in front of his men. This was something completely different.

If he could wrap her in a bubble and protect her from the world, he would. His chest was tight and it felt like there were rocks in his stomach. It was a tough spot to negotiate, because she was more than capable of taking care of herself and wouldn't appreciate him trying to fight her battles. It didn't mean he'd stop trying.

He walked over to her. "How long you been stretching, Jules?"

"She's been at it about fifteen minutes." Delilah glared at him. "I told her she should stretch for at least twenty. My soon to be ex wound her up pretty good. He has that effect on sane people everywhere."

Cade saw something flash in Delilah's eye at her mention of Brian, which made Cade oddly protective of Tess's friend.

"Yeah. He's a dick. Gotta say Dee, you were kind of a bitch to Tess growing up, but you are way out of that asshole's league."

"You're telling me. That's the last time I go through with a pity marriage." The pain that was now clearly visible in her eyes didn't match her sarcastic tone.

Cade laughed, somehow knowing she needed him to leave it alone. He had to hand it to Delilah, she was a play through the pain kind of girl. It was a sight to see. Her friendship with Tess still gave him pause, given their past, but he was smart enough to know that any interference from him was a losing battle.

After Tess finished stretching, he told her to take pass through the course at half speed.

"Watch your ass with her." Delilah stood behind him, eyes focused on the course and the woman running it.

"I don't know what you mean." He knew, but he sure as hell wasn't going to talk to her about it.

"Yeah you do. You two are doing the nasty with a side of mush."

"What?" That was Delilah, give her a pass and she pushed back too far.

"You know. You're in a re-la-tion-ship." She drew out the last syllable and used air quotes, irritating the shit out of him.

He wasn't going to do this with her. "Our business."

"Wrong." She flicked the back of his ear with her finger-nail.

What the ever-loving fuck?

He wasn't going to put up with this shit. "Wrong?" He looked at her.

"Yeah tough guy, wrong. That." She pointed her annoying talon at Tess who was easing through the circuit board. "That's my girl. I'm the first one to admit I treated her like crap when we were growing up. I don't deserve her friendship. But she found me at the lowest point in my life. Anyone else with our history would have kicked me while I was down. Not just kicked, mashed into the ground. Not her." She nodded toward Tess. "She got down in the dirt with me and helped me stand up. I'm still not on my feet, yet, but with her help I'm getting there. So, I'm going to be pissed off if you mess her up."

"I'm not going to mess her up."

"You don't want to mess her up. There's a difference."

Cade didn't know what to say. Fortunately, he didn't have to say anything because Delilah sauntered off and went to her car.

"She's like one of those little dogs that you think are all yap, and no bite until they sink their teeth into your ankle."

Cade laughed. Nick's description was pretty apt.

253

"She's not wrong, though." Nick stayed focused on Tess.

"About?"

"You not hurting her" Nick tipped his head toward the woman currently making her way toward the warped wall.

What was with everyone warning him away from Tess? "Did I suddenly become an asshole, and nobody told me?"

"Nope."

"Then why does everyone think I'm going to hurt her?" Was it that obvious to everyone that he was no good for Tess? Did his mother take out an ad somewhere for the world to see?

"Don't think you are. Pretty sure you're the one who's not seeing this straight."

"You a shrink now?" The last thing Cade needed was to be analyzed by his friends.

"Nope."

Cade rolled his eyes. He was used to not talking much with his buddies, but Nick took it to a whole new level.

"Should have tried to talk to Delilah about her ex before she took off."

"Yeah." Cade agreed. "Got a feeling that moment Tess saved her from had to do with him."

"Probably. Guy's a dick."

254

"Always assumed he was harmless." Gill has always been like a gnat to him. Buzzing around but not being able to do much to Cade.

"Guy who'd go after a six-year-old? Not harmless." The anger in Nick's voice was almost alive.

Cade could understand. The thought of anyone bullying Tess was intolerable. The thought of a fourteen-year old, or worse, his father, going after her when she was six was incomprehensible.

Tess made it up the wall at the end of the course and stood there, hands on her knees, taking deep breaths. He left Nick standing there and walked over to the wall and leapt up next to Tess.

"Show off." She smiled.

"You okay?"

"Yes." She looked like she was focused on breathing. "I'm a little winded, but it's not bad."

"Maybe we should call it for the day."

She straightened to look at him. "If I train at this rate, I'll never be ready for qualifiers."

"Jules. You can't over do it."

"Pushing myself and over doing are two different things. You can't be afraid to push me because we're…whatever we are."

A pink color spread up her neck, which was cute as hell. "Whatever we are?" Why did he want her to define it? "Well, it's...we..."

He leaned over and gave her a quick kiss. "You ran that in twelve minutes. Go back and see if you can shave at least two minutes off that time."

She smiled, slid down the pole and jogged back to the start of the course. He and Nick watched her carefully for the next two hours to make sure she didn't push herself too hard. She was right. Holding back her training because they were together, whatever that meant, wouldn't help her.

After dinner, Nick took off. The animals were all settled, and Tess curled up next to Cade on the couch. She was a burrower, which normally would have bugged the crap out of him. With her, he liked feeling the weight of her curled into his side. She smelled like vanilla and apples. It was a combination of her shampoo and shower stuff. Who knew he would be fascinated by what went into a woman's scent? But here he was, trying to covertly sneak a sniff of her hair now and then so he didn't seem like a perv.

"Want to watch a movie?" She ran a hand down his side massaging as she went. The feel of her hand, kneading his scars made his heart beat in double time. Knowing she didn't see him as less because of them, made him feel something he couldn't identify and doubted he'd ever felt before.

He wasn't thinking of movies at that moment, but strangely enough the thought of sitting with her on the couch watching a movie was more appealing than going straight upstairs. With Tess, anticipation was sexy as hell. "Sure."

"What do you want to watch?"

"Dealer's choice." He would sit through a chick flick for her. No matter how crappy the movie, at least he'd be sitting next to her.

She rose and went over to the cabinet next to the television. It was a seventy-inch flat screen, which surprised him. He figured it was more of a single dude television as opposed to one for a single woman. She opened the cabinet and he did a double take. There had to be a couple hundred movies in there. She didn't even hesitate. Clearly, she was in the mood to watch something specific.

Tess put the movie in and came back to the couch. She burrowed into him again and pushed a few buttons on the remote. The screen lit up and the movie started.

"What are we watching?"

"Towering Inferno. It's kind of long, but totally worth

it."

"Seriously?" It was a kick ass movie. Not one he'd peg her to pick.

She looked up at him, smiling. "Paul Newman, Steve McQueen, flames, action, heroics. Plus, they save the cat. Everything you need in a movie."

With that pronouncement she focused on the movie. He wasn't sure, but right then, maybe, he fell a little bit in love.

Tess went through the chart again. Her brother had the handwriting of a serial killer. She rested her forehead on the desk for a minute. It was awesome to have TJ there, mostly. Getting to know each other better was good.

Watching him try to change things was not good. He and his partner ran their fancy clinic totally differently than Tess and their dad did things here. What was worse was that he didn't seem to remember what things were like here in King's Folly. Maybe he was too big city for them now. Which was a depressing thought.

A screech from down the hall drew her attention.

She bolted toward the examination room the scream had come from and found Mrs. Dalrhymple beating TJ over the head with her ginormous purse.

"How" *thwap* "dare" *thwap* "you" *thwap*.

"Mrs. Dalrhymple." Tess grabbed the purse on an up-swing to keep her from braining TJ. Again. "Why are you beating my brother?"

"He wants me to…" she laid a hand across her ample chest. "He wants me to…I can't even say it." She rested the back of her other hand on her forehead and swooned for a moment before catching herself.

Tess hid her smile. Mrs. Dalrhymple had been in a Broadway show for a whole three weeks. She took every opportunity to "emote."

TJ was propped against the examination table, holding his hands in front of him, a glazed expression on his face. Mrs. Dalrhymple's prize pug sat on the table wheezing with, what Tess always believed, was a shit eating grin.

"What did you say to her?"

"I just suggested she consider walking —"

Tess slapped her hand across TJ's mouth. She shook her head, hoping he understood that the rest of the words coming out of his mouth would be no good for anyone.

She took her hand away from her brother's mouth. "Why don't you let me finish up with Mrs. Dalrhymple and Mr. Pugglesworth."

259

TJ gave a curt nod and left the room, giving the glowering woman, and her over-sized purse, a wide berth.

"I'm sorry, Mrs. D. Clearly, he's been practicing in the big city too long. Let's have a look at your little man."

"I understand you need some time off, but you need to make sure your brother remembers the way of things here if he's going to be treating your patients."

"You're absolutely right." She leaned into the older woman as she examined the pug's hips for signs of dysplasia. "Between you and me, daddy sat him down and gave him a good talking to about treating our hometown pets as opposed to those snooty cats and dogs he sees in the city. I'll make sure he does it again."

Tess could practically feel the molasses dripping off her own tongue. But Mrs. D was old school south and insisted on things being done a certain way. Tess would have to make sure TJ memorized the color-coding system in the charts if it killed him.

After Mrs. D and her snarky pug were on their way, Tess went back to her office, which she guessed was TJ's office too, until their parents left for the cruise. She found him lying on the couch a cold pack on his head.

"You okay?" She felt sorry for him. Kind of.

"What the fuck is in that bag?" He didn't move.

"Trust me, you don't want to know."

He shifted the pack so he could open one eye and focused it on her.

"What was that about?"

"She doesn't take Mr. Pugglesworth for walks."

"Obviously. That dog is at least ten pieces of kibble past obese. She should take him for walks."

"She's a southern belle. In her world, southern belles recline with their dogs under shady trees. They don't take them for walks."

"She could use a walk through the magnolia trees herself."

Tess laughed. "You've got a lot to re-learn about a small practice, city boy."

"I think she gave me a concussion." He rubbed his head.

She shook her head. "When did you turn into such a baby?"

"Seriously? Has she ever hit you with that thing?"

"No, because I've never been stupid enough to call her dog fat."

"I didn't call him fat. Exactly."

She shoved his legs off the couch and sat down. He sat up, still holding the cold compress on his head. "Watch it. I'm injured."

261

"Oh boo hoo. I told you to check with Dad or me before you saw any patients with a purple tag on their chart."

"What's with the purple tags, anyway?"

"You grew up here, TJ. You should understand that we have some locals who are pretty particular about how they live their lives. The ones with pets are even more particular about how their pets are treated. The purple tags get special treatment, because they are" she looked at the door to make sure it was shut, "nuts. One wrong move and you get a bag to the head."

He shifted the bag of ice, wincing as he did. "How do you stand it?"

"Stand what?"

"Staying in this town. You're a freaking genius. You could be doing amazing things with research. Could have gone to any college in the world. Hell, Davis was calling Mom and Dad twice a week trying to enroll you in their program. But you stayed here for all of it. Have you ever left this tiny town?"

She heard the confusion in his voice. It baffled her that anyone wanted to live anywhere other than King's Folly. "I leave every year for three weeks. Vacation."

"Let me guess. Myrtle Beach, same hotel every year." He chuckled.

As if he was funny.

"Lot you know smarty pants. Last year I spent my vacation in New Zealand." She wasn't going to tell him that she'd hiked the locations where they shot the Lord of the Rings Trilogy.

"Really?"

"Really. I went to school here and stayed here because this is the life I want. Doesn't mean I don't know there's a big world out there, or that I don't want to see it." Getting to know her youngest brothers made it obvious she'd spent too much of her life keeping people at a distance. It was a painful adjustment, realizing what she'd been missing by being so aloof.

"I still don't get it."

She sighed. "I don't know if I can explain it. I like my life."

"What's with this ninja stuff?"

"It started as a way to spend more time with the Trips. Turns out it's something I enjoy doing. How's your head?" She gently touched the lump forming on the right side of his head.

He flinched. "It hurts."

She pulled the pack off his head and gently explored the area of his skull underneath. "You're going to have a hell of a lump. Any blurred vision, nausea, dizziness?"

"No, just a headache."

"You should probably take it easy for the rest of the day."

Their conversation was interrupted by their father walking into the office, without knocking.

"Heard Mrs. Dalrhymple kicked your ass." He smiled at his oldest son.

"She gets an A for effort." TJ grimaced.

Trevor laughed. "Beating you senseless was probably the most exercise she's had in years."

TJ sighed. "That little bastard pug of hers was grinning at me the whole time."

"Sounds about right. You need to take the rest of the day? Your mom and I are leaving in a couple of days, take advantage of having an expert here while you can."

"No. I'll just take some aspirin." TJ leaned his head back on the coach.

"Did you need something else, Dad?" Tess could tell he had something else on his mind.

"Well…"

"What is it?" She was already figuring out how she could move her schedule around to accommodate whatever his request was.

"Your mom wants to have dinner with you and Cade before we go."

"Me and Cade?" She emphasized the word "and."

"You two aren't fooling anyone."

TJ snorted. Warmth rose up her neck and she knew she was turning red.

"I don't know. I'm tired after training. I don't usually feel up to going anywhere."

"That's all right. We'll bring dinner to you. We'll come by tonight. I'll go let your mom know we're on."

Their father left the room, leaving Tess alone with her brother, who was laughing.

"Tess and Cade sitting in a tree…"

Sometimes brothers were a total pain in the ass. She hit him in the head with a pillow, causing him to yelp. She smiled. They were fun to torment, though.

Chapter 17

Cade had never been a meet the parents kind of guy. He hadn't even met the parents the one time he'd been thinking of making a relationship permanent. When Tess announced that hers were coming over after training to have dinner with them as a couple, Nick had laughed his ass off.

It wasn't as if he hadn't met them. Hell, they'd been through the trauma of a wait in the emergency room together. But that was as Tess's trainer and Ed's protégé. This was dinner with the parents as their daughter's man.

He swallowed and eyed the door. Tess was upstairs in the shower. These days he usually joined her, but with her parents due any minute he had to stay downstairs and greet them. Not to mention, Tess wasn't crazy about the idea of her parents showing up while they were having sex in the shower. It wasn't number one on his list either.

He usually didn't care what people thought of him, but this was different. She was different. His biggest fear was that he wasn't.

A knock on the door had him shaking off his deep thoughts, well, deep for him. He moved to the door, pushed his shoulders back, then answered it. Tess's parents were standing there.

Her mother held up a bag. "Bella Luna's. It's my girl's favorite." Tess's mom emphasized the "my girl."

He stepped back and motioned for them to come in. Her father gave him a look he knew well. It was the *stay the fuck away from my daughter look.* He'd never been on the receiving end of it since he'd never met any dads of the women he'd dated, but he'd seen it directed at some of his buddies. It was funnier when it wasn't aimed at him.

"Tess is taking a shower. She should be down in a bit."

"Did she have a good workout today?"

Cade took the bags from Tess's mother and moved toward the kitchen.

"She did. The strength training with Nick is already helping. She's looking fine. I mean she looks good, I mean…" Every word he used to describe her had another meaning he didn't think her parents wanted to know about.

I sound like an idiot.

"She's not overdoing it is she?" Tess's father's gruff question was a welcome interruption to Cade's verbal diarrhea.

"No, she's not." Tess's voice came from the doorway.

They all turned. Cade was still surprised at the way his pulse raced and his heart hammered every time she walked into a room. He watched her glide to her parents and greet

267

them with hugs. Despite all the misunderstandings, her family was tight.

He wasn't sure what to do with himself in that moment. Then she turned and focused her smile on him. His doubts disappeared when the power of her smile sliced through him.

"Your folks brought Bella Luna's." He couldn't think of anything else to say.

"Yum. I'm starving."

Together the four of them set the table. Dinner passed quickly. On a discomfort scale of one to ten, Cade put it at about an eight. Tess's mom was sweet as hell, but her dad had clearly put Cade on a watch list because of their relationship. Add to that the fact that Cade had never been a big fan of talking about himself and the conversation got a little tense.

Since Tess was also insistent that they couldn't talk about the plan he was working on with her grandfather that meant that one of the few topics that was open was his life. He'd never bullshitted his way through so many awkward silences in his life.

Later, after they shut the door on her parents, she moved into his arms without any prompting from him. She fit perfectly there.

"Thank you."

"For what?" He didn't want to ruin the moment with some talk about feelings.

"For sitting through that. I know it's not your thing."

"It was fine." His voice was more clipped then he wanted it to be.

She smiled. "Liar. You looked like you would have preferred having a root canal."

"I've never been a relationship guy. I've never met the parents before."

"Not once?" She pulled back.

"No."

"What about that girl you dated senior year? Lana?"

He narrowed his eyes. "What do you know about her?" He'd never mentioned Lana's name to her. Who had?

Pink rushed up her neck into her cheeks. "Well, I may have noticed that you spent an awful lot of time with her senior year."

His insides turned to ice. "That wasn't what it looked like."

To anyone.

"Her loss." She pressed her palm to his cheek.

Her hand on his face calmed something inside him and melted the cold. He rested his forehead on hers. "I want to

269

try, you know I do."

She chuckled. "There is no try, only do."

He leaned back and noted the glitter in her hazel eyes. "Did you just quote Yoda to me?"

She shrugged. "I thought it was appropriate."

He laughed. "You would."

"What do you want to do now?"

The night was still young. The menagerie had adopted Sonny and Sam and the whole group was passed out on the family room floor, an overfed pile of fur.

Tess followed his gaze. "I think my mom got them their own helpings of steak."

"Yeah. I saw her sneaking them bits when you and your dad were talking about that new surgical technique."

She smiled. "She's always done it. Fed the animals behind our backs."

"Your parents are pretty awesome."

"Yeah. They really are." She tilted her head. "You never talk about your mom."

He pulled away from her and ran a hand through his hair. "Nothing much to say. She left when my brother and I were kids. Did flybys after that, but we don't have a relationship."

"You have a brother? You've only ever mentioned your

dad."

"Kyle's two years younger. He's a marine."

"He didn't go Navy? Isn't that sacrilege in your family?"

He laughed. "Yeah. The old man hit the roof when the runt announced he was going jarhead. It was a pretty epic night in the Maguire house."

"Are they speaking now?"

"Sure. It was touch and go for a while. Kyle enlisted right out of high school and his unit was deployed not long after finishing boot. When your son goes to war, and you know what he's facing, day to day bullshit is easy to let go of."

He hoped she would stay on the topic of his brother and leave his mother out of the conversation. That couldn't lead anywhere good.

"That's all well and good, but how big is his dick?" Delilah all but shouted to the entire bar.

Heat spread up Tess's neck. Her friend wasn't just being inappropriate. She was being inappropriate at maximum volume.

"I'm not sure they heard you in the men's room. Try it a

little louder next time." Charlie's words were slurring.

Olivia was turning redder the more Charlie and Delilah had to drink. Or, more accurately, the more Charlie and Delilah talked. It was girls' night out at Mooneys' Pub and Tess, as the designated driver, had been drinking club soda. Olivia was only two drinks into the evening. Tess could tell she wasn't entirely comfortable with Delilah and Charlie who had bonded after Tess's collapse and now viewed themselves as a united front on "Team Tess."

She leaned over to Olivia. "They're harmless."

Before Olivia could respond, Delilah took another opportunity to embarrass them. "Seriously, Tess. How big is his dick?"

At that point, given the volume of their conversation, half the bar was listening to them. Including a red-faced Brian Gill, who had been watching them for most of the evening. He sat at a table towards the back of the bar area, probably in an attempt to hide from them.

Obviously, he hadn't considered the mirrors around the room, because his table was at the perfect angle for Tess to watch him watching her. It had taken all her strength to stay seated when she wanted to go over and tell him to knock it off.

She decided to do the next best thing. "I know you are

obsessed with this topic because your ex has a micro-penis, but I am not going to talk about how extremely well-endowed Cade is."

Olivia's eyes widened and Charlie and Delilah both started laughing like it was the funniest thing they'd ever heard. Tess watched Brian in the mirror as he turned almost purple. He threw some cash on the bar and stormed out. Hopefully, he'd left a tip.

"You knew he was there." Olivia stared at the door Brian had just disappeared through.

Tess nodded.

"You don't like him."

"He's a jerk."

"He really is an asshole." Delilah leaned over toward Olivia. "But his father is the devil. Males with the last name Gill are to be avoided at all costs."

Olivia bit her lip. "You're going through a nasty divorce. It's reasonable that you wouldn't get along with him or his father."

There was something in Olivia's voice as she defended Brian that made Tess twitchy. "Olivia. How do you know him?"

Olivia blushed.

"Oh shit. You're screwing him." Delilah threw back another shot.

"Delilah. Dial it back a minute." Tess took Olivia's hand. "Are you dating him?"

Olivia nodded. "He says we can't be seen in public because Delilah is contesting the divorce, and she would use our relationship against him."

Charlie slapped her hand over Delilah's mouth. "We're going to the restroom." She dragged Delilah away before she could break free from Charlie's iron grip.

"He's lying to me, isn't he?" Olivia's whisper drew Tess's attention back to her embarrassed friend.

"Yes, honey. He is."

Olivia dipped her chin toward her chest. "He's been using me."

"Using you?" Tess was almost afraid to ask.

"We met a little over a month ago. He suggested I make my proposal to the Board."

A lot of pieces fell into place with that single statement. "Oh, Olivia."

"I really thought he liked me." She squirmed in her seat.

"Are you two…" Tess didn't want to have this conversation, but she needed to know how deep into this relationship Olivia was.

"We haven't slept together. I wanted to wait."

"Wait for what?"

"I don't know. I didn't like the secrecy. I wanted us to be out in the open before I got more serious with him." She looked up and met Tess's gaze and swallowed.

"Do you have feelings for him?"

"I don't know. Men don't usually pay attention to me. He was charming. He said he liked the fact that I was so smart. He was lying the whole time." Tears pooled in her eyes and drifted down her cheeks.

Tess grabbed a cocktail napkin and to dry her tears.

"That mother fucker." Delilah bellowed as she approached the table, Charlie on her heels.

Delilah came up next to Olivia and put her arm around her. "He hurt you, didn't he?"

Olivia sniffled and nodded.

"I am going to cut his dick off and serve it to an ant colony."

Tess put her arm around Olivia's other side. "So, the good news is you found out before you slept with him. You didn't have to fake a single orgasm."

Olivia laughed and put her hand over her mouth.

Delilah plopped down on her bar stool, barely managing to stay on it without sliding off the other side. "It's true.

I was Sally Albright for years and I never even got a sandwich for faking it." There was a look in Delilah's eyes that Tess couldn't identify.

"Sally Albright?"

"*When Harry Met Sally*," Tess, Delilah and Charlie said in unison.

"Oh."

"You have seen that movie, haven't you?" Delilah tilted her head.

Olivia shook her head.

Delilah looked at Tess and then back at Olivia. "Oh my, God. She's another you."

"What does that mean?" Tess and Olivia said in unison.

"You're as smart as Tess."

"Smarter." Tess smiled at Olivia.

"But I bet she didn't have a me." Charlie leaned into the conversation.

"I don't know what you're talking about." Olivia wouldn't meet the eyes of any of the three women at the table.

Tess took her hand. "I had Charlie growing up. She attached herself to me and made it a little easier for me in social situations."

"Oh. No, I never had a Charlie." Olivia glanced at the

woman in question. "I think I would have liked to have one."

Delilah slapped her hand on the table. "No."

"What do you mean no?" Charlie turned to Delilah and almost slid off her own stool.

"I mean you're Tess's Charlie. I'm going to be Olivia's Charlie."

Olivia had a look of horror on her face. Tess squeezed her hand.

"She's a lot, I know, but she's a good person and she means well."

"Of course, I'm a good person. I saw Mrs. Wheeler in the grocery store today and I smiled at her."

Olivia leaned in to Tess. "Why does smiling at Mrs. Wheeler make Delilah a nice person."

"Have you met Mrs. Wheeler?" Delilah leaned in.

Olivia leaned back and shook her head.

"Mrs. Wheeler is a bit of a grouch," Tess said.

"Bit of a grouch? Bit of a grouch?" Delilah's voice rose with each word. "She's a mean old biddy. Every time I see her I want to yank her purple wig off and feed it to her stupid dog. But I didn't do that today. Did I? No. I smiled and walked by. Do you want to know why?" She leaned in toward Olivia, pointing her finger. "Because I'm a nice person and I deserve to be your Charlie."

"Ummm." Olivia studied Tess then nodded at Delilah. "Thank you?"

Delilah burst into tears and threw herself at Olivia. Tess stepped behind her and braced her to keep both Olivia and Delilah from tumbling over the edge of the stool.

"I'm going to be the best Charlie ever."

Tess's eyes met Charlie's over the sobbing Delilah and the bewildered Olivia.

"What the hell?" Charlie mouthed.

Tess shrugged. She couldn't explain what had just happened. It was definitely time to leave. It took the promise of not only more drinks at her house, but also joining them, to get everyone in the car.

I'm probably going to regret this in the morning?

Chapter 18

Cade didn't know what the aftermath of a girl's night out was supposed to look like, but he wouldn't have thought it would look like this. Tess hadn't shown up at the gym, so he told Nick to meet him here to see what was going on.

He'd been a little concerned but had managed to avoid all out panic by reminding himself that she had been out with her friends last night and had gotten in late. There was no way he was going to acknowledge the fact that he'd expected her to text him when she got home. That was too clingy for his conscious brain to handle.

He let himself into her house. Truth was he spent more time at her place than his lately and last night, sleeping in his own bed alone, had felt alien. Wasn't that a kick in the ass? He looked into the family room and did a double take. He sensed Nick come in behind him and stop short.

"What the hell happened in here?" Nick whispered. They both tried to stay quiet, but it didn't help.

One second Delilah was passed out in a chair, the next she sat straight up and shouted, "micro penis."

Cade focused on Tess who opened her eyes and pulled a pillow over her face in the next second.

"Please turn off the sun."

Cade chuckled. Based on their condition, and the empty glasses on the table, girls' night out had involved a lot of alcohol.

He wandered over to the couch and hunched down in front of her. "Sorry, Jules. We can't do anything about the sun." He tried to keep his voice calm and even.

"Please do not yell. I can hear you just fine."

Cade heard Nick trying not to laugh behind him.

"She wouldn't tell us exactly how big your dick is." Delilah tried to stand up and plopped back down on the chair. "I might toss my cookies."

Cade thought he might throw up, too.

"My dick?" He wasn't sure he wanted Tess to comment. She mumbled something behind the pillow.

"Jules. Why were you talking about my dick?"

"We weren't." A voice he didn't recognize drifted from behind the couch. "We really only talked about Brian's."

Cade looked at Nick who moved over to the couch and looked over the back of it. "Professor Valenti? You okay?"

"Delilah volunteered to be my Charlie."

"Bet your ass I did. I'm going to be the best Charlie ever."

"Bullshit." Charlie mumbled, face first on the couch, her legs tangled up with Tess's.

"I think they're still drunk." Nick was staring behind the couch with an expression Cade had never seen on his friend's face before.

"If we were still drunk I don't think I'd feel this bad. Someone knit a sweater on my tongue while I was sleeping." Tess moved the pillow and looked at Cade. Her eyes were hazy and unfocused.

He gently lifted her into his arms and stood up. "Let's clean you up."

"Where's my knight to carry me up the stairs?" Delilah called out as they left the room.

"Can't help you with that." Cade carried Tess out of the room then up the stairs.

He helped her into the shower. She stood there immobile as the hot water rolled off her body. Her gorgeous, naked, glistening body. Cade cleared his throat.

"You going to be okay in here alone?"

She nodded. "I feel better already."

He left her to the shower. She seemed steadier to him, so he went back downstairs to see how the rest of the ladies were faring. They were all in the kitchen, sitting at the table, heads resting on their forearms. Nick was moving quietly around the kitchen making coffee and something else.

"What's that?"

"Hangover cure. What'd you do with Tess?"

"She's showering."

"Oh fine, she gets a shower and the three of us are propped up at the kitchen table like zombies," Delilah mumbled.

"If we were zombies we'd be shambling around the kitchen, not propped up at the table." Olivia lifted her head and looked Nick, who was glancing at her.

"You know a lot about zombies, Professor?" Nick put something in the blender and closed the lid.

"I read Pride and Prejudice and Zombies."

Nick smiled, which creeped Cade out a little. His buddy wasn't a smiler. He turned around when he heard Tess approach at his back. Her hair was still wet and hung around her head in curls the color of milk chocolate. He really wished they were alone right now and she was feeling better.

All four women winced when Nick turned the blender on. Tess pressed her forehead into Cade's chest. "Make it stop."

"No worries, ladies," Nick said over the sound of the blender, making the women wince even more. "A slug of this and you'll all feel much better."

"Is that a hangover cure?" Olivia eyed the concoction in

the blender with curiosity. "Is it a family recipe? I studied folk cures and family recipes in college for a semester."

Nick poured the mixture into four glasses and handed them out to the ladies. Delilah belted hers back right away. Tess and Charlie took sips and then drank theirs normally since they didn't mind the taste. Olivia sniffed and studied hers until Nick got frustrated.

"It won't do you any good if you just look at it." He lifted the glass to her lips.

She took it from him and drank. "I can't figure out what's in it."

"Not supposed to analyze it. Supposed to drink it." He stepped back. "Looks like we aren't working out today."

Cade wouldn't call off a practice if one of his players showed up hungover, but Tess was different. He was about to agree with Nick when Tess set her drink down.

"No. I'll go change and we'll head in to the gym."

"Tess." Cade took her hand.

"Would you let a player out of practice if he showed up hungover?"

Since her question mimicked his own thoughts he decided it was a good idea not to answer. He shrugged.

"No, you wouldn't." She answered for him. "I'll go and change, then we can go to the gym." She left.

"You ladies have rides home?" Cade turned back to the others.

"I parked my car here last night." Charlie lifted her head. "I'll take Olivia and Delilah home."

Tess's workout was lighter than usual. He and Nick tried to make it look like they weren't going easy on her. Fortunately, she felt so horrible, she didn't really notice it.

That evening, after her second workout, he ordered Chinese. She'd showered and collapsed on the couch. Wanting to be close to her, he picked up her legs and slid down to sit next to her. He pulled her legs onto his lap and rubbed them absently.

"So, girls' night…" He was curious as hell about what happened, especially since his dick was apparently a topic of conversation.

"It was going pretty well until Delilah asked me how big your dick was." Her arm was thrown over her eyes like it was still too bright for her.

"Why the hell would she ask that?"

"It appears we're not all that stealthy with the relationship stuff. They knew something was going on between us. Even Olivia knew and she's less observant than I am. So, Delilah, who was already drunk asked how big your dick was, only she basically yelled it."

284

She filled him in on the rest of the evening, including that Gill had been there, and he was behind the alternate proposal that Olivia was making to the Board.

"He's up to something." The fact that he'd used Olivia to play his game made Cade want to punch him. Repeatedly.

She moved her arm and her gaze met his. "Well that's perfectly obvious."

"We need to find out what he wants."

"Whatever it is, he won't get it." Her tone was confident.

"How can you be so sure?"

"He's never been able to beat you before. He doesn't stand a chance, no matter what's up his sleeve."

Her quiet words humbled him and terrified him at the same time. No one had ever had that kind of faith in him, ever. His team followed him because they knew he could play. His men followed him because they knew he could fight. The kind of simple, all-encompassing acceptance Tess had just offered him was new.

I wish I was worth it.

The next couple of weeks passed so quickly and there

was so much to do that Tess barely noticed that Cade was pulling away from her. It was subtle, she'd give him that. So subtle it took her a while to catch on to it. Instead of spending every night at her place, he came up with reasons why he had to spend a few nights a week at his cabin. He also came up with reasons why she couldn't join him. Gradually their conversations became about nothing but her training.

Tess didn't want to bring it up to the girls because she knew what they would say. Confront him. She couldn't talk to the Trips because they idolized Cade. That relationship was important to her brothers and she didn't want to interfere with it. Since she didn't know who to talk to about it, she fell back on old habits and didn't tell anyone anything.

She was in the best shape she'd ever been in, and one thing she was happy about were the other relationships in her life, particularly her friendships with Nick and Olivia. Nick was slowly taking over more and more of Tess's training. Cade was doing some traveling trying to line up other potential coaches for their program.

Today he was in Texas. It hadn't helped her relationship with Cade that she refused to talk about the football program. The more enmeshed he became in the program and the closer it got to the vote, the more he obviously resented not being able to share such a big part of his life with her.

"You're not thinking about what you're doing." Nick's voice came from up above her.

He was right since she was currently lifting her bodyweight and thinking about Cade. "Sorry."

"Don't be sorry. Stop."

She pushed the weights up again. Nick was still a man of few words, but he had become more talkative with her. For the rest of the workout, she focused on his instructions and her movements.

Nick handed her a towel after her last set of reps. "Your form is looking good. Strength is good too. Keep it up and you'll kick ass in qualifiers."

She smiled. "I've had good coaching."

"Hit the shower. Lunch is on me."

She nodded and headed toward the locker room. True to form, she was showered and ready to go within fifteen minutes.

In a replay of what happened a few weeks before, she found Nick waiting for her with Brian taunting him.

"Your plan can't win. A bunch of doddering old hasbeens and inexperienced never-weres can't lead the team. You need real coaches to win."

Tess went from content to pissed in a split second. She

was tired of Brian's lurking around. Truth was she'd been tired of it for twenty-two years. It was time to do something about it. She stormed down the hallway and pushed between Brian and Nick.

"Back off." She pushed Brian forcing him to step back.

A look of surprise crossed his face. It was clear he wasn't expecting her to get physical with him. Their history had never gone beyond verbal skirmishes before and Tess didn't think he would push her back now. But she knew if Brian was stupid enough to try something, Nick would kick his ass before Tess had a chance to take a swing.

"What the hell? Have you lost your mind?" His eyes widened and his mouth fell open.

"I'm tired of covering for you."

Whatever messed up relationship he had with his father couldn't excuse his behavior anymore. He was a grown man. It was time for him to stand on his own or accept the consequences of always doing the dirty work for Senior.

He flinched. "I have no idea what you're talking about."

"Yes. You do. I know enough of your secrets to make life very difficult for you."

He stiffened. "I don't know what you mean."

"Oh, I think you do. You need to think very carefully about how far you want to push. You've got your board meeting and the Board will vote on the three proposals, fairly. Whatever else you're trying to pull needs to stop."

"Is that a threat?" Brian took a step closer.

Nick's hand latched on to the back of her belt. Any second he was going to toss her behind him and take on Brian himself.

"It's a fact." She refused to be intimidated and leaned forward to poke Brian in the chest. Nick's grip tightened. "You've gotten away with a lot over the years because people are either afraid of your father or they're not on his radar. I've looked the other way as much as I could because I didn't want to deal with either of you more than I had to. But now, you're messing with my friends, and it stops here and now."

"You have no idea what I can do to you."

"Face it Brian, you've never done anything but run interference for your father. He runs the show. Without him, you can't do anything."

She heard a bark of laughter behind her, but she didn't take her eyes off Brian. His face was getting redder and redder. After a moment he stalked away.

"You've got guts. Probably not a good idea to poke a snake like that."

She turned to him. "As long as I don't take my eyes off

him, I'll be fine. Besides, it's long past time for me to take a stand against the Gills. Especially Senior."

"You going to tell me what happened with them?"

"You going to tell me what happened to keep you from playing college ball?"

He thought for a few seconds. "We'll trade stories over lunch."

She nodded. It was time to let go of a few of her secrets.

Chapter 19

Cade trudged into the cabin to find Sonny and Sam waiting for him on the couch. They bounced toward him to welcome him home. It had been a bitch of a trip. His meetings with Frankie and Ben Coleman had gone well. Both of them were ready to sign up, if they got the plan past the Board.

At least the traveling was done. They had solid commitments from most of the people on his and Ed's list. The rest of them were interested, but not ready to pull the trigger on ending their military careers. They'd all agreed to make a final decision at the beginning of the year. With Ed's team in place, and the upcoming season cancelled, they could get through the fall with five or six other coaches on Cade's side of the fence.

"Nick?" Cade called.

"He's not here." Tess's voice came from behind him.

He spun around and lost the ability to speak.

Tess stood in the doorway to his bedroom, wearing nothing but a white button-down shirt. His shirt. Was it possible to swallow his tongue?

She smiled. "Hi."

"Hi." There had to be something else he could say. Maybe he'd think of it when his brain started to function again.

"Welcome home."

"What are you doing here?" He blinked.

Her smile faded. "I thought I'd surprise you."

He didn't know what to say. Being apart from her was torture. The more attached to her he got the more it would hurt when she realized he was a bad bet and left.

"I can leave." She stepped back. Away from him.

"No." He leapt forward. Maybe he should let her go, but he wasn't sure he was strong enough to do it. "I'm happy you're here." Whatever the future held, he'd never regret any time they spent together.

She tilted her head. "You're not acting like you are."

"I had a long flight. I'm wiped." That was mostly true.

"Should I let you sleep?" She smiled a siren's smile that told him she wasn't going to give up.

He reached for her. "We can sleep later." As long as she didn't know who he really was, he could lose himself in her.

A few hours later, he stared at the ceiling. Tess was pressed close to him. Her snore was still the cutest sound he'd ever heard.

What am I doing?

More than anything, he wanted to believe he could

make this work. He looked down at her. Maybe he could do this. She was unlike any woman he'd ever met. Because of her, he wanted to be a better man, one who could go the distance in a relationship. If he gave it everything he had, was it possible he could fix whatever was broken inside him? For her, he would do anything.

He got out of bed, careful not to wake her. Sleep felt miles away and he didn't want to disturb her rest. Tess did more work than any other person he knew. If anyone deserved a solid night's sleep, it was her.

Sonny and Sam were asleep in their beds in the living room. They raised their heads when he walked through, heading into the kitchen. He pulled a beer out of the fridge. A moment later, Sam came into the kitchen and pressed against Cade's leg.

"I know, buddy. I kind of want to keep her, too."

Maybe he could make it work. He just needed to take things slowly.

His phone buzzed, pulling him from his thoughts. He glanced at the screen, but didn't recognize the number. The smart thing to do would be not to answer. Best case scenario it was some fake tax collector calling with threats to arrest him.

The decline button on his phone was saying "push me."

Curiosity killed him, and he pushed "accept."

"Yeah."

"Is that any way to greet your mother?"

Fuck me. I should've hit the decline button.

"What do you want?" Whatever it was, he didn't want to hear it.

"I heard you're back at your old school."

"And?" He didn't like the idea of her keeping tabs. Fourteen years wasn't enough time away from her and her mind games.

"Can't a mother call to wish her son good luck?"

"No." Especially not his mother. "How did you get this number?"

"A little birdy called me. Said you could use a pep talk from your mother. A reminder of where you came from."

"Generations of Navy men. That's where I come from."

"Not a football hero or happy husband in the bunch." The venom in her voice was sharper than he remembered.

He was done. Whatever he was, whoever he was, it was because of his father and his own hard work. "Are you calling just to mess with me?"

"I heard you were getting in over your head. Thought you could use a little encouragement."

"From you?" The thought of her doing anything positive for him was laughable.

"I am your mother."

"A fact you remember when it's convenient or you need something." Or when she wanted to mess with him for some reason.

The silence on the other end made him do something he'd never done before. "Why did you even have kids?"

"What kind of question is that?"

"An honest one." One he'd been wondering about since she'd walked out on her sons thirty years ago.

"People got married and had kids back then. That's what they did."

"So, when you left, why didn't you stay gone? You clearly don't want to be a mother. You haven't even seen Kyle since he was four."

"Are you sure?"

His stomach seized. Kyle would have said something if she'd been harassing him too, wouldn't he?

"Relax." She laughed. "I haven't been bothering your precious baby brother or your father."

He blew out a breath. "You didn't answer my question."

"You look just like your father. You know that?"

He did. It was something he'd heard when he was

young and something he could see for himself as he got older. "So?"

"So, torturing you was the closest I could come to torturing your father."

It was too honest not to be true. "I'm not doing it anymore. You need to get a new hobby."

The sudden intake of breath on the other end of the phone told him he'd scored a hit. He felt Sam press closer to him, anchoring him to this place, this moment, the woman in his bed, and he knew why his mother had called. What her agenda was.

"Tell your little birdy that they aren't going to make me run. Don't call me again."

He disconnected the call, too keyed up to go back to bed. His mother wasn't going to win this time, but he wasn't stupid enough to believe she would go away for good. Some people let life poison every good thing they got in their lives until there was nothing left but bitterness and bile.

Cade didn't want to follow her down that path. He sat on the sofa, looking around the room and scrubbed his hand down his face. Sonny curled up next to him and Sam padded over and put his head in Cade's lap.

"I'm okay." He was as far from okay as he could be. All

he wanted was to crawl back into bed with Tess and be the man she deserved. The truth was it wasn't the fear that he as the next generation of Maguires that was keeping him awake. It was the fear that he had too much of his mother in him rolled through his gut.

What if my happy ever after turns into Tess's nightmare?

The next day after lunch, Tess sat at her desk trying to, once again, decipher her brother's writing. She was going to have to talk to him. As much as she appreciated his help, he was acting like he was slumming it by helping his father and sister out with their clinic.

Every time she turned around he was talking about how things were done at his practice in Chicago. Like they would ever do anything in King's Folly that way.

The object of her irritation walked into her office.

"You rang, oh brilliant sister of mine."

She wasn't in the mood for his attitude. "You have the handwriting of a serial killer."

"I do not." He ignored her tone, if he heard it at all, and flopped onto her couch, a couch he was taking over even though he was using their dad's office for work.

"I can read and write thirty languages, including two

dead ones, and I can't decipher this scribbling you call handwriting. Were you absent when they taught penmanship?"

"I think I had Suzie Jenkins doing my homework that year in school." He smirked.

She stared at him, really looking at him for the first time. "Do you take anything seriously?"

"Do you take everything seriously?" He countered.

"I take this practice seriously. I know dad started it, but I've helped him build it for the last eleven years and I don't appreciate you coming here and treating us like we're the village idiots, and you're the big city vet come to save us."

TJ sat up. "I don't —"

"You come here, ostensibly to help, but you can't take the time to write a legible note in my patients' charts so I can track their cases. You do know I'm the one who'll still be here treating them long after you've brushed the dust of this tiny town off the soles of your shoes and left us behind again."

"I'm not —"

She was on a roll. "I'm sick of you acting like a small-town practice isn't as important as a big city one where you treat a bunch of neurotic pets who are only nuts because of their insane owners."

"You —"

"We aren't some backwards, clingy group of hillbillies that you can look down your nose at, and you aren't the re-incarnation of Christ here to save us all from our own sins."

"Holy shit." His jaw went slack.

Tess was out of breath after her diatribe and a little be-wildered. She had no idea where that came from, and wasn't sure it was entirely about her brother. Cade had acted very strange this morning and mumbled something about seeing her later before he disappeared.

"Want to tell me what that was about, sis? Because I'm pretty sure that wasn't about me."

She gave him a look.

"Well it wasn't all about me. Want to help me unpack that so I can figure out why you're pissed at me and whose ass I need to kick?"

"Why would you kick anyone's ass?" She frowned.

He patted the seat next to him on the couch. She got up from her desk then moved to the coach, flopping down next to him. After a moment, he put his arm around her shoul-ders and pulled her close.

"One thing that's been clear to me since I came to help out is that I've been a pretty piss poor big brother. I as-sumed that because you were so smart I didn't have to look

299

out for you the way most big brothers look out for their little sisters. I thought your intelligence insulated you from the stuff that other kids dealt with, and when Charlie attached herself to you it seemed like you had the insight into the rest of the world that a lot of geniuses don't have. I was wrong, wasn't I?"

She shrugged. He was pretty spot on. Her throat felt tight at the thought that people she loved could finally see her. Really, truly see her.

"You held back from the world because you didn't trust it, not because you weren't interested."

Tears pooled in her eyes, but she didn't know what to say. So much had been happening lately, and she didn't really know how to deal with any of it. In her confusion, she'd retreated to old patterns. Most of them involved hiding.

"Dammit. I'm not trying to make you cry." He sounded panicked.

"I'm not crying." She burst in to tears.

Her brother pulled her into his arms and held her while she cried. He made soothing noises but didn't try to stop her tears. After a few moments, when Tess's tears finally started to dry up, he leaned back.

"Feel better?" He awkwardly patted her on the back.

"No. Now I have a headache and my eyes are all puffy and gross."

He laughed.

"Why is that funny?" She could barely think past the throbbing pain behind her eyes.

"Because it's such a you comment."

"What does that mean?"

He paused for a moment, as if trying to choose his words carefully. "I have this image of you that I've carried with me my whole life. At first, when I came back, I thought that image was totally wrong, and I felt like a shitty brother. I've realized my image of you wasn't wrong, it was incomplete. Still makes me a shitty brother, but not a completely shitty brother."

"I wasn't easy to get to know." Hiding the things that made her insecure seemed a simpler course of action.

"It's nice to know that I wasn't completely oblivious to who you were growing up. You can still be way too literal sometimes. When you are, it's kind of funny. Makes me feel even worse that I wasn't a better brother to you. We both missed a lot because I was a self-involved asshole."

"It wasn't just you." She let out a huff of frustration. It was time for her to meet people halfway. "Remember when Tabby got in that accident last year, we were all sitting in the waiting room at the hospital?"

He shuddered. "No need to remind me."

"I sat there watching everyone, as usual." She sniffed. "I saw that I was sitting in a room filled with my family and I was alone."

"Sis."

"It was my own fault. I was always so focused on projecting this image of not needing anyone. It put a wall between me and the world, including my family. I didn't know any of my brothers and sisters. Not really. The triplets were off in one corner. You and Tony were sitting next to Mom and Dad. Tiffany, Trish and Trudy were huddled together. I was sitting there watching it all, on the outside looking in."

"Shit. That's —"

"It was what made me approach the Trips about spending more time together."

"What's that got to do with me being a shitty brother?" He sounded confused.

"You aren't responsible for everything."

"We could've tried to spend more time with you."

"I didn't let any of you close to me." Maybe Cade was pulling away because she couldn't let him in.

Where did that come from?

"You let Charlie in." He pointed out.

"Have you ever tried to stop Charlie from doing something she wanted to do?"

"No." He laughed.

"I have. I tried to make her stop being my friend." All she'd wanted was to be left alone. She hadn't understood Charlie or her attitudes, and what Tess didn't understand when she was growing up, she'd ignored. Or tried to.

"Seriously?"

"Yes. She confused me. She was loud, and she always talked without saying anything at all. But, no matter what I said, or did, I couldn't shake her. Finally, I just accepted her presence and taught myself to handle it."

"That's…" he seemed to be looking for the right word "…messed up."

She laughed. "That's not a bad description of me."

"Why didn't you leave? Go somewhere…that could give you more?"

"Everyone thinks that because I'm so smart I should've left King's Folly, gone to some big program focused on research. No one understands how much I love this town. It's my home. I've always wanted to live here and go into practice with Dad. I like having roots."

He motioned for her to continue.

"I've been happy. Charlie's helped me out of my shell from time to time. I never knew anything was missing from my life, until that night at the hospital. When we knew Tabby was going to be all right and everyone went back to their own lives, I got depressed and went to a bar to get drunk. I didn't tell Charlie. I wasn't in the mood for company."

TJ took her hand. It was as if he knew interrupting her would make it harder for her to say the words.

"I went to The Dive."

He sucked in a breath.

"Delilah was there. Drunk. She saw me walk in and insisted on sitting with me. She ordered our drinks and I proceeded to get drunk with one of three people in this world that I actively disliked. Before long we were spilling our secrets." She shivered at the thought of what her friend had endured in her life. "Hers were way worse than mine."

"So that's when she attached herself to you."

Tess nodded. "The day after, when I could drag myself out of bed, I called the Trips and asked them if they wanted to hang out at my house. I'm not sure why they agreed at first. They were as uncomfortable around me as I was around them. I almost gave up on my plan to get to know them better. But we turned on American Ninja Warrior and suddenly we were having an actual conversation about something. So, we started watching the show together and then we had the idea to build obstacles in the back yard and train together."

He chuckled. "You and American Ninja Warrior. Still can't believe it, and I've seen you kick ass on the course."

The hair rose up on the back of her neck. "Well then I met Cade and this whole thing started with the plans for the football program and the Board vote. Then you were here, then Brian Gill and his father started threatening me again, and now my life is a mess." The last few words came out in a rush.

"Hold on a minute. The Gills threatening you? Again? When the fuck did they threaten you the first time?"

Tess leaned back. She was used to Cade and Nick cussing. She'd never heard her brother use that word.

"Umm."

"No umm. When did they threaten you the first time?"

"Well, Brian was just an ass. The threats were more his father's thing."

"When?" He repeated, a vein pulsed in his forehead.

"When I was six."

"What the ever-loving fuck?" TJ burst off the couch and started pacing.

"You remember when I was tested as a genius, and Mom and Dad took me to that counselor?"

"Vaguely. I was fourteen and had just discovered the girl I liked actually liked me back. I was distracted."

"Esther Lang." Tess didn't have the heart to tell her brother that his fantasy girl had liked TJ's best friend and was using TJ to get close to her actual crush.

"You knew?"

"I was observant. I knew everything. I didn't always understand it, but I knew what was going on around me."

"Don't distract me with stories of my first crush. What happened?"

"When Mom and Dad took me to the counselor, Brian was there with his father. The procedure is that the counselors meet with the parents first and then with the kids. So. Brian and I were alone in the waiting room."

Her brother's face started to turn and odd shade of purple. "What happened in that room?"

"He wasn't there because he was gifted. He was there because he's dyslexic. I offered to help him. He was rude but didn't say anything. Then his father came out and said some things."

"What exactly happened?"

She shivered. "I don't want to talk about it again."

"Again?" He stopped his pacing and stared at her.

"I told Nick at lunch."

"You'll tell some random guy, but not your brother."

"Nick isn't some random guy. He's my friend."

"Fine. You'll tell your friend, but not your brother?" He rejoined her on the couch.

She really didn't want to repeat the words Brian had said to her that day. But TJ was right. If she was going to trust Nick with her secret, she could trust her big brother.

"He was embarrassed about a six-year-old offering to help him and told me to leave him alone. Neither of us heard his father come out of the counselor's office. One minute I was talking to Brian the next his father was in my face. He said if I ever told anyone about his son he would ruin our whole family, make sure we lost everything and everyone would know it was all my fault and no one would want me. He'd see me in an orphanage on the other side of the country." Her brother's eyes were filled with a mixture of horror and rage. "I was terrified."

"You didn't tell anyone."

"He said he'd destroy our family." She shivered at the memory of the rage that Senior had directed at her that day. "I didn't know if he meant it or not, but I didn't want to risk it."

"I am going to go find those bastards and kick their asses." He started to stand.

She grabbed his arm and pulled him back down. "No. You're not."

"You're right. I'm going to go find Nick and we're going to kick their asses. More damage that way."

Tess held onto his arm when TJ started to stand again. "No."

He looked at her hand on him. "Holy shit, you're getting strong."

"I've been training." She flexed her left bicep, hoping to take his mind off his sudden need to make the Gills bleed. It was time to change the subject. "I really am sorry. It's entirely possible that tirade wasn't all about you."

"But it was partly about me. Do you really think I'm treating your practice like it's inferior to mine?"

She shrugged. "You do mention what you do in your practice a lot."

He ran a hand through his hair. "I don't mean to. Truth is I like the way you and Dad manage this place. Being here is reminding me of why I became a vet."

"What's your practice like?"

"You kind of nailed it. It's exclusive. Most of the pets are treated like accessories. Hell, most of our clients are so rich we don't ever see them personally. The animals are brought in by assistants, maids, butlers. Some of our clients hire personal assistants for their animals. It's mostly pure breed dogs and cats with the occasional exotic animal. They're almost all high strung and spoiled. Some of them are total nightmares."

"I bet there's no one whacking you with a purse because you suggested taking her dog for a walk."

"No." He laughed. "Even getting beaned on the head, I've been happier here in the last few weeks than I've been in a long time."

She smiled. The thought of him enjoying working here made her want to do a little dance. "You should stay then."

"That simple."

She nodded. "Pretty much."

"It's a small town. You don't really have room for three vets."

"Sure, we do." She and her father had agreed it would be a challenge to accommodate him at first, but they had already figured out ways to make the arrangement beneficial for the practice and everyone involved.

"Is there some waiting list for veterinary care you haven't shared with me?"

"No. Dad would like to do more teaching than he does,

but I can't spare him from the practice and Mom really wants to travel more, but Dad doesn't want to leave me in the lurch. She got him to agree to this cruise because it was already paid for and Gran needed them to take the tickets."

She got up and paced the room. "I have other projects I want to look into after the competition. If you came home and joined the practice, between the three of us we can make sure all our patients are cared for, and we'd all have time for a life outside of the practice."

"You think Dad would go for it?"

"I was instructed to make it happen while he was away." She smiled.

"My practice —"

"Is very successful and your partner is rich. He can afford to buy you out and then hire a couple of vets to take over your share of the workload. He strikes me as the kind of guy who would jump at the chance to be the big boss."

He was silent for a few moments. It was a comfortable silence. She was starting to get the hang of this human interaction thing and knew that silence wasn't always bad.

"You've only met him twice." He sounded skeptical.

"Yeah, but he was true to form both times."

His eyes narrowed. "What do you mean?"

"He hit on me by describing how rich he was."

"Really? Son of a bitch."

"He wasn't gross, just kind of a douche."

"Still, you're my sister. You don't hit on a buddy's sister like that."

She shrugged. Her lessons in human interaction hadn't really penetrated the rules of male bonding and friendship.

"You sure Dad's on board?"

"Yeah. We talked about it right before he left. He wanted me to see if you would be interested. He'd be thrilled if we had all the partnership paperwork ready to sign when he got back from the cruise."

"Well then. You need to call whoever is preparing that paperwork for us and I need to call my soon to be former partner about buying me out."

"Just like that?"

"It'll take some time to move my life here completely. I have to sell my condo, pack up my stuff, but yeah, just like that."

He got up and left the office. She smiled.

I wonder when he'll remember he wants to go kick the Gill's asses?

Chapter 20

❞ You're fucking this up."

Cade sat in his living room and looked at Nick over the top of the beer he'd taken a swig of. He wasn't going to have this conversation. Especially not while he was staring at a wall full of pictures from his military days that he'd put up because of Tess.

"Don't know what you're talking about." Under normal circumstances, that would be enough to get his friend to back off.

"Yeah. You do." Nick crossed his arms.

Damn it. Not normal circumstance. "I'm not talking about this."

"She's the best thing that ever happened to you."

Cade agreed, but it didn't change anything. "Doesn't matter."

His friend wouldn't let it go. "It matters."

"Fine. She's the best thing that ever happened to me." No use in denying it.

"Then why are you fucking this up?"

"Because I'm not the best thing that ever happened to her." Cade picked up his beer and threw it across the room. Every nasty word his mother had ever said to him rang in his ears. The noise of the bottle shattering against the wall

312

startled Sonny and Sam sending them out of the room.

"That's bullshit." Nick almost spat the words at Cade.

He scrubbed his hand down his face. "It's true."

"Dude, not to get all girly here, but you're the best man I know. You're the best friend I've ever had."

Cade was overwhelmed. He knew Nick's history better than anyone but the man himself. That Nick considered him his best friend was an honor he hadn't expected.

"Nick."

"Known you for more than thirteen years. Never met a better leader, a better man. She's good for you."

"But I'm not good for her." Cade held up a hand. "All the stuff you know about me, you know from playing ball with me, serving with me. The things that make me a good leader, good player, even a good friend, aren't things that make me good for a woman. I'm a Maguire. We aren't built for relationships. Fucking them up is in my damn genes."

"What kind of bullshit is that?" Nick sounded incredulous.

"There isn't one successful relationship in my entire family."

"What the hell are you talking about?"

"My mom walked out on us when I was six. I've seen and talked to her a handful of times since, and every damn

313

time she told me all the reasons my father fucked up her life and how I'm bound to fuck up any woman's life who was stupid enough to give me a shot." He wasn't even going to bring up Lana. It pissed him off that the one woman he'd thought he had a shot with after his mother spent sixteen years messing with his head had teamed up with his mother to take him for a ride made him want to hurl.

"Sounds like your mom's a bitch and you were all better off without her."

"My grandmother left my grandfather when my dad was ten. My great-grandmother refused to live with my great-grandfather after my grandfather's fifth birthday. The list goes on. Going back as far as you trace my family line the Maguire men are Navy men whose wives leave them, even back in the day when wives didn't leave husbands."

"Are you serious right now?" Nick shook his head.

"Deadly. Maguire men make great sailors, we're leaders of men. We also make the women we love miserable. I'm trying to save Tess that pain."

Cade got up and started pacing the room. "I know what will happen. It's the same story that's been playing in my family for generations. I'll think I'm the exception to the rule, Tess and I will get married and for a while we'll be happy, maybe even have a couple of kids. Then the

Maguire blood will kick in and I'll start to make her misera-ble. I won't mean to, but I won't be able to stop it. Then she'll walk out and everything will be fucked."

Nick stared for so long Cade thought he might come out of his own skin. Ever since his mother and Lana had dropped their bombshell on him, he'd played the family history over and over again in his mind. There was no way to escape the curse. He ran his hand through his hair. Funny how it hadn't felt like a curse until he met Tess.

"That's the biggest load of bullshit I've ever heard."

He whipped around and faced his friend. "What?"

"You heard me."

He'd expected a little more support from his friend. "It's my family history."

"It's your mother's bullshit."

"Watch it."

"Fuck that. I'm watching you walk, no run, from the best thing that ever happened to you because you've been told the men in your family have historically been dumb shits by an unreliable source."

"What the fuck, man?" This was the most talkative Nick had ever been. Cade didn't like it that much.

"Let's assume your mother's telling the truth and every story you told involves a woman walking out on her man

315

and her kids. Right? When the women in your family all left, they left their kids behind."

"So?"

"So? I'll bet the women in your family were the hottest things going in their time. The most popular chicks. Hooking themselves to the most popular guys."

"Again, so?"

"So, your family history is filled with men strong enough to serve and women too weak to stand by them. Anything about Tess say weakness to you?"

"Of course not."

"You bet your ass. That woman is the strongest woman I've ever met. The shit she's been dealing with from the Gills alone for twenty-two fucking years would probably have had a woman like your mother in a loony bin."

"What are you talking about?" Cade didn't like the fact that Tess had clearly confided in Nick when she wouldn't confide in her man. "Why's she talking to you about the Gills and not me?"

"You're getting pissed that Tess is talking to me instead of you, when you've been pulling away from her for weeks now? Your head is so far up your own ass I'm surprised you can't see through your mouth. She's exactly what you need. Get your act together."

Nick stomped out the front door and slammed it behind him. Cade stood there his muscles shaking and his heart beating a mile a minute. Tess had been talking to Nick and not him. He grabbed his keys and headed out himself.

I'll be damned if I take this bullshit.

Fifteen minutes later he pulled up in front of Tess's house. The pounding in his ears sounded like the rotors of an Apache helicopter. He found her sitting on her back porch.

"What the ever-loving fuck?" The instant the words were out of his mouth he knew he'd gone off the deep end. He had one chance to reel it back in and, maybe, not blow the best thing that had ever happened to him.

Her eyes widened. "What the ever-loving what?" She sounded confused, which somehow pushed him over the edge.

"You and Nick?" Definitely over the edge. It was like he'd stepped outside of his body and was now watching a total moron fuck up his life for him.

"Me and Nick what?" Her expression went blank.

"I turn my back and you start —"

She froze. "I would be very careful how you finish that sentence."

He'd never seen that look on her face before today and

317

he could swear an icy breeze slide down his spine. "Confiding in him. You've told him things you refused to tell me, the man you're fucking."

She flinched. "I'm admittedly not good at reading signals, but —"

"Will you for once stop hiding behind the bullshit that you're socially awkward?" He was getting tired of her using that excuse whenever she messed something up.

"Why are you so angry?"

"Because I went out of town for business, on a trip I can't talk to you about because you're so fucking rigid, and I find out that you're cozying up to one of my best friends." Why couldn't he shut himself up? Every time he spoke he made this worse.

"Rigid? You told me you understood why I couldn't talk to you about your program."

"Tess, half the town knows we're sleeping together. Do you honestly believe they don't think we're talking about the plan your grandfather and the guy you're screwing are putting together?"

"Is that all we're doing? Sleeping together?" Her skin was flushed and mottled and she was shaking.

Even seeing the effect his words had on her he couldn't stop the train. "I never made any promises to you." That sounded lame, even to his irrational, rage-soaked brain.

"I'm not talking about promises." Her hands clenched.

"Then what are you talking about?"

"What are you talking about? I don't understand this whole conversation."

"Why are you confiding in Nick and not me?"

"You weren't here." She stood up and backed away, putting distance between them.

"I was here last night." The space between them felt like a chasm.

"Not really."

The accusation stung. "What's that supposed to mean?"

"You've been pulling away for weeks. I didn't want to say anything because I didn't know what to say. I'm not completely clueless about relationships. When we first started seeing each other, we were together all the time, unless I was at work or you were with Grandpa. I don't know what happened, but sometime after dinner with my parents you started spending less and less time with me. The only reason we saw each other last night was because I blindsided you."

"I've had to travel to meet with potential coaches. With our plan up in the air, they don't have a reason to travel to us." He knew it was a lame excuse. She was right, and he

319

didn't want to tell her why, to admit that he would fail her in the end. It was inevitable. The Maguire curse.

"I know that. Again, not stupid. But the last few weeks, even when you're in town, you're barely with me. When we're together, your mind is a million miles away. You don't even show up for all our training sessions, even when you're here. I've been spending more time training with Nick than I have with you."

"So, that's your thing. Fucking the trainer. You want me to step aside so you two can go at it?" There it was. One second he'd been over the edge, but still dangling by a thread, the next the thread had snapped and he was hurtling into the abyss.

She looked like he'd slapped her. He wanted to take it all back. The whole conversation had gone sideways the second he stepped out of his truck. Hell, it had gone sideways back at his house when he'd overreacted to the conversation with Nick.

"You need to leave and stay away. I won't ever repeat this conversation because I know what it will take for you to be able to work in town, but I can't see you for a while."

"Your training —"

"Nick and the Trips can help me finish. They've been handling most of my training the last few weeks anyway."

320

"Sonny —" Bringing his dog into it was a reach and he knew it. He had fucked up royally and now he was scrambling to keep her from cutting him out of her life.

"Is fine. His cast comes off in a couple of days and he likes TJ. He can handle the rest of Sonny's care."

"Tess —"

She held up a hand. "You know, more than most how hard it is for me to open up to people. To let myself be part of things. I let you in. I made myself a part of something. Us. Now I have no idea why. You need to go."

She turned around and went inside. The quiet snick of the door closing was louder than any explosion Cade had ever heard.

Dear God. What did I just do?

Tess stood in the middle of her front hall. Numb. Frozen in a place she didn't understand. Lost without a map to lead her home.

If she was honest with herself, she'd been expecting him to break things off for a while and had tried to brace for it. But the gentle "it's not you it's me" speech she thought she'd prepared herself for hadn't come. Instead he'd all but accused her of cheating on him with Nick.

She was hollowed out and trapped in a place she couldn't navigate. Her first thought was to go upstairs, crawl into bed and stay there for the next million years or so.

That was impractical.

Retreating to her safe distance and never speaking of him again might work.

That made her chest ache and her throat tighten.

There was the option of calling the girls and getting drunk while she bitched about Cade.

That was the most appealing of her options, but also the most dangerous.

The vote was in eight days. If Delilah went off on Cade and the nastiness of their fight became public, it could impact the vote, or at least give the Gills more ammunition to make it an uglier fight than it was shaping up to be already.

Tess went to the kitchen to grab a beer out of the refrigerator. The back porch called her. Maybe watching the sunset would help stop the world from spinning out of control. Within minutes her animals packed themselves around her, tight. Her last option was to sit and brood on her own and talk to people when she was damn well ready.

Door number four it is.

It looks like the only person she'd manage to fool with

her insistence on equal treatment for the various plans was Cade. She'd looked through the preliminary materials submitted for all three proposals and knew that Grandpa and Cade's was the best plan, hands down. Olivia's simply wasn't practical, and the Gill's rogues' gallery of coaches would lead Cormac further down the road it was already on now, thanks to Delano.

There hadn't been time to tell Cade what Gill had been up to in the last few weeks, other than recruiting a questionable group of coaches. She held the cold beer to her forehead, hoping it would ease the ache that had started at the bridge of her nose and was now spreading towards the back of her head.

"You okay?"

She opened her eyes and saw Nick standing at her back door.

"Not really. Cade stopped by and said a few things. He's gone now." Just saying it made the emptiness inside her grow.

"Afraid of that." His shoulders drooped.

She nodded at the screen door. "The door's unlocked. You can come in and grab a beer if you want."

His look of indecision told her that Cade had shared some of his crazy ideas with Nick, too.

"He's mad about something and taking it out on us. Even I know that. Given the situation, we can keep each other company and minimize the impact his stupidity might have on the proposal to the Board."

He nodded and let himself in to the back porch. Nick disappeared into the house and returned a few moments later with his own beer. Since none of her animals made a move, he settled himself on the chair next to the couch.

They sat together in companionable silence for a while. Neither of them seemed to have anything to say. Tess doubted their respective silences were for the same reasons.

"He's going to figure out he fucked up." Nick broke the silence.

"Maybe." She was too numb to care.

"No maybe about it. Question is, did he say something you won't be able to forgive him for?"

His deep blue eyes held a question she couldn't answer. Not now.

"I don't know." She wished she could say yes. It would be so easy to believe Nick and know for sure that Cade would come back and want to try again. A happy ending for them was all she'd wanted for weeks now. But their argument aside, Cade had spent a majority of their relationship, such as it was, pulling away from her. She deserved to have someone in her life who would fight to be with her.

"I hope the answer to that question is yes when you figure it out. You're good for him."

"But is he good for me?" She'd thought so at first. He was the first person who knew her on every level and seemed to like her no matter what. That made what he'd implied a little while ago even worse. If he didn't know she'd never do the things he'd hinted at, he'd never known her at all.

"Deep thoughts."

"He had a lot to say." She wished she could erase the entire conversation from her memory.

Nick hesitated before he spoke. "Got a worm in his brain."

"What?" She leaned forward, alarmed. "He's sick?"

Nick reached out and settled her back with one arm. "Not a real worm. He's got this stupid idea in his brain. Been there since his mom left. It's not going to work its way out overnight. Got a feeling it will, though. I'm hoping you can be there when it does."

"Are you going to give me a clue?" She'd known Cade had issues with his mother, since he'd changed the subject whenever she came up.

"Not my story to tell. All I can say is he's a good man.

325

He can be every bit as good for you as you are for him."

"Recent evidence to the contrary."

Nick shrugged.

"Let's assume you're right. He figures out he made a horrible mistake and comes back here looking for forgiveness. What am I supposed to do? Say it's all right that he behaved so badly, treated me horribly? Isn't that a bad precedent for a relationship? Delilah would tell me I was giving him all the power."

"Not about power. The real thing, kind of thing that lasts? That's about love and forgiveness. You two find your way back to each other? There's going to be more days ahead when you have to forgive him. Probably some days when he'll need to forgive you. Making it work means leaving the bad shit behind and moving forward, every damn day."

She tilted her head. "You sound like an expert."

"Seen couples that made it work and couples that didn't."

"Taking notes for your future Mrs.?" She teased.

He shook his head sadly. "Not going to be a Mrs."

"Why not?"

"The other thing you need to make it work is trust. Got none of that left in me."

"You trust me." He'd never said as much, but given the stories he'd shared, she knew it was true.

"That's different."

"Why?"

He shifted in his seat and stared at the ceiling.

"Why, Nick?"

"You can't get mad."

"Why would I?"

"You're a woman."

"So?" Would she ever understand these tangential conversations?

"Sometimes stupid stuff pisses women off."

She had to smile. He wasn't wrong, and she had often had trouble over the years figuring out why the women in her life were mad at the men in theirs.

"You're not wrong. But I think all my anger is reserved for Cade right now. You should be safe."

"I never thought of you as a real girl."

She drew back. "I…does my intelligence make me a fake girl to you?"

"No. I like the way your brain works. It's just…when I got here it was clear which way things were going with you and Cade, even if you guys hadn't figured it out yet. So, you were firmly out of the hot chick category to me."

327

"Oh." She must have looked as confused as she sounded because he let out a huff of frustration.

"You're hot. No doubt. I don't think about you like that because you're Cade's. So, I can be myself around you. No worries about the future. Since we're never going to be romantic it was easy, well easier, for me to learn to trust you."

Tears pricked the back of her eyes and she blinked them back. She didn't want to make him uncomfortable with more emotion than was already filling the air of the back porch.

"I'm glad. It's nice to have friends you can trust with your secrets."

"Yeah. It is." He held out his beer and she clinked her bottle against it in a toast.

"To friends."

"To Cade getting his head out of his ass." He clinked their bottles again.

She didn't drink. If that happened, she wasn't sure what she would do, what she would want to do. There was a lot to think about. But first, she just needed to make it through the Board vote. Then, whatever Cade did, she would have to focus on the rest of her life.

If it included him or not.

Chapter 21

Cade signaled the bartender for another round. The last time he'd been to The Dive he'd been eighteen and flashing a fake ID. Nothing had changed in the last eighteen years. It was still the kind of place that didn't look too carefully at the patrons' IDs and it was still the place people in King's Folly came to when they didn't want word getting back to anyone in town about a bender.

The bartender left the shot and the beer in front of him with a nod before moving back to the end of the bar to entertain two bleached blondes with some bar tricks. Someone sat down next to him. The warning tingle at the base of his spine told him he wasn't going to be happy with whoever was sitting there.

A glance to the left confirmed his suspicions when he caught sight of Gill looking a little less put together than usual.

"Backup." He turned slightly so he could appear to face forward but keep the bastard in his peripheral vision.

"Maguire." Gill sneered. "Where's your girlfriend?"

Bringing up Tess was the wrong thing to do, which Cade proved a moment later when he wrapped his hand around Gill's throat. He squeezed, not enough pressure to leave a mark, but enough to make his point.

"You don't look at her. You don't talk about her. You don't think about her."

Gill didn't answer. Cade knew he wasn't pressing hard enough to interfere with the bastard's voice. There was something in his eyes. It wasn't fear. It was almost like resignation.

What the fuck?

He let go of Brian, who didn't flinch. Didn't even rub his neck. All he did was lean against the bar and nod at the bartender, who sidled over with a shot and a beer.

"Don't recall asking you to stay."

Brian threw back the shot. "Free country. Thanks for helping with that by the way."

There was no sarcasm in the other man's voice, but Cade wondered if it was a dig. "What's your game?"

"No game. Tonight." He sipped his beer.

"Have you ever been able to do that? Not play games?"

"I have my moments." The other man seemed to consider his next words. "I'll admit not many of them are around you. But, I have them."

Cade thought about moving. It's not like he wanted to spend any time with this douche bag. Maybe he deserved it. For hurting Tess, he should be punished with Brian's presence.

"I meant what I said. Stay away from Tess."

Brian sipped his beer. "I'm not the one you have to worry about."

"What's that mean?"

The other man rubbed the back of his neck. "You ever been so fucking tired you can't sleep?"

"What's that got to do with Tess?"

"I've been tired for a long time. This whole thing with the team just makes everything worse." Brian stared at his beer.

It was like he was looking at a complete stranger. "What's going on, Brian?"

Gill turned to him, his blue eyes looked tortured. "In the eighteen years I've known you, you've never called me Brian."

Cade blinked. "That can't be true."

"You think I don't know what everyone says about me? What everyone thinks about me? I'm not stupid." He took a sip of his drink. "All evidence to the contrary."

"What's going on?"

"You hear from your mother lately?"

The question hit Cade so hard it gave him whiplash. Was Backup the little birdy that told his mother to call him? "What do you know about her?"

"Lana."

"What do you mean Lana?" He wasn't jealous that Brian was bringing his old girlfriend into the conversation. Thanks to his meltdown with Nick, Cade understood that nasty emotion all too well.

Brian stared at him for a minute. "You really never figured out that we were fucking behind you back our senior year?"

"What the actual fuck?"

"Bitch couldn't shut up after sex. Told me all her plans with your mommy dearest when I was done banging her."

Cade didn't know what to say. A part of him wanted to beat the shit out of Brian on principal. The other part of him wanted to find out what the hell the bastard was up to.

"What the fuck does my mother have to do with this?"

"I may be my old man's lackey, but it looks to me like you're still your mother's. My old man's an evil prick with a stranglehold on my life. What's your excuse?"

"What the hell does that even mean?" This conversation was so far out of left field it was in another time zone.

"It means it's obvious to a blind man you're fucking things up with Tess because of that shit with your mom. Which makes you a bigger dick than me."

"You're giving me relationship advice?" He could swear

the theme from *The Twilight Zone* was playing. Was Rod Serling going to step out from behind the bar soon?

Brian shrugged. "She tried to do me a solid once when she was too young to know it would put her on the wrong radar. She's going to need you before this is through."

Brian's phone pinged. He pulled it out of his pocket and glanced at the screen. "Got to go." He signaled to the bartender. "My friend here's buying."

Cade grabbed his arm. "Was that a threat?"

"That was a statement." Brian yanked his arm free and leaned closer. "We're all doing what we have to do to survive. You don't fuck with me. I won't fuck with you. But I can't speak for my old man."

With that comment, Gill strode out of the bar.

"What the hell just happened?" Cade asked a room full of people that didn't give a shit.

Later that night, Cade tried to put his key in the lock and kept missing. He could hear Sonny and Sam on the other side of the door, but since they hadn't yet mastered the art of unlocking doors they weren't going to be any help.

His booze-soaked brain told him that there should be someone else there, but he could barely remember his own name much less the details of his current living situation.

333

He was lucky the bartender was a local and a die-hard Knights fan. Instead of going home with the bleached blondes, he'd called his brother to help him make sure Cade and his truck made it home in one piece.

God bless the fans.

The door snapped open, and for a minute he was wondering what he could do with his duo of door opening dogs, when he saw Nick standing in the doorway, arms crossed. He glanced over Cade's shoulder and relaxed a little. Clearly, he saw the taillights heading down the driveway.

"At least you weren't stupid enough to drink and drive."

Cade shrugged and wondered why he was suddenly seeing two Nicks in the doorway. He burped. The force of it almost sent him toppling onto his ass. Nick, well one of the Nicks, grabbed him and yanked him into the house, a look of disgust on his face.

"Man, you reek. What the hell were you drinking?"

"Didn't care what it was. Just wanted it to keep coming."

"Yeah. Got news for you, brother. You won't be able to drown your stupid in booze."

"Fucked it up." The only thought that was clear in his

334

brain was that he'd messed everything up with Tess.

"Yeah you did."

"The two of you don't have to yell."

Both Nicks chuckled. "Time for you to go to bed. No use talking tonight."

"Good idea." Cade stood in the front hall, swaying slightly. A split second later he went down like an imploded tower. The last thing he heard was Nick, one of them anyway.

"Fuck me. I'm not carrying you to bed.

The next morning, Cade woke slowly. Every inch of his body hurt, and someone was using tiny jackhammers inside his skull. Licking his lips might help, but instead of relief, he got a mouth full of fur. He sat up, too quickly and had to fight back the vomit that rose in his throat.

It wasn't supposed to be this bright. There were blackout shades in his bedroom. It took him a minute to figure out he wasn't in his room. He was still in the front hall with Sonny and Sam, who had kept him company after he passed out on the floor. The vague memory of drinking, a lot, drifted through his muddled brain.

Shit. Tess.

He'd been downing shots and beers because he'd fucked everything up with her. Way ahead of schedule.

Worse, he'd done the last thing he wanted to do. Hurt her.

"Morning, sunshine." Nick stood in the doorway, freshly showered and holding a cup of coffee.

Cade cleared his throat. "Don't suppose you have one of those for me."

"You know where the kitchen is," he responded loud enough to make Cade wince.

"No pity then."

Nick shook his head. "Not from me." He turned and walked back into the kitchen.

When Sonny and Sam followed his friend into the kitchen, Cade knew he was screwed. He sat in the front hall trying to find the energy to move off the floor. It was like he'd gone ten rounds with an MMA fighter and lost. When was the last time he'd been that drunk or this hungover? Never. Turns out losing Tess was the worst thing that had ever happened to him.

It took him longer than he'd ever admit to stand up and walk into the kitchen. Nick was sitting at the table, reading over the latest draft of the presentation, Sonny and Sam at his feet. Traitors. Cade staggered over to the counter where the coffee pot was, thankfully, full. He poured himself a cup. After taking a sip he turned to Nick.

"Don't suppose you'd make me some of that hangover

cure you made the girls."

"Nope." Nick kept studying his papers.

"You've talked to Tess."

"Had dinner with her last night while you were out pickling your liver." Nick pinned Cade with his glare. "You going to accuse me of fucking her?"

Cade winced at the venom in his friend's voice. Too bad the booze didn't erase the memory of what he'd said to her yesterday.

"I crossed a line."

"You didn't just cross it, you jumped so far over it you couldn't even see it anymore."

Nick's berating, deserved as it was, wasn't going to help Cade fix it. "What am I supposed to do about it?"

"There's this new thing called an apology. You could try that."

"Wouldn't change anything." He set his coffee down and went looking for some aspirin.

"Might start fixing things between the two of you."

"I'm still no good for her. Better it's really over now than later when it'll hurt more." He sounded like an idiot, even to himself. Nick's snort made Cade wonder if he'd said the idiot part out loud.

He finally found the aspirin and swallowed four and

washed them down with coffee. He would have preferred whatever Nick's hangover cure was, but it didn't seem like he was going to get that any time soon. Looks like he would have to settle for a shower. He trudged down the hall wondering how everything had gotten so completely messed up.

I fell in love. The beginning of the end for a Maguire male.

Seven days later, Olivia finished her speech to a smattering of applause. Tess reviewed the summary again confirming what she'd known all along, this plan didn't have a chance of passing. It was a testament to Olivia that she hadn't been laughed out of the room. This was a football school. The question before the board was whose plan would be best for the football program, her grandfather and Cade's or Gill's.

Grandpa and Cade had done an inspiring presentation. She knew it would be good, but some of their choices for the next generation of coaches were positively inspired. Not to mention their program's stated philosophy on the importance of education for the players. Tess had stolen a glance at Professor Ryan, chair of the Women's Studies Program, when Cade mentioned one of the new coaches would be a woman. It was obvious she was torn between her academic leanings and the opportunity to continue to break the gender barrier.

Tess had to keep herself from laughing during Brian's presentation. It was dull and uninspired. He'd given them a list of coaches who were "ready to go." The presentation had gone off the rails during the questions and answers. A stranger in a suit, who introduced himself as Mr. Lacks, indicated he would act as a liaison and stepped forward to answer the first question about Coach Sorenson. It was clear, Brian wasn't aware he was being given an assist. Just as it was clear that Gill Senior had hired the suit. Junior was pissed. If looks could kill, Senior wouldn't be the Board's headache anymore. Or anyone else's.

Before they took the vote, Gill Senior cleared his throat.

"Before we take a formal vote. I move to have Tess Gallagher recused from voting."

His motion started an uproar in the room. Tess narrowed her eyes and stared at Senior. She noted the calculating gleam in his eye.

"On what basis?" She looked from father to son.

"Your grandfather is putting forth one of the plans."

"Your son is putting forth another. Are you recusing yourself?"

"I think I can be more objective." His sneer seemed to be fixed to his face.

"Why?"

Senior looked at his son, who crossed arms and shook his head. Senior turned red and looked at the suit.

Mr. Lacks shook his head. After a few signals from Senior, the other man grimaced and cleared his throat. "Because you're having an inappropriate relationship with Mr. Maguire, and it's clear you cannot be impartial," the suit said.

Tess gasped. She smiled a second later when Gran smacked the slimy bastard over the head with her purse.

"You low-down son of a snake." Delilah was being held back by Charlie, who also had a hand out to try and prevent the Trips from going after the stranger, who obviously wasn't prepared to face the consequences of his forced statement.

Junior sat in front, arms crossed, smiling at his father.

What was that about?

Cade stood immobile. Their argument still rang through her head and she knew he wouldn't say anything. He was convinced she was better off without him. This little display from Senior and his lackey was going to add fuel to that fire, and she was done. She had better things to do with her time than sit here and take this from anyone, especially Brian Gill, Senior.

She loved Cade enough to stand up for both of them, no matter what happened.

"I'm not going to deny I was involved with Cade Maguire." She was careful to emphasize the word was as she tried to give Mr. Lacks a glimpse of exactly what he'd stepped into by taking Senior's orders. Mr. Lacks flinched and she felt satisfaction roll through her.

Tess was careful not to look at Cade. She didn't want him to feel she was pressuring him to come to his senses. "But your employer, and clearly you, are a pair of unscrupulous weasels. You can force me to recuse myself, you can kick me off the board." There were murmurs in the room that let her know Gill might have pushed too hard. Time to really drive that point home.

"I don't think —" Gill Senior cleared his throat.

Tess pinned him with a glare. "You started this. Are you man enough to finish it?"

Gill Senior sat back in his chair, clearly unprepared for what he had unleashed. She looked around the room making eye contact with every member of the Board.

"So far, I'm the only member of this Board who hasn't been treated a mini-vacation by the Gills." Some of the

Board members had the grace to blush. "I believed we could all be impartial, listen to the plans with open minds and do what's best for the university."

Tess turned to her friend. "Olivia, I admire what you wanted to accomplish, but this is a football school. They're never going to eliminate the football program, and I personally believe it was bordering on cruel to raise your hopes. The only reason your presentation went forward was to give the academic members of the Board an option other than Grandpa's."

Olivia was obviously crushed, even though Tess had tried to warn her about this.

"I think you have some wonderful ideas for the university and I believe we can make them happen, but not right away and not by getting rid of the football program."

Olivia nodded and held her head up higher.

Tess admired her grit. She glared at the Board members. "We all know this is a football school. Forcing Professor Valenti to present her innovative ideas in this context is disrespectful and disgusting. It's beneath the dignity of this institution."

There were more gasps from the audience. Some of them had known Tess her entire life and had never heard her talk like this.

"If this is the influence Maguire has on you maybe we should —"

"Maybe you should shut it, Gerald." She had to keep herself from saying something worse to the Board member who served as Gill Senior's number one toady for decades on the Board and off it.

"Now see here —" Gerald tried to take control of the situation.

She wasn't going to give it to him. "This whole room knows you're going to vote in lock step with Gill. I don't know what he's been blackmailing you with for the last twenty years, but you should just let the secret out because I seriously doubt it could be worse than what the gossips are speculating." She heard several more gasps in the room. This time they were joined by some coughs, which appeared to be people masking their laughter.

Some of the other Board members chuckled and Tess went for them. "You should keep your mouths shut. He may not have had anything on you, but you've let Gill run roughshod over this Board for years, before he was even on it. He's the reason we're in this position in the first place."

"Now just a damn minute —" Gill Senior's face was red, and he stood so fast his chair fell over.

"You were the one who encouraged Delano to force

Grandpa into retirement. You engineered the vote that got him ousted and you were behind every dirty deal he made that led to the sanctions." She wasn't kidding when she told Brian she knew about all his family's skeletons. It wasn't their business if how many conversations has been had with the local authorities. Yet.

President Adams stepped forward. "Now hold on Dr. Gallagher. Those are some serious accusations."

"I'm sure this is where my father wants me to ask you if you can spell lawsuit, Dr. Gallagher?" Gill Junior sneered, not taking his eyes off his father.

"Better than you can spell cat, asshole." Delilah had broken free from Charlie's grip and smacked Junior on the back of the head.

"He's right Dr. Gallagher." Senior had suddenly found his voice again. "I will sue you and your —"

"My little dog too?" It was Tess's turn to sneer at the older man. "I'm a genius, Gill. Do you think I would make such a public statement if I didn't have proof?"

"Do you really?" President Adams stepped forward.

Tess nodded at Charlie who reached into her pocket to grab something, which she threw to Tess.

Tess reached up and caught it. She handed the small flash drive to President Adams. "This is a copy of all the proof you need to confirm that not only did Gill and his cronies push my grandfather out, but they also profited on all the Delano deals that brought down this program." She turned to Gill Senior. "You can read all about it in The Dispatch. I'm sure you know that Maggie Slater's cat is one of my patients. You remember Maggie don't you? She broke the story about Delano last year, with Quinn Wilder's help."

"I've also given a copy of all these documents to the authorities. True, most of what I've seen just looks unethical to me, but I'm sure they'll be able to find anything illegal." She took a beat. "Now that enough people are looking."

The older man sat back, red faced and sweaty. "You can't hurt me."

"I had no intention of hurting anyone. I just wanted to stop you from bringing the university down with you."

She turned back to President Adams. "You wanted to restore the football program. More importantly, you wanted to restore this university's reputation. By letting Gill propose a plan and implement it, you're just allowing him to drag this university further into the mud."

"But your grandfather's plan..."

"Is bold and innovative and insane. It's also the best thing for this university and the football program." She walked over to Nick and put a hand on his shoulder.

"You've all made a big deal out of this man's past. He made a huge mistake and lives were forever changed because of it." She smiled at him before focusing on the rest of the room again. "He paid his debt to society. He lost a chance to play college football and a shot at a professional career. He could have done a stint in juvie and become a statistic. Instead, he chose to enter the military and worked his ass off to earn a second chance."

She tightened her hands in to fists and met Cade's gaze. "Cade Maguire was destined to be a first round draft pick. Everyone said he had the potential to be the greatest quarterback to ever play the game. He could have stayed with football. Instead, he chose to withdraw from the draft and serve his country. He devoted fourteen years of his life to the Navy and came back a hero. There is more honor in his little finger than a lot of people in this room have in their whole bodies."

"She means you, dickwad." Delilah smacked Gill Junior.

"Now, thanks to Grandpa, he has a second chance to be part of the game I know he loves." She made eye contact with each of the Board members and President Adams. "This isn't about bringing inexperienced people onto the coaching staff. Grandpa's plan is about bringing men and women who know what pride, sacrifice, honor, and hard work mean to the program, to teach that to the next generation of Cormac football players. Their plan brings together a group of coaches and a group of former players who collectively know more about this sport than anyone else in the universe. They can build a program that can restore this university's reputation and football team. Not to mention they could lead the way for athletic academic programs that have been in the news more often than not. It's audacious and untested. It's also beyond brilliant. When it works, we can all take pride in the Cormac Knights again. If you idiots don't force my recusal I'm voting for this plan, and if you all have the sense that God gave a monkey, you will too."

She picked up her bag and stormed out of the room. It was impossible to stay.

Chapter 22

Cade watched Tess storm out of the room. He couldn't take his eyes off the doorway she'd walked through with Delilah and Charlie hot on her heels. She was magnificent. The room was filled with a stunned silence.

"That's my girl," Delilah called out as she and Charlie went rushing after Tess.

Cade turned to look at Ed. "What now?"

Ed shrugged, his eyes on President Adams. "Coach Maguire's got a point. What now?"

"He's not a coach, yet," Gill Senior snarled.

Junior sat in the front still staring at his father and smiling.

Why was Backup smiling?

"He should be." The room slid back into stunned silence at Olivia's announcement.

"Professor Valenti?" President Adams raised his brow.

"I would like to withdraw my proposal and I urge anyone who was considering it to support Coach King and Coach Maguire's proposal." She stared at Junior with a frosty glare.

"May I ask why?" Professor Connor, the head of the biology department and a member of the Board tilted his head.

"I have to admit something that embarrasses me. I prepared this proposal at the urging of Mr. Gill, Junior."

"Olivia." Gill Junior jumped out of his seat.

Nick stood up and moved to Olivia's side. He crossed his arms and stood there, daring Gill to make a move.

Olivia blanched, but continued. "I went to a bar one night for a drink, why doesn't matter now. I met Brian and we started dating." She blushed.

Cade heard Nick growl and took his eyes off the pretty professor to focus on his friend. Sensing things could go sideways, Cade shook his head and relaxed when Nick gave him a slight nod.

Olivia took a deep breath to continue her story. "He told me that the university was trying to figure out what to do about the football program. I may have said something about all that money being put to better use on the education programs of the university. He encouraged me to put together a proposal. He said I had a new perspective the university needed. I see now what he was doing." She ducked her head.

"What do you think he was doing?" President Adams stared at Gill Senior.

"There are ten members of the Board. He assumed the academics would vote for my proposal, which is three votes. Gill Senior clearly has two votes in his pocket. There are three that are clearly in Coach King's favor, leaving Tess as the deciding vote. If they got Tess recused, then there would have been a tie. If there was a tie, then the bylaws state that the Provost is the deciding vote." Olivia turned to look at the man in question, who was trying to slip out the side door. "I'm assuming, since he was also the deciding vote when Coach King was forced out, that Gill Senior would have four votes and push his proposal through."

The Provost stopped when all eyes were on him. He turned back to the room, red faced. The truth of Olivia's words written were all over him.

"That's ridiculous." Gill Senior sneered.

Olivia stared at him. "Maybe it is and maybe it isn't. Either way, I am going to withdraw my proposal, and I am urging anyone who would have supported it to vote for Coach King and Coach Maguire's proposal. They do have some innovative ideas for student athletes. I believe it will be a good thing for the entire Cormac University and King's Folly community. Excuse me."

Olivia rushed out of the auditorium. Cade noticed Nick had to stop himself from following her. They might have to talk about that. Who was he kidding? His own love life was in shambles. He had no business overseeing anyone else's.

The look Tess had on her face the last time they'd talked was tattooed on his brain. He rubbed his chest. The terrible things he said to her echoed in his brain like they were on a twenty-four-hour loop. Even if he could figure out how to move past his insecurities, he doubted she would ever forgive him.

"I have something I would like to add," Brian said, his gaze focused on the doorway Olivia had just left through.

"I think you've said enough." President Adams stared at him.

"No. There's one more thing." Brian turned to the Board and faced his father. "I'm withdrawing my support for my father's plan." He emphasized the last three words. "I won't be a part of any team at Cormac. You can look to Lacks here to implement it, if the board is stupid enough to vote against Coach King again."

Brian walked out of the room like he hadn't just dropped a bomb into the proceedings.

In the end, the vote was nine to one in favor of his and Ed's plan. Even Senior's lackeys jumped ship after his son walked away. In that moment when everything he'd been working for came to fruition, he understood that the coaching program wasn't the second chance he really needed. Now he had to figure out exactly how to convince Tess to give him the only second chance he really wanted.

That evening, Cade threw the stick from his back-porch step for Sonny and Sam. He knew that Ed was having a celebration at his place, but he wasn't up for it. The last week without Tess had been the worst of his life. Her absence carved a hole in his chest. He wanted to fix what he broke more than anything, but he knew he was right to push her away. It was better for her, no matter how much it sucked for him.

"Thought you'd be celebrating."

The sound of his father's voice startled him. He'd been so miserable he hadn't heard a car pull up. Cade stood at attention for what felt like the first time in a lifetime. "What are you doing here, sir?"

"At ease. We're not military anymore, son. You can call me dad again if you want."

"We're not military?" Cade emphasized the first word.

His dad motioned for him to sit then sat next to him. "Retired last week."

"Didn't think that would ever happen."

His dad shrugged. "It was time."

"What's next for you?"

"Not sure. Thought I might spend some time with you. Figure it out."

"Sure." He wasn't sure what else to say. This was unexpected. Not as unexpected as Brian turning on his father, but close.

His dad reached into the cooler next to the step and grabbed a beer. "So, I heard you fucked up."

"Don't know what you're talking about." His father had spent the better part of the last two years in a sub. What could he know?

"Tess Gallagher."

Apparently, his dad could know plenty. "What'd you hear?"

"That you were good for each other and you pushed her away, hard." His father took a swig of his beer and stared straight ahead.

"She's good for me. I'm not good for her." He grabbed the stick Sam dropped and threw it again.

"Why not?" His father sounded confused.

"How can you ask with the Maguire history?"

His father raised his eyebrows. "What Maguire history?"

"Maguire wives all leave. They end up hating us and they leave. We're not fit for a real relationship."

His father stared at him for what felt like hours but was

353

likely only a minute or two. "Who fed you that line of bull-shit."

Cade's neck warmed. "Mom said —"

"First rule. Never listen to your mother. Listen to every person on the planet and most of the animals before you give that woman the benefit of any doubt."

"She —"

"What exactly did she tell you and when would she have told you? You were six when she left." His dad studied him.

"The day she left and the times she came to see me after."

"Came to see you? How many times?" His father grabbed his arm.

"Every couple of years she showed up. Played nice for a while. Then spewed a bunch of nasty shit about how Maguires make terrible husbands before she took off." He couldn't look his dad in the eye.

"Are you serious?" Dad looked dazed.

"She told me that you were a horrible husband like your father was and his father. She said that there hadn't been a single successful Maguire marriage from the jump, and I was just like you, only fit for making women miserable when I grew up."

"You were six when she left." His father's voice was little more than a whisper.

"I know." He still couldn't look the other man in the eye.

"She said that shit to you when you were six?" His dad squeezed his arm. "Your mother?"

Cade shrugged. There wasn't anything else to say.

"And you saw her every couple of years after? She kept spewing that garbage?"

"Right up until I was twenty-two in person. Then a phone call about a few weeks ago."

"Twenty-two. She have anything to do with why you pulled out of the draft?"

This wasn't something he wanted to talk about with anyone. Ever.

"Son?"

Cade's chest tightened. "She hooked up with the girl I was seeing. Wanted me to go pro and spend some of that money on her."

His father closed his eyes. "And that's why you didn't go pro."

"I always wanted to be in the Navy."

"You wanted to play football, too." There was a tone in his father's voice as he turned to look out over the forest that Cade had never heard before.

"I don't regret not playing professionally." That was true. He would never regret his time in the Navy.

Cade's father ran his hand through his hair. "Marrying her was the stupidest thing I ever did. I could never regret it because I got two sons any father would be proud of out of the deal. But still, putting up with her was a steep price to pay for the two of you."

"Dad —"

Cade's father held up his hand. "You need to hear this. All of it."

Cade nodded, watching his father cautiously. He'd never seen him so angry.

"I was a decorated officer when I met your mother. Four years out of Vietnam and I was on my way to my own command. She was the most beautiful thing I'd ever seen. Before I knew it, we were married, and she was pregnant. A second later it seemed you were here, then your brother. I was on my way up, so I had some pretty plumb assignments during those years."

"I remember Hawaii and Italy." There were a few other big deal commands, too.

"Yeah. Your mother loved being an officer's wife on those bases. Then we got transferred to Norfolk. Not nearly as glamorous for her."

"Pretty choice assignment for you." Norfolk was the world's largest naval station.

"It was, but your mother wasn't happy. When she wasn't happy, nobody was. I don't know if she messed around before that, but the first time I went out to sea after that transfer she started dating someone. Openly. He was an aviator and she decided she'd rather be a Naval aviator's wife. She thought that douche bag was Richard Gere and she was Debra Winger. Ink was barely dry on our divorce when they got married."

"You kept track of her?" He'd never heard his father mention her.

"Navy's big, but some news spreads everywhere. She's on husband number five now, Coast Guard."

"Seriously?" She'd mentioned a couple of husbands the few times she'd blown into his life like a hurricane.

"Your mother is the type of person who's never happy with anything she has, and she's got to make everyone around her feel her pain."

"Still the Maguire marriages —"

"What she told you about the Maguire marriages was total horseshit. She really made it sound like we were cursed?"

Cade shrugged.

"Bitch," his father spat. "Cade, my divorce is the first divorce in Maguire history. We're usually pretty good at choosing the right woman."

"She said —"

"I've tried not to say anything about her over the years, because whatever she was to me, she was your mother. I kept thinking she might show up some day and I didn't want my problems with her added to yours. If I'd known she was showing up and messing with you, I would have mentioned a few things." His father sighed. "Probably should have told you anyway."

"You think?" Cade cracked his knuckles. All he'd done the last few weeks was try and protect Tess from what was inside him, what his own mother had told him was inside him. To think that was a lie made his blood run cold. He'd walked away from the best thing that had ever happened to him because of a lie.

"She's a liar to the bone. I meant it when I said she wanted to make everyone else around her miserable and she didn't like being a mother. I used to talk to some of my buddies who had kids and they would tell me stories about how their wives were with their kids. Hell, I'd see it at family barbeques. Your mother wasn't like that. She barely hugged you. Didn't have it in her to be a mom. Honestly, I just thought she didn't give a shit about you or your brother. I didn't think she'd actively fuck with you on her way out the door, or after."

"She said Grandma left Grandpa and Great-Grandma refused to live with Great-Grandpa. She said Maguire marriages didn't last."

"My mother didn't leave my father. She died when I was ten. We didn't talk about her because it hurt too much. Losing her damn near broke me and your grandpa. She was an amazing woman." He stopped talking, the pain on his face made it clear why he'd never talked about Cade's grandmother before.

"I'm sorry." Cade wished he'd known that kind of love existed in their family but feeling Tess's loss he understood the need to avoid talking about the pain.

"Your great-grandmother didn't live with your great-grandfather for a while. That much was true. But she didn't leave him. Her parents were sick and so she went to stay with them to take care of them since her husband was out to sea so much. He was at that house with her and their family every chance he had."

Cade's father reached out and put his hand on his son's shoulder. "There's a kernel of truth in every lie your mother told, but the only reason the Maguire marriages before mine didn't last was death. We're warriors by nature, son and when we love, we love fierce and true. When we love the right woman, she gives that same thing back."

Cade put his head in his hands. What the fuck had he done?

"Why would she try and make me believe —"

"You boys were mine to the bone. She wasn't a good mother and she resented me being a good father. Hated that even though I was gone months at a time you two would still rather be with me than her. I guess she thought she could stick it to all of us by fucking with your head."

"But she's my mother." What kind of mother would do that to her own son?

"Yeah and some mothers in the animal kingdom eat their young. Plain fact is, not every woman wants to be a mother and not every woman who is a mother is meant to be one. Your mother was better than some, worse than others."

"Better than some?"

"Stories I've seen in the news? I am fucking grateful you two survived her."

"Did I?" Cade wondered.

"What do you mean?"

"I thought I was protecting Tess. I pushed her away. Hell, I threw her away and hurt her in the process. I don't see how I can fix this. If I can't I might as well be dead. She's it for me."

"Screw that, son. You're a Maguire."

"What does that even mean?" His father's tone sounded so sure.

"We have a history of happy marriages in our family, doesn't mean we have a history of smooth sailing to the altar."

"Huh?" Cade had no idea what the man was talking about now.

"Haven't you looked at any of the family pictures?"

"What pictures?" Cade had never seen any."

"Those boxes your grandfather sent you. You must have them."

"I've never looked inside." He'd thought about it when he was with Tess, but since he'd started to push her away, he hadn't had any interest in digging through his family history.

"Tell you what. Let's go in, you can grab your old man another beer. We'll look at some pictures and I'll tell you some stories I should have told you a long time ago. Between the two of us we'll come up with a plan to get your woman back. You do want her back, don't you?"

"More than anything." For the first time since he'd started to pull away from Tess there was hope. If his dad was right, maybe this was fixable.

"Anything?"

"Yeah. Anything."

"All right then. Let's go."

"Are you sure I'll be what she needs?" Cade's voice was raspy and hoarse.

"Son." His father put his hand on his shoulder. "I look at you and see the man you are, and I see the man you'll be. I'm glad I'm going to be here when they meet. Because that man is going to be a hell of a husband and father." His father walked into the cabin.

Cade followed his father inside. Maybe he could be everything Tess deserved. She sure as hell was everything he wanted.

Tess stared at the course in front of her. She had gotten lucky and drew one of the last slots in the qualifiers. While it meant she had to stand around watching the others compete for hours, it also meant she saw exactly where they went wrong and exactly what she needed to do to make it to the finals. Only the top five women would and she needed to make sure she was at least in the top four. The last woman running the course after her was a legend.

The qualifying course was tough, and they'd added new, tougher obstacles. It wasn't unexpected. Rationally, she knew that they added new obstacles every year. The new used to be something that threw her off. Thanks to the last few weeks of her life, she'd learned to roll with the punches a little more.

She thought of Cade, missed him. For what felt like the millionth time she pushed him out of her mind and focused on what was in front of her. Ever since he'd broken up with her that was all she could do, put one foot in front of the other. Right now, there were six obstacles and at least six minutes between her and the city finals.

The starting signal blared and she raced forward then jumped onto the floating steps. It was five steps, but much farther apart than the ones she'd practiced on at home and each one was higher up than the last. As they raised in height their angle got much steeper. After clearing the fifth step, jumped to the hanging rope and swung to a platform clearing the obstacle.

As the crowd cheered her on, she moved on to a new obstacle, the spinning bow-ties. She stared at the handles in front of her. All she had to do was jump from the platform, swing for a while and fly six feet through the air to grip the second set of handles, then dismount. Easy. Except the obstacle had taken out twenty-percent of the competitors and most of the women tonight. She took a deep breath and jumped. Her grip slipped a fraction when she grabbed the handles but didn't let go. All she had to do now was build up momentum. She swung her body, thinking of the swings in a park. After a few swings, she let go of the first handles and reached for the second set. For a second her heart stopped as it felt like she was gong to miss, but she grabbed them at the last moment and held on. Time to get off this obstacle. After two more swings she flew to the platform and landed with a thud.

Two down four to go. It was straight on to the swinging bridge. The series of vertical pads, hung at varying heights and were hung from wires, meaning they moved with each step. This one was all about balance and being light on her feet. One wrong shift and she was water bound. Tess took a deep breath and raced forward, barely feeling the steps beneath her feet as she kept her focus on the platform in front of her. On the second to last step, she felt the movement of the pad go sideways. Instead of taking the next step at a bad angle, she bent her knee and propelled herself off the step, hurdling the last step and rolling on to the platform.

She laid there for a second to catch her breath. The roar of the crowd cheered her on and she rose to her feet.

The ring swing was next. She grabbed a ring and swung it to a post halfway across the water and managed to hook the ring on the first swing. The cheers around her sent a jolt of excitement zipping through her body. The only thing better than this was being with Cade. At the thought of him, she almost lost her grip when she was transitioning to the second ring. But she recovered, hooked it over the post, and swung to the landing platform.

Halfway there.

She stood on the platform in front of the fourth obstacle. It was another new one. The lightning bolts. She had to grasp a bar, hop it onto the other side of a cradle, then leap with the bar to another cradle about four feet away. Then she had to repeat that two more times.

She used the mini-tramp and jumped to a bar resting in the front cradle. After making a quick calculation in her head, she hopped and braced as the bar rested in the second cradle and the entire mechanism shifted with her weight. She checked her grip and began to swing. When she had enough momentum, she moved hurling herself and the bar to the second cradle. With every jolt of the bar land-

ing in the next cradle her muscles rebelled. As she made the

transition to the back of the second cradle and then the

front of the third cradle, her muscles screamed at her to let

go. Her hands started to cramp as she made the jump to the

second part of the last cradle. All she had to do now was

swing and dismount. She took a deep breath, closed her

eyes at the last second and went for it.

Her feet connected with the platform and the crowd

screamed. She smiled at her cheering section. Her grand-

parents and all her brothers and sisters were there follow-

ing along the side of the course as she progressed. Charlie,

Delilah, Nick, and Olivia were right up front in the stands.

TJ was holding up a tablet, so her parents could watch her,

too. There was only one person missing.

Dammit. When am I going to stop thinking about Cade?

She gave a wave to her family and friends and turned

back to the course. One more to go.

The warped wall was a concave quarter-pipe and she'd

have to run up and grab the top of the wall. Next to it stood

the mega wall, an eighteen-foot wall. If she tried that and

made it, she'd win ten thousand dollars, which could go

straight to her mother's animal shelter. If she missed, she

would only have one shot at the regular wall, instead of

three.

The old Tess would have played it safe, stuck to the regular wall and given herself the maximum number of chances to finish the course. Something she'd realized since her melt-down in front of the Board was that she was a new person now. Cade had blown into her life, and almost as quickly he'd blown out. But he'd changed her. Loving him had made her stronger, more self-assured, and more willing to take a risk. In the few weeks since the Board meeting she hadn't seen him, but he'd never been far from her thoughts. He likely never would be.

The crowd screamed "beat that wall" over and over again. She looked at the Trips, smiled and pointed at the mega-wall. They all held up their hands and screamed "yes." Tess blew them a kiss and turned back to the wall.

Nothing ventured, nothing gained.

With a whoop she made her move running full out and scaling the wall. For a second, she thought she wasn't going to make it, but the fingers of her right hand latched on to the edge of the wall and she refused to let go. She grabbed the top of the wall with her left hand, grateful for all the times Cade and Nick had made her scale the wall at home over and over again. Even when she was too tired to think straight.

Tess kept her grip on the top of the mega-wall with her hands, and with a burst of energy from somewhere, she pulled herself up over the edge to the platform.

She laid there for a moment, gathering her strength for the last task today, hitting the button. The distance to the button was ingrained in her memory, and, without looking up, she reached up and hit it, securing her place in city finals. The crowd roared its approval, as the announcers screamed that she was the first woman to scale the mega-wall and had just won ten thousand dollars.

She didn't really know what she expected after hitting the button, she wasn't prepared for his voice.

"I knew you could do it, Jules"

Her head snapped up at the sound of Cade's voice. He stood on the edge of the platform, eyes shining, grinning from ear to ear. It took her a second to register that he was waiting for her at the top of the mega-wall and not the warped wall.

He knew I'd take the chance. He believed in me.

The roar of the crowd faded as she pulled herself to her feet. When she steadied herself, he went down on one knee. She barely registered the sounds of the announcers talking about college football legend and Navy veteran Cade Maguire.

"What are you doing here?"

"I had to come see my girl kick American Ninja Warrior ass."

Her eyes filled with confusion. "You said I wasn't your girl."

"I think we've established that you're the brains of this particular operation." He smiled. "I was an idiot. Sonny and Sam stopped speaking to me, the Trips threatened to kick my ass. Nick wouldn't make me any hangover cures. Hell, Ed wanted to fire me."

"I doubt that." She smiled.

Cade grinned. "Well, maybe not fire me, but he was pissed."

"That I can believe. What are you doing here?"

"It took me a while to, as Ed put it, pull my head out of my ass. I needed a little help from my dad. I thought I was bad for you because my parents had a crap marriage and I thought all Maguires were built to be bad husbands. He told me he was the exception, not the rule. The curse I thought I was saving you from was bullshit. Usually, Maguire men have excellent taste in wives."

"Is that so?" She was worried this was a hallucination brought on by dehydration and over exertion.

"That's so. Turns out I thought I was saving you from

the wrong thing. The Maguire curse isn't about marrying the wrong woman. It's about almost losing her. Well, I don't want to lose you. Ever. I figured out we were made for each other. I'd be an idiot to walk away from that. I may be slow, but I'm no idiot."

Cade pulled a small blue velvet box out of his pants pocket, opening it to reveal a perfect Marquise cut diamond.

"I know this is just the first step, and there's a lot more groveling in my futre."

She laughed. "Who said you weren't smart?"

"I'm smart, but without you it's all brains, no heart." He took a deep breath. "Tess Gallagher, I love you more than I ever thought I could love another person. I know that I will love you more every day we spend together. Will you follow in your gran's footsteps and be the wife of a football coach?"

She should make him grovel more right now, but the truth was she didn't have it in her. It sounded like he intended to do more atonement in the future.

He took her moment of hesitation the wrong way and went on. "I know I hurt you. I was an asshole and I'm more sorry than I can ever say. If you'll have me, I'll spend every day of my life making it up to you. Will you marry me?"

She threw her arms around him. What more could she ask for? "You bet your ass I will."

Cade's smiled turned into a grin as he slipped the ring on her finger, stood, and pulled her into his arms with a whoop. The crowd roared its approval and Tess turned her focus to her cheering section. Her brothers were front and center high fiving each other and laughing like loons. Her friends had come out of the stands and Charlie and Delilah stood next to them crying and holding hands like they hadn't spent the better part of three weeks coming up with creative ways to have Cade killed. Next to them were her grandparents, holding on to each other and looking on with such pride.

Her sisters were smiling and giving her the thumbs up. She was looking forward to spending more time with them. She could see her parents' images on the tablet, arms around each other. Nick was standing next to Olivia and a man who had to be Cade's father. Every last one of them were cheering for the couple. She could hear the announcers talking about another American Ninja Warrior first.

Tess turned to her fiancé, the love of her life, a sly smile on her face. "So, we're one step closer to Vegas."

"Bet your ass we are." He moved closer to her. "Finals are going to be a breeze. Then it's on to Vegas."

"I've just decided that I hate long engagements."

His smile slipped for a split second before it grew larger, if possible. "That so?"

"Yep."

"I hear your whole family's coming to Vegas once you qualify."

"Think the coaching staff could be there?"

"I think we can arrange something." He pulled her close. "How about it. You, me, Elvis, and you win this whole damn thing as Tess Maguire."

"I do love a man with a plan." She pressed her forehead to his. "And I do love you. You help everything make sense."

He tightened his arms, lowering his head to whisper in her ear. "You know coaching at Cormac wasn't my second chance, you are."

He kissed her making the tingling start in her toes and work its way up to her heart, which beat only for him, the man who saw everything she was and loved her for all of it.

The Beginning…

Thank you for reading *Second Chance Option*. I hope you enjoyed Cade and Tess's story. If you did, please leave a review.

Want to get the latest news on King's Folly and Cormac University? The world keeps getting bigger and bigger and there are lots of happy endings yet to come.

Interested in who's up next? Sign up for my NEWSLETTER (http://elizabethspaur.com/landing-page-newsletter/)

BOOKS BY ELIZABETH SPAUR

<u>Gridiron Knights</u>

Second Chance Option (http://elizabethspaur.com/books/second-chance-option/)

Shotgun Romance (http://elizabethspaur.com/books/shotgun-romance/)

Romancing The Receiver (http://elizabethspaur.com/books/romancing-the-receiver/)

Love In The Zone (http://elizabethspaur.com/books/love-in-the-zone/)

Bootleg Love Affair (http://elizabethspaur.com/books/bootleg-love-affair/)

ABOUT THE AUTHOR

When her physics teacher gave her detention for reading a romance novel during class, Elizabeth Spaur knew she was destined to be romance writer. Her journey from physics class to published author as gone from coast to coast and led her through multiple industries, including film and television, banking and the law. Every step along the way has enriched her life and helped her tell stories that always come with a happily ever after and, usually, a side of snark. Elizabeth writes contemporary, historical and paranormal romance. She lives with the love of her life and two pairs of cats and dogs, all of whom are named after television crime fighters.

Elizabeth loves hearing from her readers at elizabeth@elizabethspaur.com

You can also finder her on the web:

WEBSITE (http://www.elizabethspaur.com)

FACEBOOK (https://www.facebook.com/elizabethspaurauthor)

TWITTER (https://twitter.com/spaurromance)

BOOKBUB (https://www.bookbub.com/profile/elizabeth-spaur)

AMAZON (https://www.amazon.com/-/e/B06WGNTV5L)

www.ingramcontent.com/pod-product-compliance
Lightning Source LLC
Chambersburg PA
CBHW060152260626
47160CB00001B/226